I0580852

Also by J.M. Holmes:

Retrievers: A Kat & Jerry Anthology

Falling From Space: Kat & Jerry Return!

Ice, Ice, Baby (*with* Prodigy *and* Time Trial)

They Left Me for DEAD: A Crime Noir thriller

Beautiful, Naked, Rich… and DEAD

The Fruit-Eating Cat

A Deep Breath of Water

Pro Tem: The Amazing Year *(nonfiction)*

Scan this code to view or purchase any of these books

All titles available in paperback, hardcover, and large print editions

J.M. HOLMES

ADVENTURE IN ASTEROID CITY

A Kat & Jerry mystery

LITERATI INTERNATIONAL

~ SINCE 1981 ~

TORONTO • NEW YORK • LONDON

Scan this code to correspond directly with the author at: jm-holmes.com

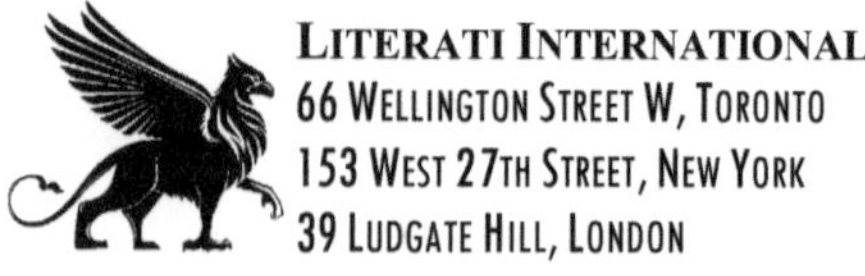

LITERATI INTERNATIONAL
66 WELLINGTON STREET W, TORONTO
153 WEST 27TH STREET, NEW YORK
39 LUDGATE HILL, LONDON

Library of Congress Control Number: 2025905805
ISBN 978-1-956784-15-2

for Alex

who thinks he is smarter than me

MEET OUR HEROES

First encountered in *"Retrievers"*, an anthology of their earliest adventures, Kat, Jerry & Batman return in another exciting mystery in search of a missing treasure.
This stand-alone novel is third in the sequence of adventures of these two clever fortune-hunters (and their cat).

Not takin' any guff

THE FEMME FATALE:
A creature of the real Space Age, when cheap, accessible lightspeed travel is available to everyone. A formidable foe, armed with nothing but her wits and a powerful quantum computer housed in her eyeglasses.

Smarter than he looks

THE MASTERMIND:
A relic from the distant past.
A former titan of industry rejuvenated in a regeneration tube, firmly rooted in the earthbound twentieth century. He relies on Kat to make his complicated plans work.

It's not complicated

THE CAT:
A player with no hidden agenda, secret allegiances or devious plans, Batman is refreshingly honest.
All he wants is smoked salmon.

If this is your first time encountering Kat, Jerry, and Batman, strap-in and prepare for a wild ride as they solve mysteries, dodge bad guys, and fight for their lives. Enjoy!

CONTENTS

PART I:

WELCOME TO ASTEROID CITY

Life is either a daring adventure, or nothing.
— Helen Keller

O THE RIGHT! The *right*, Kat! Starboard! Oh, for God's sake! *Three o'clock!*"

Kat leaned forcefully into the joystick and the ship banked hard, sending Jerry tumbling sideways into the forward bulkhead behind her co-pilot's chair. He looked past her shoulder to see an endless expanse of craggy rock sweep across the viewscreen in a dizzy arc. As the ship twisted away from the massive asteroid, the stars swung back into view in a stomach-churning clockwise spin.

"I thought your glasses were navigating this part," shouted Jerry, launching himself into the pilot's chair beside Kat.

"Even my Slimlines need proper sensor data, Jerry. They don't have psychic abilities. But the ship's sensor array isn't picking up all these rocks – there's an insane amount of voromite on their surface. Seems like this ship's designers kind of dropped the ball on that one, if you ask me."

"Kat, it's a pleasure yacht, not a mining ship! Voromite is so rare, the chances of ever encountering it in normal space are essentially nil."

"Tell that to the rocks outside," grunted Kat, pulling back forcefully on the joystick as another wide expanse of sharp protrusions disappeared beneath the belly of their ship.

A long, throaty yowl from the cat nook behind them betrayed Batman's unhappiness with the roller coaster ride.

"I give it five minutes before he's coated that cathouse in cat yack, Jer."

"Don't worry, baby. I'm sure he'll still have enough left in his stomach to deposit a hefty load on the carpet when we're done."

A crowd of battleship-sized asteroids encircled their ship, each rock leisurely rotating in its own private pattern. Kat gritted her teeth and leaned forward into her chair, deftly tapping and alternately pulling, pushing or twisting the joystick, dodging their ship around the tumbling obstacles.

In a desperate effort to avoid one huge asteroid directly in their path, Kat forced the ship to the side – and directly into a massive brown cloud.

A thick rain of cantaloupe-sized rocks peppered their viewscreen and hammered down onto the hull. Angry red lights started flashing as the hail of debris increased in intensity. With a sickening thud, a rock the size of a beach ball cracked the viewscreen, leaving a nasty gash in its wake

"Oh my God!" cried Kat. She pressed her hand against the crack, only to yank it back when she felt the tug of vacuum on the other side of the screen.

"Yo! Kat!" Jerry yelled, throwing her a roll of wide tape.

She grabbed the tape midair and yanked off a long, gooey strip, which she pasted down onto the gash. As the vacuum outside sucked the goo into the crack, thin tendrils of ooze spread along the outside of the viewscreen and immediately solidified in the airless void.

The barrage of rocks continued unabated, driving furrows and deep dents into the ship's hull. Three antennae were snapped off and spun away silently, joining the other rocks flowing past their ship.

Kat tossed the tape back and resumed manually navigating through the cloud and away from one particularly large asteroid dead ahead. Jerry fumbled the catch, and as he bent down to retrieve it, a marble-sized rock pierced the cracked viewscreen and punched through the center of his seat-back, burying itself into the decking behind the chair.

Jerry straightened up and spotted the new hole in the viewscreen. He slapped a patch of tape over it, then turned and saw the puncture in his chair. The blood drained from his face.

"Looks like being a klutz saved your life, Jer."

Dropping back down into his chair with a dazed look, Jerry said, "You throw like a girl."

Kat laughed loudly. "And you catch like one, boss."

Spiraling away from a trio of mammoth boulders, their ship burst out of the thick cloud of smaller rocks. Taking a deep breath, Kat cranked the joystick and resumed dodging the remaining asteroids in their path.

"Say Jer, what was that again about asteroid fields being 99% empty space? You know – 'the likelihood of a collision is a million to one'. Remember that conversation?"

"That was for a normal asteroid field, Kat. This is a man-made collection. The mining companies tag these rocks, then drag them here and park them in their own orbit in range of the mining facility. Like a bunch of planes circling an airport, waiting their turn to land, or ships lined up at a port."

Jerry paused, as the blank look on Kat's face reminded him that most of the common experiences of his 21st-century life were no longer common, if they still existed at all. Airports and shipping terminals had been the first casualties of the transportation revolution in the mid-2000s, when traveling the globe became as cheap and easy as it had been for his parents to drive to the corner store.

"But like I was saying," he continued, "even in the endless void of space, when someone purposely drops a few hundred mountain-size moving objects in one tiny sector, the neighbourhood starts to get a bit crowded. That cloud of debris we just escaped is probably the remnants of a collision between two of these monsters."

With one last twist, duck, and spurt to the side, the ship passed beyond the cluster of asteroids and emerged into relatively clear space. A light flashing on the viewscreen's display indicated their destination.

"There's the mining settlement, Jerry. I hate to say this before we're safely parked, but it looks like we made it in one piece. Almost. I still don't know why we couldn't approach from another direction, though – like from one of the other 359 degrees in the compass that don't go through an obstacle course of flying death."

"Which we could have done if we'd completed a few extra orbits of the planet, but I didn't think we needed to. I figured your glasses could navigate for us – I had no idea there was voromite in these rocks to mess up the ship's sensors.

"And don't forget that the natural ring of asteroids we're heading toward is orbiting the planet at 30,000 kilometers per hour. That limits our approach options, since we need to match its speed and attitude before touching down on the asteroid housing the settlement."

Jerry tapped a button on the ship's console and waited while the mining settlement's computer processed his landing request. A few seconds later, a light on the console flashed green. Kat and Jerry both heaved a sigh of relief, unbuckled from their command chairs, and staggered into the main cabin.

"Thank God for auto docking," said Kat, flopping back onto a couch. "I need the break. I feel like I've just run a marathon."

A pitiful meow from behind caught her attention. She tapped her teeth together twice, and the grill on the cat nook popped open, releasing an extremely annoyed black and white cat.

"Here," said Jerry, holding out a tall glass of orange liquid. "This should dull the pain."

"I feel numb already," grinned Kat, draining half the glass in one swallow. "I'm not sure life would be tolerable without orange juice and vodka."

"You better add cats to that list, babe. If you don't want to find a reminder on your pillow, that is."

As if to punctuate Jerry's comment, Batman leapt up onto the couch and tucked himself into Kat's side. Then promptly threw up.

AT OPENED the ship's hatch and skeptically peered out. Sniffing the air as if checking for nerve gas, she tentatively placed one foot on the ramp. And then stopped.

"Come onnnn, Kat," moaned Jerry. "What are you afraid of?"

"Um, oh, I dunno – being sucked into the endless void of space, perhaps?"

"You can't be serious. Did you not just witness our passage through a double-door airlock? And I know you've debarked at literally dozens of spaceports before."

"But never onto an airless, gravity-free asteroid, with nothing more than an invisible bubble between me and eternity. There's Earth-standard air pressure in here. Under that kind of force, this flimsy dome could pop off at any moment and fly away into space. And where will that leave us then?"

"In an alternate universe, that's where. That only *looks* like a dome. It's really the top half of a sphere 15 kilometers in diameter anchored into a specially carved crater.

"It's two layers of a transparent nanofiber polymer grown in microgravity, with a thin sheet of acrylic between them. I think they got that idea from the way they used to make car windshields back in the 20th cen—"

A blank look on Kat's face snapped Jerry back on topic.

"Anyhoo… the lid can't 'pop off', as you so colourfully phrase it, because it's not a lid. And whatever air pressure is in the top half of the sphere is nothing compared to the 900 cubic kilometers of rock filling the lower half beneath our feet.

"There's a graviton grid buried beneath our feet, too, which gives the entire settlement Earth-standard gravity. Very elegant work, all-in-all."

"Uniform gravity settlement-wide? That makes no sense, Jerry. Why insert Earth-standard gravity into places it's not needed? Like in the ore refineries. Surely it would be more efficient to do that work in reduced gravity."

"It was done on purpose. It's a galaxy-wide requirement from the labour unions for any settlements built by the mining consortium. They didn't want to end up with gravity ghettos in the settlements, where the bosses could extort extra fees for gravity."

"So they build one continuous gravity grid," said Kat. "Waste a perfect opportunity to fine-tune working conditions in the refineries—"

"Because it's the only way to guard against the inescapable greed of the wealthy and powerful."

"I weep for humanity."

"That's not all you'll be weeping about, honeybuns, if you don't move your ass down this ramp right quick. I'd be happy to introduce my foot to your butt so you can experience the inefficiency of this station's full gravity first-hand."

Kat shot Jerry a snarl, but scampered down the ramp nonetheless.

"What were you doing while I was reading-up on this place, Kat? Probably playing with the cat, right? And thinking you don't need to be prepared because those glasses of yours will cover for you."

"Don't be silly – why would I need to memorize a bunch of boring specs when you're all too happy to do it for both of us? My glasses I save for *important* things."

They headed across the hangar and entered a glass-walled office beneath a large sign reading: "REGISTRATION".

There was nothing inside except a waist-high counter holding several little desktop dispensers with rolls of stickers and foil seals and hologram tags. And standing behind it, a young man in chinos, wearing a shirt with the name "Billy" embroidered on the breast pocket.

"Checking in," said Jerry.

The clerk looked up from the tablet he had been studying. "You the one who just set down on Pad 27?"

"If that's Pad 27, then yes," said Jerry, glancing at the bay.

Billy craned his neck to look into the hangar. Their beat-up ship sat crookedly on the pad, with little vents of steam escaping from random points. Various puddles were forming beneath the ship as fluids leaked from the underbelly. The hull was extensively marred with ugly, football-sized dents, a huge crack bisected the front viewscreen, and the external antennae were all missing, except for a large dish hanging halfway down the starboard side, dangling from a tangle of wiring.

"Looks like you ran into a bit of trouble," the clerk said.

"What? That?" said Jerry, shrugging. "No biggie. Those marks'll buff right out. You offer repair services here, right?"

"Yup. But we'll have to move her over to the repair bays."

Billy looked expectantly at Jerry. Jerry stared back.

"Um, your auth token?" the clerk asked.

"Oh! Damn!" exclaimed Jerry. "Sorry, I wasn't thinking. I'll have to go get it from the ship."

"That's okay – I've got mine," said Kat, and slid a small silver wedge of metal across the counter.

Billy chuckled good-naturedly. "Thanks, Miss. A lot of people forget to bring in their tokens – they're so used to their ships recognising their DNA, they stop thinking about it.

"You wouldn't want to see what we do to ships we have to move when we don't have this little guy. It's not a pretty sight."

He pulled a barcoded ID tag from one of the countertop

stands and clipped it onto the token, then waited while Jerry swiped his phone over it.

The clerk craned his neck forward and looked down at the carrier Kat was holding. "You have some sort of animal in there? Is it a pet?"

"Hush. You'll hurt his feelings," said Kat. "He's more of a traveling companion. 'Pet' is so feudal-sounding."

"I don't care what you call him. He can't enter the settlement until he's cleared quarantine."

"But he just cleared a 14-day quarantine on Benson II," Kat lied. "Surely you can't expect him to go through that again."

"Can and do," said Billy implacably.

"Are you suuuuure there isn't there something we can do?" asked Kat suggestively.

The subtlety of her question flew over his head.

"Not without documentation showing he's clear to enter the settlement. Period."

"Well, why didn't you say so sooner?" asked Kat, reaching into a small pouch she pulled from her pocket. "This should have more than enough documentation on it for you."

She pushed a coin across the counter and left it in front of the clerk. "Read it all you want. Memorize the words. I'm sure you'll find what you're looking for."

The clerk's eyes bulged when he saw the coin. It was a red Gold Drachma from Aristotle Majoris, and easily worth more than he made in a year. His eyes moved from the coin, then up to Kat, then back to the coin. He bit one of his lips, then squeezed his fingers together until his knuckles were aching. He was the perfect picture of a man in turmoil.

Kat decided to give him the teensiest little push to put him out of his misery.

"Here," she said. "Let me help you." Reaching across the counter and pulling on a roll of foil seals, she unpeeled a seal reading "CLEARED", and slapped it down onto the carrier.

"There," she said sweetly, flashing him a sexy smile. "I knew we could figure something out."

Billy managed to salvage enough composure to discreetly sweep the coin off the counter, cleared his throat and examined his tablet. "Okay, then. And I see you've already uploaded your payment details. You folks are good to go. You can access the bays anytime. Your phone will show you where to find your ship after we've fixed her up."

Jerry and Kat headed over to an access platform for the settlement's maglev transit shuttles, then boarded a waiting commuter car and settled in among a dozen other passengers.

Looking up at the transit map above their heads, Kat said, "This is quite the place, Jerry. They have a lake, two golf courses, shopping malls – the whole shebang."

"Even a racetrack," added Jerry. "They probably need it all, too. Even though the settlement covers almost 170 square kilometers of ground, I think it's still pretty easy to get cabin fever locked up on this rock for any period of time. And some people live here for years on end."

Kat looked at the other riders. There was nothing to distinguish them from countless other commuters in cities across the galaxy, slumped in their seats, staring at their phones.

"I'm glad I don't have to carry one of those things," she said. "My glasses are so much easier."

Jerry nodded. "A couple of centuries ago we all thought so, too, and phones nearly ended up on the scrapheap of history. Implantable devices became the thing to have. But the cyber wars in the 2040s put the fear of God into all the early adopters. People couldn't get their implants removed fast enough – some even tried cutting them out of their heads themselves. It was mass panic."

"I remember hearing about that," said Kat. "But isn't that when everyone switched to wearables?"

"Yep. So the hackers targeted those, and people's clothing started bursting into flame or they were blinded by their smart glasses. After that, carrying around a small slab of glass suddenly didn't seem so bad after all."

Kat frowned. "So what would induce the Slimline Corporation to create these glasses?"

"It was a corporate gamble," said Jerry. "It's true that most people are still too scared of wearing computers, despite a century of technological advances. But your glasses were designed from the start to be a ridiculously expensive niche item. Wide acceptance in the marketplace was never part of the marketing plan."

"No one ever talks about the cyber wars," said Kat. "Even the history vids barely mention them."

"I don't think we like to dwell on our more foolish behaviour. Makes us question our self-anointed status as the only wise and all-knowing species in the galaxy."

"Speaking of which, Jerry, tell me more about this friend of yours who's brought us to the extreme edge of that galaxy. In what nefarious way do you suppose he'll get us killed, tortured, maimed, or pushed out of an airlock?"

"Who, Howard? Never. He's perfectly harmless. He's a computer nerd. He just needs our help finding something. He wouldn't go into details when he called, but I think you can put away any fears you might have of impending skullduggery."

"Says the man who has jeopardized my life on practically every trip I've taken with him."

"Hey, we didn't have any problems on Plebus IX at the galactic music convention."

"Except that if you had spent even five more minutes debating the merits of vinyl records – whatever the hell those are – versus the fidelity of digital storage, I was going to go lie down in the hot tub and slit my wrists. That trip was the longest two weeks of my life."

"We only spent two days there."

"Exactly."

The shuttle lurched to a stop and Jerry looked up.

"This is us," he said.

Kat and Jerry stepped out into a deceptively normal street scene that could have been the downtown business district of any one of thousands of cities across the galaxy. A few multistorey office buildings rose above an unremarkable stretch of storefronts. People were strolling along the sidewalks, running errands, shopping, or stopping to buy food and coffees from street vendors. In a small park facing them, a low, wide fountain glittered in the sunlight while three children carrying ice cream cones chased each other in circles around the water.

Kat craned her neck to look up at the sky.

"Why can't I see space, Jerry? It looks like a normal sky."

"Because from this spot the dome roof is about seven kilometers above us, and light works the same way here as in any other atmosphere – the particles in the air refract the sunlight and appear in our vision as blue light."

"What do you mean, 'sunlight'? You mean that spotlight? How do they make it look like the sun?"

"Because it *is* the sun, Kat. It's this planetary system's star. This asteroid – the whole ring, in fact – is locked in geosynchronous orbit with the planet, which completes a rotation about every 27 hours. So we do, too."

"How do they compensate for the 27-hour day?"

"They don't. Apparently, it's not hard to get used to. At the very least, you get an extra three hours to sleep in, every morning."

Kat looked at him with wide eyes.

"Jerry," she whispered reverently. "This must be what heaven is like. I'm never leaving."

Jerry chuckled and patted her on the back. "Come on, Sleeping Beauty. We got people to see."

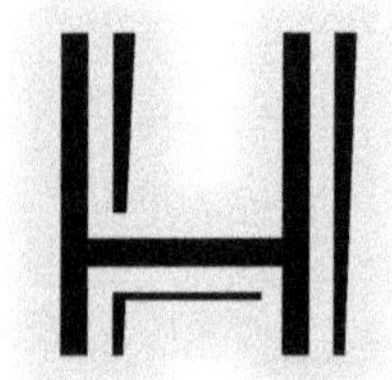OWARD WAS DELIGHTED to see Kat and Jerry, but apparently not enough to feel compelled to rise and greet them. He shouted a hearty "Welcome!" at their arrival, and buzzed them in without leaving his desk.

From what little she could deduce from his seated form scrunched behind his workstation, Kat figured he was one of those roly-poly kind of guys, egg-shaped and flabby from years spent hunched-over at computer terminals. She guessed he was somewhere in his late thirties. His face was round, with a pale, pasty complexion hiding behind a curly brown beard, which matched his curly brown hair. Behind little round rimless glasses his bloodshot eyes blinked rapidly as he squinted at them.

"You two look hot and tired," he said, and before they could reply he hollered, "Suzie! Hey! Sue!"

They turned to see a trim young woman in her twenties, short blonde hair bobbing above her shoulders, emerge from a doorway carrying a tray of lemonades.

"I'm way ahead of you, Howie. Got refreshments for everyone.

"Hi. I'm Suzie," she said, smiling at Kat and Jerry. "As you might have figured out."

Jerry could not have been more surprised. "Ah, hi – hello. I'm Kat – I mean, this is Kat. We're Jerry. Oh— DAMN!"

Suzie laughed broadly.

"I get the same reaction whenever any of Howard's friends first meet me," she said, grinning.

"Go ahead and say it, Jerry," chuckled Howard. "Never seen me with a girl before, have you?"

"Well, uh, I guess that's right. I suppose I just never expected – I mean, you don't really get out much, do you Howard? How did you two meet? Was she delivering a pizza?"

Laughing, Howard shook his head.

"Not quite. There was a tech conference in the hotel across the street, and Suzie was an organizer. I was making a presentation on eliminating redundancy in recursive factorial functions when programming for self-contained wastewater treatment systems."

Jerry and Kat looked at him wordlessly.

"I have no idea what that means, either," said Suzie. "But I found him on the mezzanine level after his speech, manhandling a vending machine that had eaten his credits, and we ended-up connecting over a couple of power bars and coffee."

"She's good for me," said Howard. "Makes me leave my lab at least once a day. That's a first."

"I hope you guys aren't allergic to cats," said Jerry, setting the cat carrier down on the floor. "We had a little trouble with our ship and this poor fellah got all shook up. Kat didn't want to leave him by himself." He unclipped the door of the carrier and a small black head emerged, tentatively sniffing at the air.

"Oh, how cute!" cooed Suzie.

"I'll be fine," said Howard, "as long as I don't get cat hair up my no—"

Howard looked up from his desk console suddenly and said, "Is one of you running a spy program right now?" He looked alarmed.

Jerry was puzzled, but Kat said, "Oops, it's me, Howard. I'm wearing a quantum computer. Its default programming is to infiltrate any computer network in the vicinity, in case I need to access that network for any reason. I don't even think about it anymore – I guess I just take it for granted."

"It must be a pretty sophisticated piece of machinery, Kat. I thought my system was bulletproof."

"And kudos to you for spotting the intrusion, Howard. Normally that doesn't happen."

"Well, I'm feeling a bit more paranoid than usual these days, Kat. I have sniffer programs continuously monitoring every byte of information passing through my network."

"Here, let me turn off my program," said Kat, and she made a little movement with her jaw.

"What did you just do?" asked Suzie.

"Oh, the computer is in my eyeglasses. They're called 'Slimlines'."

Suzie shuddered. "I'd be too scared to wear a computer over my eyes. How do you operate them?"

"Well," said Kat, "I can talk to them, but I've also programmed commands associated with certain jaw movements and teeth tapping. Or I can control them with my eyes. The glasses monitor my face at all times and the lenses mask my eye movements for anyone I'm talking to."

"That's so cool," cooed Suzie. "What other tricks can they do?"

"Well," said Kat thoughtfully, "they're also set to cloak my appearance – and Jerry's, too, of course – on any security system I can access. Which is essentially every one. They don't wipe us from the video, but replace our images with a random set of other humanoid profiles. We might appear as children, men, women, or any combination. That way any humans monitoring the video feeds don't get suspicious at the sight of other people interacting with empty space.

"It's all automatic, and I don't even think about it anymore. But in our line of work, it can come in pretty handy."

"I have no doubt," said Howard.

"What's really useful, though, are the macros I've programmed to communicate with Jerry. With a single movement of my jaw or a flicker of my eye I can send him a variety of different alerts, share calls with him, and intercept other people's calls and redirect them to his phone."

"Howard," said Jerry, "do you know a local number – for a takeout joint, maybe?"

"Of course," said Howard.

"Call it now."

Howard lifted his phone and tapped on an entry. Kat blinked twice and immediately Jerry's phone rang.

"Beautiful!" Howard exclaimed. "And with just a blink of an eye. Those glasses are pure magic, Kat."

"Well, Howard, you know the quote," said Jerry. " 'Any sufficiently advanced technology is indistinguishable from magic'. I guess this proves the point."

"Hey, I know that one, too," said Suzie excitedly. "It's from the guy whose book got made into some famous old movie – one with apes and a flying mattress. Howie made me watch it."

Kat laughed. "You're a girl after my own heart, Suzie. I feel your pain." The two girls high-fived, giggling.

"Do you guys have a hotel yet?" asked Howard. "I can recommend a very nice one near here."

"No need, Howard," said Jerry. "We'll just return to our ship each night – it's only about a ten-minute ride."

"But we're open to suggestions on restaurants and bars – especially bars," said Kat. "Come to think of it, you can skip the restaurants."

Howard chuckled and said, "You'll like it here, I think. One thing this city has plenty of, is bars. Miners and refinery workers make up a big percentage of our population."

"So what are *you* doing here, Howard?"

"I'm a system administrator for one of the settlement's many computer systems. Just a tiny cog in a big wheel, I'm afraid, surrounded by dozens of other wheels. The number of people it takes to keep a city running in an artificial environment is mind-boggling."

"But I take it the reason you called us has nothing to do with your job," said Jerry. "You made it sound very mysterious in your message. Which was pretty clever of you – curiosity was just about the only thing that could have dragged me and Kat all the way out to the far edge of the galaxy."

"I figured as much," said Howard. "This rock is the virtual definition of exile. And that's why – well, jeez, it's complicated. I don't know exactly how to explain all this. I suppose I should start with a bit of background about this asteroid and the planet."

Kat and Jerry flopped down into two empty office chairs in front of Howard's workstation. Suzie disappeared into the other room in search of fresh drinks. Howard cleared his throat, then began talking.

"You know already that the planet we're orbiting is called New Terra. As the name clearly implies, it was one of the very first habitable planets discovered outside Earth's solar system. In fact, they hadn't even established the Planetary Registry yet, because no one expected we would be finding so many usable planets. So the planet's 'ownership' – for lack of a better word – was recorded in an electronic deed and deposited in a bank vault. And promptly forgotten."

"Forgotten?" asked Kat. "Who forgets about a planetary deed?"

"Well, in this case, everyone. New Terra is an ugly place. Calling it habitable is generous. The air is only one step short of toxic, with a noxious smell that makes it misery to breathe. The flora is unremarkable and as unpleasant as the air – stinky, thorny, and virtually inedible. There's not a lot of nutritional value in it, either, as most of the plants absorb dangerous amounts of heavy metals from the planet's surface.

"The fauna is equally unappealing. Mostly reptilian, vicious, and very aggressive when encountered. The water dwellers – one hesitates to refer to them as 'fish' – are little more than hosts for colonies of parasitic burrowing worms. They tunnel under your skin and breed if you so much as touch them in the water.

"There are a few other land-based species but there's nothing to recommend them. There are no cute bunny rabbits or furry teddy bears. Everything we've found is scaly and covered in noxious secretions that burn skin on contact. Even if humans still ate animals, no one would willingly eat these. There's a mammal similar to deer here, but I'm told that consuming even one bite leaves a foul aftertaste that lingers for days, outlasting even the taste of your vomit."

"Okay, I'm starting to understand why this place didn't become the next Paradise Planet," said Jerry.

"To say the least. And add to all that the fact that this planet was too far off the beaten path to be worth developing for its natural resources, and you understand why its value was dismissed and the deed of ownership abandoned in a bank vault."

"Wait," said Kat. "What do you mean by 'too far off the beaten path'? That makes no sense. It may be at the edge of the galaxy, but it's still well within range for every Langstrom Drive ship. It's just inconvenient, is all."

"You've put your finger on it, Kat. By today's standards, this planet is an easy jump, but when it was discovered, our understanding of Langstrom Drive travel was incomplete. It took several weeks and multiple jumps to get here from Earth.

"But that was well over a hundred years ago, and all that's important right now is that this previously-repellent, once-useless planet we're orbiting has become one of the jewels in the interstellar mining industry.

"It has one very special attribute, which is the asteroid belt we are currently camped on.

"The key lies in the new standards of Planetary Ownership, which apply retroactively. They deed ownership of all other planets, moons, asteroids and celestial matter found within one AU of the registered planet."

"An Earth AU?" asked Jerry, who was still unclear about the minutiae of planetary ownership rights.

"No," said Kat. "I learned this in Day One of Retriever training. It refers to the planet's own AU – its distance from its own star. Which covers everything from its sun to the planet, and an equal distance outward from the planet."

"Right," said Howard. "It was a logical way to prevent claim-jumpers from grabbing other pieces of the same system. It is very helpful in preventing system-based wars. Once you own the rights to a planet, it effectively locks-out your competitors so you can develop the target planet in peace, using nearby resources as necessary.

"But even after the new laws were instituted, this planetary system was so thoroughly forgotten that it took another 50 years before someone decided to take a second look.

"This ring of asteroids we're on is the remnant of a previous planet that broke apart and ended up orbiting New Terra. And it's a gold mine. Actually, much better than gold – there's tritonium, callesium, and mile-wide chunks of virtually pure halladium circling the planet in a beautiful microgravity environment.

"It's a mining company's dream come true. No environmental concerns or indigenous lifeforms to tiptoe around. Minimal refining necessary, no gravity well to pull the ore up out of, and an almost endless supply.

"We're orbiting the planet at 120,000 kilometers above the surface, in a ring that's almost 800,000 kilometers in circumference. It would take over a decade to fully mine even just one medium-sized asteroid in the ring. And there are literally thousands of such hunks of metal orbiting this planet. The potential riches can't even be estimated. Computers can't count that high."

"I'm starting to get the picture," said Jerry. "And who owns this little piece of heaven today?"

"Right now, no one. So far, over three hundred mining companies have set-up shop on various asteroids in the ring. It's the Wild West. No royalties to pay, no local labour laws, no planetary regulators to fight with – or bribe – and no limits on what they can do. Without a deed of ownership, the original discoverers are powerless to control these companies. They can only sit by and watch while their resources are sucked dry in front of their eyes."

"There must be records showing who discovered it," said Kat.

"Sure. There's lots of 'em. But the law is specific – planets discovered pre-Registry need the original deed."

"Don't tell me that access to untold riches all hinges on the possession of some moldy old piece of paper," said Jerry.

"Almost," answered Howard. "It's electronic. Disk of some kind, from the late 21st century."

"And no one made a backup copy?"

"Wouldn't be any good. You need the original, authentic digital file."

"Hey, I think I remember something like this from when I was young," said Jerry. "There was a brief spate of activity centered on something called NFTs – "Non-Fungible Tokens". They were supposed to be authentic, original versions of digital artwork."

"Exactly. This deed is a direct descendant of that technology. It's the only possible means of proving ownership of the planet."

"Could someone else claim the planet if they possessed the deed?"

"Yes. The document is more like a Bearer's Bond. It was designed that way on purpose because when it was created there was still no official way to register planetary ownership. Anyone who comes forward today and produces the disk simply needs to present it to the Registration Board, which would then properly record them as the new official owner, once and for all."

Jerry took a deep breath and rose to his feet. He looked around at the cluttered lab and the myriad machines and computing units.

"So tell me, Howard, how does any of this concern you? Don't tell me you have the disk, because if you did, I imagine you'd already be on the first ship to Earth to register your new planet."

"You're right, Jerry, I don't have it, but I think I know who does, or at least someone who found where it is. There's a small problem, though, and that's something I think you can help me with.

"You see, guys, this fellow who found the disk, well… he's dead."

HEN YOU SAY 'dead'," said Kat, "is that a euphemism or expression? As in, 'You're dead to me'? Please say yes."

Howard chuckled.

"No, Miss Kat, I'm afraid I'm speaking literally. If we had daisies anywhere on the station, the man would be pushing them up."

"So maybe you can explain, then, how you think Jerry and I can help you. Do you think we can commune with spirits? Because I gotta tell you, Howie, the only spirits I'll be communing with are currently in an icy cold vodka bottle in my ship's freezer."

"I don't need you to talk to the fellow, Kat. I just need someone who can be very discreet and make some inquiries on the QT. I want you and Jerry to find where he put the disk. I thought that was kind of your specialty – you know, finders of lost objects."

"Howard," said Jerry, "tell me more about this dead guy. I want to know how he fits in to the picture, and why you think he has the disk. How did you find him, anyways?"

"I can't take credit for that, Jerry. He found *me*.

"About three weeks ago I got a call here in the lab from someone asking if I had any equipment which could read a mid-21st century data disk. Now, that's a pretty vague request, sort of like asking a mechanic if he can fix 'an old car'. The first thing you'd do is ask for more details, like the year, make and model.

"I did the same thing with my caller. I tried to get at least the disk's brand name or decade of manufacture, and what kind of computer it had been used in, but the fellow was evasive. I got the impression he was holding back, not because he was technologically ignorant, but because he didn't want to give away any identifiable details."

"That would set off alarm bells with me," said Jerry.

"And with me, too," agreed Howard. "But before I could squeeze anything useful out of him, he ended the call. I must have spooked him. Maybe I pressed too hard.

"But something about the call made me feel it was worth digging into, and after all, what else do I have to do around here?"

He swept his eyes over the cluttered lab, and for a brief moment Kat saw the cramped space not as an office, but as a depressing, suffocating prison cell. She shuddered to think of living here, stuck in a dark corner of the galaxy, breathing canned air and eating synth food, never seeing real sunlight. *Of course* Howard would jump at any chance to break the monotony, and would be even more motivated if he thought something might present a way off this barren rock.

"So then what?" asked Jerry. "Did he call again later and fill you in?"

"No, I never heard from him again, as it turns out. But I didn't just sit on my hands while I waited for him to call back.

"That one call piqued my curiosity enough that I decided to track him down. I thought maybe if I could reach out to him again I could find out what he was up to.

"I have pretty broad access to the settlement's network, and one of the fringe benefits is being able to track internal station communications. When I discovered he'd called from a public booth in a transit station, I really got interested.

"I ran a core-level scan of all the settlement's network searches from the last two months involving ancient data disks or computers, and I found a treasure trove of inquiries conducted the day before he called me. The searches were all performed from a workstation in the National Archives building that houses this planetary system's operational records."

"National Archives?" asked Jerry.

"Yeah, think of it as the local City Hall. Even without a planetary regulatory body, these operations still need to keep records, file paperwork, and maintain a support system for tens of thousands of workers. The Archives houses all that paperwork, along with historical records, the original planetary scientific surveys, you name it.

"But the Archives has its own set of security protocols, and I hit a wall. No way to find which of the several hundred employees made the inquiries."

"But you persevered and eventually hit paydirt," said Kat.

"Sadly, no," chuckled Howard. "I actually gave up. But I guess the Universe had other ideas.

"Two days ago, an article in the local newsfeed caught my eye – actually, it caught Suzie's eye. She pointed it out to me. It mentioned a run-of-the-mill burglary that tragically resulted in the death of the dwelling's resident, but the last paragraph said that the deceased was an employee at the Archives building. They identified him as one Hector Belasky."

"You said there are hundreds of employees there," said Jerry. "That's a pretty weak link, at best."

"Until I dug into the network and scanned his emails. The fellow had been religious about deleting his messages, but a glitch in the system allows an administrator to see the subject lines of trashed emails. I found several messages with the title, 'Re: Disk'."

"He was looking to sell the disk," said Kat.

"I think so. And I think he found someone. One of the messages was entitled 'Offer attached'. I think it was from a broker, maybe a middleman of some kind."

"Then it's got to be long-gone by now, Howard. No one would sit on something like this."

"I might agree, except my guy had one final unread email titled, 'Re Friday meeting'. It came in on Thursday afternoon, the day he was killed.

"He missed that meeting, obviously, and I think the disk was never delivered, and all we have to do is find out where he stashed it. If we can do that, we'll all be richer than God."

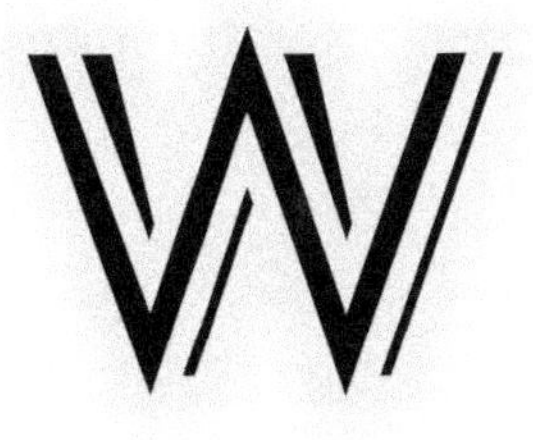**HEN KAT AND JERRY** returned to the Port Hangar complex, their ship's location showed as 3 levels up and about half a kilometer away.

"I suppose we should be grateful that they at least parked us on the same asteroid," grumbled Kat, leaning against the handrail on the moving walkway.

"I don't think a lot of private craft come through this place," said Jerry. "Most visitors likely arrive on commercial transports. They probably stuck us somewhere that's not in the way of the cargo vessels this facility is designed for."

Their ship was easy to spot when they finally arrived at the right section. It was the only craft in sight.

"At least we don't have to worry about noisy neighbours," said Kat.

Jerry set the cat carrier down and opened its door. Batman dashed out and ran over to the ship, then stopped in front of the entry hatch and turned to look back at them.

"I see someone's ready for his own bed," said Kat.

"That's for sure. And apparently, Batman is, too."

"I've never actually owned a whole solar system before," said Kat, dangling her feet over the edge of the hot tub. "It might be cool."

"Be careful what you wish for, babe," said Jerry, handing Kat one of the two highball glasses he carried, before carefully stepping into the tub and sliding down opposite her. "The sums of money we're talking about will bring the nastiest kinds of vipers out of their hidey-holes. We already know at least one person has been murdered—"

"Maybe…."

"—*Probably* murdered over it. I'm not eager to join that club. It's not like we need the money."

"Since when are you such a pussy, Jer? Time was, you'd be champing at the bit to toss your hat into the ring."

Mistakenly thinking that he was the pussy being discussed, Batman jumped onto the edge of the tub and looked expectantly at Kat. She giggled and reached out a soapy hand to scratch him behind the ears, but seeing the foamy appendage heading his way, he expertly ducked her grasp and scampered back onto the floor. He took up residence on the bathmat, safely out of reach, and began defiantly licking his fur.

"*That's* what kind of pussy I am, Kat. I see danger coming and I run away. Just like Batman, I prefer to keep soap suds off my fur. Life is too short to be drawn into reckless adventures. And besides – wasn't it you just a few short hours ago who was bitching about being thrust into life-threatening situations?"

"But that was before I had the opportunity to own my very own planetary system, Jer! I get to tick off another box on my Bucket List!"

"Owning a solar system was on your Bucket List?"

"It is now! And all I need is a teensy-weensy bit of help from you to make my dream come true!"

"So now it's a 'dream', is it? Well, you can dream this dream alone. Batman and I are going to sit this one out. And just like him, I'm going to completely ignore any of your entreaties. We cats are immune to your manipulations."

Kat laughed scornfully.

"Batman will get his comeuppance, Jer, and so will you. Don't forget, I know your weaknesses."

"And what might those be?"

"Well, for Batman it's smoked salmon. But yours is far more… primal," she said, and giggled as she climbed onto his lap, splashing a tidal wave of water and soap suds over the edge and onto the floor. The cat leapt out of the way and skittered across the tile, mere inches from being drenched.

"Oof," grunted Jerry, as Kat settled onto him. "Watch the drink, hon. Vodka doesn't grow on trees, you know."

"Oh, I don't know about that," she murmured, nuzzling his lips with her own. "Once we find this disk we'll have enough money to plant a whole orchard of vodka trees. Whaddaya say, Jerry baby, are you sure there isn't *some* way I can convince you to help me out here?"

As they sank lower in the water, Kat's mouth breathing hot and heavy in his ear, Jerry sighed and closed his eyes in resignation. He may not want to get soap suds on his fur, he reflected, but the prospect of the tongue bath that was sure to follow was simply too tempting to resist.

PART II:

TREASURE HUNT

The game is afoot.
– Sherlock Holmes

"First things first, Kat," said Jerry, reclining on the couch in their ship's lounge. "We need to see the police report for Belasky's murder. I'm not walking into this thing blind."

"Way ahead of you, boss," said Kat as she scratched Batman under his chin while he lolled on his cat tree. "I've already downloaded it along with all the crime scene photos and the lab reports. You'd think a law enforcement organization would have better security, but their system looks like it was set up by a high school student."

"This is just an isolated mining colony on the edge of the galaxy, Kat. Breaking up bar fights between drunk miners doesn't exactly qualify as top-secret operations. I'll bet this murder is the first serious crime this settlement has had to deal with in years."

"I'm sending the data to the wall screen, Jer."

Judging by the paucity of information in the file, the investigation into the archivist's death had been cursory, at best. The entire report was a page and a half of text and six photographs, mostly of the dead body.

"Apparently," said Kat, "the cops took one look at the scene and concluded it was a simple break-and-enter gone bad. Bet they made it back to the donut shop before their coffees even got cold."

"That's what puzzles me, Kat. You'd think they would be all excited about a break in the monotony. If I were the investigating detectives, I'd be taking this thing apart right down to the molecular level."

Kat frowned as she examined a data screen on her Slimlines.

"I think I might have an explanation for their lack of interest, Jerry. According to their personnel reports, the so-called 'detectives' on this case are just two elderly security guards culled from the local mining companies. It looks like they're still on the mining consortium's payroll, even. That would account for their sleepwalking through this case. Probably just killing time until retirement."

"It might even go deeper than that, Kat. I think I may be smelling a rat."

"What do you mean?"

"Well, we know the mining companies would rather leave the ownership of the system unresolved, right? And what better way to bury an investigation that might turn up inconvenient evidence than to assign it to two old coots whose primary loyalty lies with the people who sign their paycheques?"

"You're a cynical man, my friend."

"Cynicism is the last refuge of the optimist, Kat. I live my life expecting people to act as humans have always acted – driven by self-interest and greed – and they rarely prove me wrong. But I still hope for the best."

Kat shook her head sadly.

"What a bleak world you must live in, Jerry."

Getting up from the couch, Jerry grabbed Kat around the waist, then spun her around and pushed her down onto a pile of pillows on the floor.

Collapsing down onto her and moving his hands up under her tank top, he growled into her ear, "Oh, I don't know about that, baby. It's not so bleak when I have these to grab onto…."

Giggling, Kat turned her head and bit Jerry on his earlobe.

"I think I can feel some of that cynical optimism pressing up against me. I'm so happy I can help you with your hopeful outlook."

"See? What did I tell you, Kat? Things are looking up already."

**AT TOYED IDLY** with her espresso, pushing the tiny cup around in little circles, watching the inky liquid shimmer in iridescent colours. Jerry, focusing intently on the data pad he held, looked up and opened his mouth as though to speak, only to drop his eyes back to the screen and return to his study.

They were sitting in a little café opposite the National Archives building. Nestled in a utilitarian, grungy area of the settlement populated with various commercial sites and eateries, the tall grey building dominated the block and loomed heavily over them.

Kat watched a team of workmen erecting a gigantic colour banner over the front entrance of the Archives building. Reaching at least fifteen meters up, it displayed a curious, strangely-pixelated image of some unidentified planetary landscape. Bold text beneath the image breathlessly announced:

GRAND GALA OPENING
MYSTERIES OF THE UNIVERSE REVEALED

There was a date mentioned, which Kat recognised as this Friday, four days hence.

There was little other activity in front of the building, owing perhaps to another sign by the main entrance – this one considerably smaller – displaying the message:

ARCHIVES TEMPORARILY CLOSED
DURING ART INSTALLATION

Which had thrown a wrench into their plans. Without access to the building, their investigation had ground to a halt. Jerry, refusing to give up, had insisted they park themselves here until he could divine a means of accessing the offices.

Kat sighed, drained her espresso, and swept her eyes over the little café.

All the café's other patrons were Archives employees. The ID badges dangling from shirt pockets or lanyards advertised their association with the building across the street, but Kat could have picked every one of them out of a crowd regardless. The dead eyes, earth-tone clothing and listless demeanour all screamed "civil servant" in unmistakable clarity. Conversing *sotto voce* in small groups of two or three, heads bent together over little round tables, they imparted an air of mystery to what was surely nothing but banal workplace conversations.

Kat allowed herself to imagine them as dangerous revolutionaries plotting treason and various other nefarious criminal activities. She wished one would suddenly spring from his chair, scream *"Death to Tyranny!"*, *"Rodina! Slava!"*, or some such patriotic slogan, and start shooting up the place. Which would set off all the other revolutionaries, plunging the coffee shop into utter, bloody chaos as guns were drawn and fired, people screamed, and furniture and windows shattered all around them.

Kat was playing out in her mind the various gunfights, overturned tables and women weeping over slain compatriots, when Jerry reached over and tapped her on her arm. Startled, she nearly jumped out of her chair.

"Geez, Kat, keep it together. What's gotten into you?"

"Why did you grab me like that?" asked Kat, heart in her mouth and pulse hammering.

"I've been trying to get your attention for the last twenty seconds. You were really lost in thought. I didn't mean to startle you."

Kat exhaled heavily and shut her eyes. When she opened them again she looked calm.

"It's not you, babe. I think the six espressos I've just had might be catching up with me."

"I warned you about knocking 'em back like that. I'm surprised your head hasn't literally exploded."

"But they're such teeny cups. And I didn't know we'd be here so long. Have you got any ideas yet?"

"No such luck. I'm coming up blank. But I think if we're patient, the Universe will show us a way."

"And why would the Universe do that for us, Jerry?"

"Because we're on the side of Right. You know – 'Truth, Justice, and the American Way'?"

"Now there's a phrase I never thought I'd hear from your lips."

"It's an inevitable consequence of a childhood spent reading Superman comics. I got a million of 'em – have you ever heard 'With great power comes great—' "

"Hold on a second there, Shakespeare," interrupted Kat. "I think the Universe is calling."

Jerry turned to look out the front window, just in time to see a young couple carrying an armful of books hesitantly approach the main door of the Archives building.

"Looks like students with a research assignment," commented Kat.

"Let's see how this plays out for them – we might try the same ploy," said Jerry.

They watched as the scene unfolded in pantomime: the students attempting to pull open the entrance doors; the inevitable interception by a security guard; the explanations; the entreaties; the useless waving of student IDs; the implacable refusals; the morose retreat.

"Well, strike that one off the list of possible tactics," said Kat.

As the students were walking away they ran headfirst into a gaggle of chattering visitors coming from the opposite direction. Many wore white lab coats. They walked past the students and directly up to the main entrance, where the security guard once again began his routine. But this time something changed.

One of the visitors at the front of the line produced a letter from his breast pocket and handed it to the security guard, who read it carefully, then nodded, and finally pulled open the door and reluctantly moved to the side. He looked disappointed. The stream of visitors slowly began to move into the building.

"This is our chance, Kat. Let's roll."

Jerry hustled across the street with Kat fast-walking behind him trying to keep up. They smoothly inserted themselves into the line just as a few stragglers caught up and joined the group, falling in behind Kat.

"Ooh, can I take a look at that for a sec? I left mine at home. Thanks ever so much," said Kat to the man in line behind her, and gently pulled a colourful conference brochure from his hands. Bending their heads together over the brochure, murmuring quietly, Kat and Jerry moved with the line and stepped past the security guard and through the entrance.

"Thanks again," said Kat, handing the brochure back. She grabbed Jerry by the arm and dragged him over to the side.

"I hate to break it to you, Tonto, but it looks like that was the easy part. Check it out." And she indicated with her chin the Registration desk where the visitors were heading.

A large sign beside the desk announced, in bold red letters:

NO PUBLIC ADMITTANCE

Beneath it hung the qualification:

CONFERENCE ATTENDEES ONLY
IDENTIFICATION REQUIRED

"Piece of cake, baby. I got this."

Kat raised an eyebrow. "You sound confident."

"I've been wanting to try this one out for ages, Kat. And this looks like the perfect opportunity. Check out the girl they've got staffing the desk. Can't be more than 22 or 23 years old, poor child. Probably some post-grad Student Intern. This might be her first real job. Look how earnest she is."

"And you think that's a good thing?"

"In this case, yes. Pay attention and maybe you can try it someday yourself when you're all growed-up like me."

Kat gave him a little kick in the shin, then whispered, "Lead on, MacDuff. I'm ready to be schooled."

Jerry and Kat reinserted themselves into the line, Kat smiling warmly at the man who had lent her his brochure.

"Name, academic affiliation and identification, please," the young woman at the desk intoned to the person at the front of the line as Kat and Jerry drew within earshot. Her manner was stern and commanding. Her hair was pulled back and knotted in a tight bun, her nails were short, and she wore an understated business suit that advertised her serious personality.

The answers were provided, the information was entered, and a badge was produced. The next person in line stepped up and the cycle began anew. The process was quick and efficient. The line was moving rapidly. One man fumbled with his ID and received a sharp rebuke from the desk.

"Uh-oh," whispered Kat. "This really doesn't look good. You may have bitten off more than you can chew here. This girl ain't taking shit from no one."

"O ye of little faith. Just watch."

Jerry stepped up to the desk and the attendant looked up expectantly.

"Name, academic affiliation and identification, please!" she said unsmilingly. She obviously expected not to have to ask, having demanded the same three questions of every single previous person.

Jerry smiled broadly and exclaimed in a booming voice, "Yuss. Nimm. Ees Boris. Professor Boris Badenov. Und zees ees koligg Professor Fatale. Natasha Fatale.

"From Rossian Institute. Een glorious Rossian peeninsoola

of Kamchatka. Yu are fommeelyar with wodka, maybe? Kamchatka Wodka femmous through gellexy."

The girl at the desk lost a beat, for the first time since they'd seen her.

"… I'm sorry? Do you mean 'vodka'? — I mean, no, sorry. Um, let's start over. Name…?" She looked hopeful.

Jerry's ebullient demeanour seemed to deflate a slight bit. "BO. REES. BOREES."

Her fingers paused midair above her keyboard. "Um, you mean 'Boris'? With an 'I'?"

"YUSS. BOREES. Should not be so deefeecolt. Ees vurry common Rossian name. Yu are fommeelyar weeth Borees the Great – glorious Grand Prince of Tver? In fourteen hondreds?"

"Er, ah, yes. Of course," she lied.

"Gudd. Ees spilled same way."

If that bit of news was meant to help, it appeared to have the opposite effect. But the young woman drew on her training and soldiered on. Hoping the hardest part was behind her, she said, "Wonderful. And your last name?"

"Badenov. Ees not so common as Borees. Weel spill. BEE. HAY. DEE. EE. HENN. OH. WE."

The fingers paused midair again. It was a pity. Things had been going so well.

"Um, is that 'WE' – I mean 'V' – or is that 'W'?"

Jerry looked offended.

"Ees not 'WE' – ees *'WE'* – as in 'WODKA'."

"You mean wod— that is, *vodka*. With a 'V'. Right?"

"Yuss. Wott else yu spilling wodka weeth? Three x's mebbe?" And he guffawed uproariously, as though he'd just heard the funniest joke of his life.

There was considerably less good humour in the line behind them, Kat noted. A few impatient grumbling noises filtered up to her, along with some irritated coughing and the sound of feet shuffling in place.

"Und now, weel geev yu nimm of kollig. Professor Fatale."

Kat peeked around from behind Jerry's shoulders and glared at the girl, and then at Jerry. Before she could say anything, Jerry said, "Weel spikk for hurr. Kollig Fatale not spikking Hinglish yet."

Leaning closer to the desk, he added conspiratorially, "Ees a bit slow, but has incredible body. Was gymnast, yu know. But now ees scientist. Zees ees wott hoppen when only breenging home bronze medal."

The girl blinked at him, trying to parse the wealth of information he had just imparted. She quickly glanced at Kat, who was still glowering from over Jerry's shoulder.

"Ah, you know, Professor Badenov, perhaps this might go a bit more smoothly if I could see your ID – I can just enter your credentials directly from that. No need for any more spill— I mean, spelling."

"Yuss. Ees gudd idea. I geev." Jerry pulled out his wallet and began shuffling through an endless stack of cards tucked into its folds, and eventually extracted a bent brown card embossed with two names. There was absolutely no other information on the card.

He handed it to the young woman, who gingerly accepted it from him as though he were handing her a shred of Kleenex that he'd found on the subway. She examined it carefully and turned it over to look at the back, which was gloriously devoid of any markings.

"Um, well," she said, and was about to voice a criticism when she glanced at the long line of disgruntled conference-goers waiting behind Jerry.

"This will do fine," she said, rapidly typing the name Natasha Fatale into her system. She shuddered as she contemplated what miseries of Hell might have been in store for her had she needed him to spell it.

"But, oh, oh dear," she stuttered. "The system won't let me

enter your names without an academic affiliation. You know –
your Institute or University, or whatever you call it…."

She blinked up at Jerry in terror.

"Hoff course. Ees vurry well known Univursity. Ees
Wossamatta U. In Kamchatka."

"Right. In Kamchatka. Of course it is. Um… can you,
I mean, do you think you might…." The words seemed to
catch in her throat, but there was no way around it. "Um, that
is, can you spell it?"

"Spill which? 'Kamchatka' or 'Wossamatta U'?"

"Um, 'Wossamatta'. I think I can handle the 'U' part okay."
And she squeezed out a weak little smile.

"Ha! Ees leetle joke! Am liking yu vurry moch, yong leddy.
Hoff course I can spill.

"DOBBLE-YOU. HAY. ESS. ESS. HAY—"

"Oh dear, I'm so sorry to interrupt." The girl was so
unnerved she was biting her lower lip, which made it hard to
understand what she was saying. "I mean, you said the second
letter is an 'A', yes? So you must mean 'wassa', not 'wussa'."

"Ees wott I said. 'WOSSA'."

"WOSSA," repeated the girl.

"NO. Not 'wossa'. *WOSSA*," said Jerry sternly.

"Wassa?" attempted the girl.

"Yes! 'WOSSA'!" answered Jerry.

"Now," he continued, "for second word. Spilled—"

It was the proverbial straw breaking the camel's back. The
girl seemed to crumble in front of him.

"I think I have it," she blurted out quickly. " 'Matta', right?
EM AY TEE TEE AY?"

"Ees perfect," said Jerry in a warm, glowing tone. "Yu mosst
be part Rossian, ham I right? So smart.

"And byootifull, too," he added, in a low growling voice.
"Like Siberian snow angel."

"Ah, yes, thank you. No, no, I mean, I'm beautiful, not

Russian – oh, I didn't mean that – I meant—"

"Ees hokay," said Jerry, leering. "Am onderstanding."

By now the discontented grumbling behind Kat had reached a crescendo, and several Archives employees were looking over in concern. The young lady at the desk looked around frantically, but no help was in sight. She was not used to dissention in the ranks. Up until now, she had commanded this desk with absolute mastery, and in five short minutes everything was falling to shit. The line behind Kat continued to grow longer and noisier.

"Right," said the poor girl, determined to persevere. "Well, now I just need – oh my God – I need… your university's address…."

"Ees no problem," said Jerry. "Ees 14000 Zelenaya Roschka, Krasnoznamenk District, Pervomaiskoe Kottedzhnyy province, Kamchatka, Rossia. Are yu needing zeep code, too?"

Before the stunned girl could reply, Kat stuck her head around Jerry's shoulder again and barked, "Nyet! Eto utilsy adres! Skazi im adres pochtovyy!"

Jerry turned to face Kat, and they started loudly arguing, shouting a lot of foreign-sounding phrases at each other. Jerry was certain that at least half the things he said, he'd read on restaurant menus. Finally, their argument ceased and Jerry looked apologetically at the desk attendant.

"Kollig says yu should haff melling heddress. I geev yu stritt heddress. Ham so sorry."

Looking directly at the girl, Kat rapidly called out, "Ul'yanovskogo Lesoparka, Dzerzhinsky, Vysokinichi Okrug." And then, after a momentary pause, "Rossia."

"Perhopps am geeving yu both heddresses, am theenking ees better idea," said Jerry. "Should I spill?"

At the thought of trying to type even one of the two addresses, a synapse deep within the girl's brain sent a white-hot shaft of pain coursing through her frontal lobe.

"You know what," she said, smiling at Jerry, "I think we're okay here. *Yes.* We have all the information we need. Why don't you two just take these badges" – she grabbed two blank ID cards from a little stack on her desk and frantically pressed them into Jerry's open hand – "and you can fill them out yourselves. There's even room at the bottom for you to add an email address and phone number, if you wish. Go nuts."

Leaning far to the side and craning her neck, she called out loudly, "Next!"

Jerry looked like he was about to say something, but Kat forcefully pushed him away from the desk and into the inner foyer.

" 'Boris and Natasha'?" she asked, once they were out of earshot. "And why would you even have a business card with those names on it?"

"First rule of the game, Kat: Be prepared, and make sure you can remember what you say. I can remember those names."

"I can't believe she didn't recognise the reference," said Kat.

"Well, she might have, if her boyfriend were 250 years old and made her watch cartoons every Saturday morning, but more likely her cultural knowledge doesn't include anything before the 23rd century. I could probably have said Donald and Daisy Duck, for that matter, but I don't have a card with those names on it."

"Oops! Look out, Jerry. Someone's trying to get past."

Jerry turned to see a group of men carefully wheeling a towering display through the foyer. It was several meters tall and wide, composed of two gigantic sheets of plexiglass sandwiching thousands of coloured marbles. The men wheeled it toward the back of the building's tall atrium of a dozen open floors overlooking the foyer, with a waist-high protective railing stretching across each one.

Guy wires descended from the roof and dangled against the display, where two men in cherry pickers worked attaching the wires to hooks embedded in the top of the display.

"Say, excuse me," said Jerry, stopping a passing Archives employee. "What is that?"

"You don't know? Oh, right – you must be from off-asteroid. Here for the conference. Right.

"Well, that," he continued, suffused with pride, "is the result of sixteen long years of painstaking work by one of the Archive's most valuable employees. It's a combination of artwork and stellar cartography. Every one of those little glass balls is sitting in its own tiny cradle, and when an electrical current is applied, they rotate to display star maps and scenes from across the galaxy. Some of the images are quite breathtaking, I'm told. People will often stand and watch for hours, spellbound, when it's activated."

"It doesn't look like much now," said Jerry. "Sort of like an early Jackson Pollock before he figured out what he was doing."

"Just wait till it's turned on," said the man. "We're extremely lucky to have it. It may be one of the most valuable pieces of 22nd century art in existence."

"What's it doing here, then?" asked Jerry. "I mean, let's face it – this rock isn't exactly known as a cultural mecca in the galaxy. No offense."

"None taken. As I said, we're lucky to have it. But when the artist died – somewhere around forty years ago, I believe – his Will required that the piece be disassembled and the glass balls scrambled. And if each ball isn't in exactly the precise location, the piece won't work at all. Just sits there, dead."

"Like a string of Christmas tree lights with one burnt-out bulb, am I right?" chuckled Jerry.

The man looked at him blankly.

"Ah, sure, if you say so…. But as I was saying, the piece needed to be painstakingly reassembled after the artist's death. I think it was his way of ensuring that only a truly dedicated institution would be able to display his work. But no museum or gallery had the resources necessary to reconstruct it.

"Aside from their unique coloured mottling, the balls have no distinct identifying marks – no numbers or grid locations on them. The only way to restore the artwork was by examining a single existing photograph of the piece as it looked before it was dismantled, and then matching each individual marble with the marbles in the image."

"Shut up!" exclaimed Kat, eyes wide in amazement. "That would be like doing the world's hardest jigsaw puzzle, only a thousand times worse!"

"Precisely," said the man. "And we were the only institution willing to undertake the task. As I said, it's been sixteen long, painstaking years of tedious work, all performed by one man, often working twelve and thirteen-hour days."

"Bet he really appreciated those extra three hours of sleep," said Kat, prodding Jerry with her elbow.

"He thought he had it finished several times in the past, but each time we tried to activate it: nothing. Finally, three months ago, it came to life. And now we're about to reveal it to the public for the first time in almost half a century. It's going to be magnificent. We're going to lower it down from the upper storey and present it in all its glory before a crowd of several hundred VIPs from all over the galaxy."

"I wouldn't mind seeing that," said Jerry.

"Good luck. Tickets sold out weeks ago. In five minutes. And they cost several thousand credits each. This will be a huge jewel in our crown. The entire city is on edge."

The man directed one last admiring glance at the artwork as the workmen secured it to the guy wires, and then took his leave of them.

"I am *never* bitching about my job ever again, Jerry."

"What job?" asked Jerry, and received a sharp punch in the arm for it.

Kat pulled him over to a quiet alcove and whispered, "My Slimlines have access to the Archives' internal records, but most of the good stuff is firewalled. It's a tight system – they take their security seriously here. Even I might have trouble getting full access."

"They probably have their hands full managing the records of 300-odd mining companies and all their proprietary data. A data breach would be catastrophic. No wonder the system is locked up so tight."

"I think I've found something that might help us, though, Jer. It's a subdirectory with deleted internal information searches. The records are purged every thirty days, but I see an entry with our guy's name. Looks like he accessed Storage Repository 2711 – Original Settlement Blueprints."

"That could be where he found the disk itself. Either that, or information about where it's hidden."

"Or maybe he was following someone else's trail. We won't know until we access the box and the full set of records showing who's had access to that archive. If we're lucky."

Jerry walked over to a directory mounted on a wall beside an elevator.

"Looks like the Historical Records Department is on the third floor. Let's go. I feel lucky."

he Reception desk on the third floor was staffed by a much different creature than the attendant in the foyer.

Pushing sixty, with grey hair and spectacles hanging from a chain around her neck, she sat placidly behind her desk, greeting Kat and Jerry with a warm smile. Clearly, this was not someone who would be rattled by thick accents or fast talk. A small brass sign on her desk read "Clara Ridgeway – Archivist".

"Can I help you?" she asked, turning her gaze from the workmen along the railing who were tugging on the guy wires that descended from the roof.

Kat stepped forward and took the lead. Jerry discreetly backed away and disappeared into the stairwell beside the elevator.

"I hope so. I'm Theresa Smythe-Collins from Infrastructure and Environment – you know, over on Sixth Street across from the new maintenance depot," said Kat, eyes flickering behind her Slimlines.

"Yes, I know the building," replied Clara, still smiling.

"Well, we need to access some historical records from the early days – the original wastewater collection drain map. We might have a problem with a null-gravity purge outlet, and we need to see if there's a shunt that the original designers built in."

"That shouldn't be a problem," said Clara. Her smile was still frozen in place, but Kat sensed a fit of bureaucracy coming on. "You have the necessary paperwork with you, I assume."

"Ah, well, there's no time for that. All the clerical staff took the afternoon off – it's Heather Kraminsky's 50th birthday today and they absolutely insisted on taking the sweet dear out for drinks and cake, and what kind of monsters would we be if we said no to something like that – but where was I? Oh yes, so we didn't have anyone to prepare the paperwork and thought maybe you could let it go just this once, since it's a bit of an emergency – wouldn't want the toilets in Sector 17 to start flinging raw sewage into the tenants' faces, you know. And that's where the Mayor lives, of course. I'd hate to have to explain to him why he got a fecal shower when he only needed to take a leak...."

Kat stopped talking, and stood there blinking expectantly.

"I see…. Yes, it does sound like an emergency…." The old lady was pondering the situation, and suddenly brightened as she thought of a solution. "Maybe we can do this by phone – I think I know your supervisor. Crenshaw, isn't it?"

Kat's jaw was twitching furiously as her eyes flickered rapidly behind her glasses. "Um, yes – no, I mean, that *used* to be my boss, but he got a promotion. He's in… Conduit Replacement now. He was replaced by… ah, jeez, I'm sorry, I can never remember his name… OH! Good! I mean, yes, I have it now. Seguin! Maurice Seguin. I can give you his number if you like…."

"No, that's okay dear, I have it right here," said Clara, who had apparently already known that Crenshaw was long gone.

There's no grass growing under her feet, thought Kat. *The old biddy tried to trip me up. Shame on her.*

Kat heard the sound of a ring tone from the clerk's earpiece. When the call was answered, a faint echo of the respondent's voice could be heard from the stairwell behind Kat.

"Seguin here," the voice(s) said.

"Oh, hello, Mr. Seguin, this is Clara Ridgeway over in the Archives building and I think I have one of your operatives here with an information request."

"You mean Smythe-Collins?" came the gruff reply. "Tall redhead with an idiotic smile and ugly eyeglasses? Got more tits than brains, that one, I'm telling you. She causing trouble?"

"Oh, ah—" The old lady looked a bit rattled. "No, no. I'm just double-checking. She says it's an urgent matter and there's no time to generate proper paperwork."

"You bet your ass it's an urgent matter! And everyone else's ass, as well. We've got toilets shooting shit sky-high all over Sector 17. Drenched some lady's bathroom with enough raw sewage to fill a shuttle. At this point, the Claridge Building is basically a fountain of diarrhea. It started seeping into the hallways and now it's pouring in huge, godawful waves off the balconies, right onto the goddam sidewalk! Doorman got smacked on the head with a turd the size of a corncob. They had to evacuate the building. And over on 37th, they—"

"That's quite alright, Mr. Seguin, I get the idea. It does sound like an emergency. Thank you for your time."

Relieved to end the call, Clara looked at Kat apologetically. "I'm so sorry, dear. But we're good now. Let's get you that information."

"Terrific. According to my notes, it's supposed to be in Repository 2711, if that's any help."

The clerk tapped away on her console, and within seconds a plastic storage box whooshed into view, sliding along a conveyor belt behind her.

"Here you are," she said, handing the box over to Kat. "There are workrooms over to your right, where you can check your documents. You may take photographs, but nothing may be removed from the Archives.

"The box is electronically sealed. Take it into the workroom and place it on the table within the marked area and the box will unseal. When you're done, replace the lid on the box, and if its weight is exactly the same, the electronic seal will reactivate. Be very careful, the measurement is very sensitive, and even one gram of difference will activate the security alarms.

"Is there anything else? Um, didn't you have someone with you when you arrived?" She craned her neck to look at the stairwell where Jerry had disappeared.

"Yes, my secretary, Reese. I think he went to the bathroom – oh, here he is now. Come on, Reese! We're on a deadline here you know!"

Kat shot an exasperated look his way, then looked at Clara and rolled her eyes. "I'm telling you, Clara, it's just murder to find good help these days."

The path to the workroom took them past the workmen tugging and sweating as they guided the massive artwork to its new home. They were taking special care not to jostle the panels lest they inadvertently shake loose one of the glass balls. The sound of the winches on the top level could be heard faintly grinding as the heavy plexiglass panels inched upwards.

Jerry glanced over the railing at the foyer floor below. A nervous-looking man of about fifty – who appeared to be one heartbeat away from a massive myocardial infarction – paced rapidly back and forth in ever-smaller circles, jamming his knuckles into his mouth in a desperate attempt to hold on to his sanity.

"I think I see the guy who devoted the better part of two decades to assembling this thing, Kat."

"You mean the sweaty guy who looks like a family of weasels is loose in his pants?"

"That's the one. Someone needs to shoot him with a trank dart."

"Several darts, from the look of it."

They set their box down on a table in the workroom and began riffling through the contents. There were maps and blueprints and folders full of engineering specs, but no disk. Kat quickly fanned through the documents, letting her Slimlines scan each page, then dropped the folders back into the box.

"Damn!" swore Jerry. "No disk. I had high hopes."

"And according to my glasses, none of the documents mention any disk, or even offer hints about possible storage locations other than this facility."

"Look, Kat," said Jerry, pointing at a printout affixed to the inside of the open lid. "There's an inventory of this box and… Good Lord! Look at entry #14 – 'Data disk'! It *was* here! Belasky must have removed it. That's the only explanation."

"Unless he didn't actually remove it himself – he might have noticed the disk missing while he was doing other research."

"Then why would he claim to have the disk?"

"I'm not sure he ever did – Howard said he might only have known where the disk was. Maybe Belasky noticed the disk missing, checked the records, and found out who accessed the box before him."

"That would explain so much. He could have been killed because he was blackmailing the person who stole the disk."

"We need to find out who else accessed the box, Jer. We need to see the Archives access logs."

"I may be overly-pessimistic here, Kat, but I doubt Clara is going to share that information with you."

"Leave Clara to me. All I need is a glimpse at her monitor. My Slimlines will do the rest. But if I strike out, I'll need you to cause a small distraction. Ready?"

"Is this where I say I was born ready?"

"Only if you want me to throw up. Let's go."

Kat and Jerry left the workroom and headed back to Clara's desk. When Kat stopped to hand the box back to the archivist, Jerry kept walking and disappeared again into the stairwell.

"If they paid that fellow just for the time he spends in the bathroom he could retire today," she said grimly.

Clara nodded sadly.

"We have one like that in Acquisitions. I think he's on the drugs," Clara said quietly. "No one needs to spend that much time in the restroom."

As Clara recorded the return of the box before sending it back to its storage place, Kat sidled over to the edge of the desk, then casually leaned over to peer at the monitor.

Clara immediately spun the monitor away from Kat's view.

"Oh, sorry. I didn't mean to peek. Just bored, I guess."

"That's okay, dear," said Clara, in tones that indicated it was anything but okay. "But we keep a tight grip on security here. Information is very powerful, you know."

"So true," said Kat, then made a small movement with her jaw.

She wandered over to the railing overlooking the atrium and looked down at all the upturned faces. The top of the artwork had drawn even with the fourth-floor railing now, and the workmen were steadying it to prevent it from swaying.

"Look out!" screamed a voice from the floor.

"Oh my God!"

"NO!"

"Catch it!"

Kat looked over to the artwork, and saw that one of the guy wires had snapped. Its truncated end dangled limply just above the sixth-floor railing.

The artwork swung away crazily to the side, supported by only one wire at its left corner, then came crashing back toward the workmen, who made the tragic error of trying to catch it and arrest its momentum. The grasping, flailing hands only served to increase the artwork's runaway momentum, and it swung drunkenly inward, pulled by the workers. When they lost hold of it, it swung back outward, dangled momentarily in midair far above the horrified spectators below, and then swung

violently back towards the workers, who ran screaming from the impending crash. In the blink of an eye, the artwork impacted sickeningly with the third-floor railing and broke apart.

An explosion of little glass balls engulfed the third-floor walkway directly beneath the artwork's shattered base. Marbles bounced off the railing and the floor, skittering into open doorways, and showering down onto the crowd of shrieking observers on the main floor. A technicolor tidal wave of glass balls cascaded down the open walkway where Kat stood, and washed over her feet.

"CATCH THEM!" shouted voices from the main floor. "Don't let them fall! If they shatter it's the end! Someone catch them!"

"O Lord have mercy!" shrieked Clara, bounding from her desk and running to the railing. She fell to her knees and scooped up handfuls of marbles. Dozens of other people burst out of doorways and frantically grabbed at the bouncing, rolling maelstrom of coloured glass beads.

Kat quietly sidled up to the now abandoned reception desk, twisted the monitor 180°, then methodically scrolled down the page. She tapped an entry, expanding it to display a list of names and dates.

Spinning the monitor back around with a grim smile, she moved toward the stairwell, where Jerry was just appearing, slipping his Swiss Army Laser back into his pants pocket.

"This is your idea of a 'small distraction', is it, Jer? Or were you just pissed you couldn't get tickets to the grand gala opening?"

"I am wounded that you would think me so petty. You asked for a distraction, did you not?"

Jerry strode over to the reception desk, yanked open several drawers, and grunted in satisfaction. He pulled out a glossy sheet of paper and tucked it into his suit jacket, then grabbed Kat's arm and fast-walked her back to the stairwell.

They trotted down the stairs and stepped into the foyer on the main floor, where the scene was even grimmer than they had expected.

A frantic crowd of people was scooping up little glass balls and feeling around under chairs and tables. Two women and one elderly man had fainted straight away. Workers leapt over their prone bodies, grabbing at bouncing glass balls still dripping from the upper levels. Terrified, several Archives employees and a dozen conference attendees were stampeding for the building exit, unsure what had just happened but not wanting to stick around and find out. The Registration desk was unattended, an upended chair lying abandoned at its base. Blank ID badges littered the floor around it. The young lady was nowhere to be seen.

The nervous man Jerry had seen earlier was openly weeping, frozen in place while the crowd surged around him. His howls of misery echoed eerily through the atrium like the wailing of a ghostly apparition.

"Look what you've done to that poor man," said Kat accusingly as they picked their way through the hysterical masses.

"You mean 'given him new purpose in life'? His job was over, Kat. He was probably due to get the gold watch the day after the unveiling. He should be happy. He has new job security. At least for the next sixteen years."

"Maybe he should send you a thank-you note."

"At the very least. But I'm happy to toil in anonymity. It's my mission in life to improve the lot of the little people."

"**C**HINESE!**"** called Jerry, as he and Kat burst into Howard's lab, their arms full of steaming little boxes.

"Won Tons! Spring Rolls! Moo Goo Gai Pan! Kung Pao Tofu! Szechuan Broccoli! General Tso Rice!"

"And cold beer!" added Kat.

"Lo Mein! And Mongolian—"

"Jerry! STOP!" yelled Howard.

Kat and Jerry froze. Howard stood up.

"You had me at 'Chinese'," he said softly.

Twenty minutes later, as the last won ton disappeared into Suzie's mouth, the little group of diners exhaled an enormous collective sigh and flopped back in their chairs.

"Wow. I didn't realize I was so hungry, until you guys showed up," said Suzie, burping.

"We figured," said Kat. "Jerry and I do that, too – get so lost in our work we forget all about eating."

"Then you must have built up quite the appetite today, considering what you two have been up to," said Howard.

Jerry lifted his eyebrows in mock innocence. "I'm sure I have no idea what you mean, Howard."

"Oh, really? If this isn't your handiwork I'm a fairy princess." Spinning his desk monitor around, Howard displayed a full-screen article from the settlement's news feed, topped with a huge black headline reading, "TRAGEDY AT ARCHIVES BUILDING". Several smaller headlines below it announced various other tidbits of information, such as "Mysterious perpetrators still at large", "Utilities Manager held for questioning", and "Russian embassy placed on lockdown".

"It says here," continued Howard, "that whoever sabotaged the Archive's art installation – sixteen years in the making, they claim – infiltrated their network and removed themselves from the security video feed, wiping all traces from the system.

"They have a variety of witness reports about several suspicious individuals, but none of them match. Conflicting theories place the blame on: the Russians; rival museums; a rogue civil servant from the Infrastructure Division; even disgruntled Archives employees. But I think I might have a more likely pair of suspects in mind.'""

"Alright, Howard, you got me. But you must have expected something like this might be necessary. You can't make an omelet without breaking a few eggs, you know."

"A few eggs! Jerry, you didn't just break 'a few eggs' – you slaughtered all the chickens, destroyed the henhouse, and then burned the farm to the ground! I told you we had to be discreet."

"For Jerry, this *is* discreet," said Kat.

"Oh really, Kat?" asked Jerry. "This from the woman who caused an entire planet to be evacuated because she thought they were being cruel to a species of bloodthirsty carnivorous beasts? 'Hello Kettle? The Pot's calling – it's for you.'"

"Hey, hey," interjected Suzie. "Everyone take a breath. Okay, Howie, maybe things spun a bit out of control today, but the results are probably worth it. I'm betting Kat and Jerry got a lot of very valuable information from the Archives – and the end justifies the means, right?

"So tell us, guys," she said, turning to Kat and Jerry, "what did you learn today? Do you know where the disk is?"

"Um, no…" said Kat.

"Oh. Okay. Well, you must know who has it, then, right?"

"Ah," began Jerry. "well, we certainly have a good lead on that...."

Crestfallen, Howard and Suzie glanced at each other and sighed.

"But it's a process," said Kat. " 'Little by little, the bird builds its nest', right? 'Rome wasn't built in a day', and all that stuff. Jerry and I know the way forward, and we'll have a fix on that disk's location in the next day or so."

"Really?" said Howard hopefully, noticeably brightening.

"Well, maybe," said Jerry. "But that's a *strong* maybe, Howard. Trust me."

ATCHING THE changing numbers on the apartment elevator's display, Jerry looked smug.

"This is perfect timing, Kat. The police should be long gone by now. And management here in the building will surely have removed the police tape and seals, so we should have Belasky's apartment all to ourselves."

"I hope you're right, Jer. But we can't afford to take our time – my glasses have been picking up some chatter on the local net about a certain disk. I don't think our little secret is too secret anymore."

"As long as everyone else is one step behind us, it won't matter. Here, this is our floor."

As they stepped off the elevator Kat swore softly and tapped the side of her glasses with a fingernail.

"What's wrong?" asked Jerry.

"I can't see for shit," replied Kat. "The cops have doused this hallway in chemicals – they must have sprayed it from top to bottom in light-reactive liquids. Probably looking for traces of blood, DNA, even old-fashioned fingerprints. All the residue is wreaking havoc on my glasses. Everywhere I look is a mad kaleidoscope of psychedelic colours. This hallway looks like Walt Disney threw up all over it. I'm going to have to go analog. I'll be as blind as you."

"What a tragedy," answered Jerry, with not a little sarcasm. "However will you function? Should I take your hand and lead you?"

"Not funny, Jer."

"Sorry, babe. I'm just trying to be empathetic."

"How about I jam my fingers into both your eyes and lead *you*? How empathetic would you feel then?"

"Now, now. There's no need for violence. We still have a long way to go yet in the realm of clever repartee."

"When you finally think of something clever, be sure to let me know. In the meantime, can we please just get back on task?"

"Aye-aye, Captain," said Jerry, scanning the door numbers along the hallway.

They got to the number they were looking for and Jerry stopped and turned to Kat with a self-satisfied expression. But Kat was preoccupied, tucking away her glasses.

"Here we are, and looky-looky: no police seal. Looks like our timing is perfect. Just like I predicted."

Kat was still fussing with her glasses, so Jerry slapped his hand against the door to get her attention. He nearly lost his balance as the door swung wide open and smacked with a thud against the wall.

Immediately a voice boomed out from inside.

"WHO'S THERE?"

Kat and Jerry looked at each other in panic, unsure how to react. Before they could decide, a head came into view at the far end of the unit's entrance passageway, peering around the wall in a distinctly challenging manner.

"Yes? Who are you?" asked the head.

"Agh, well, ah…" stuttered Jerry, flailing for a suitable response.

The head, smelling a rat, adopted a suspicious demeanour.

"Look here, this is private property. I don't know what you're up to, but I assure you that Building Security is only the touch of a button away. Please leave now."

"No, no – please don't do that," said Kat quickly, pushing past Jerry and moving down the passageway toward their inquisitor. "We don't mean any trouble. It's just that, well,

I don't want to seem morbid, but a friend of mine lives in the building and heard about the recent tragedy… that poor man… brutally cut down by a thief in the night… in his own home, for goodness' sake…."

By now Kat had made her way to the end of the little hallway. The body beneath the talking head moved into view, and Jerry – who had followed Kat like a duckling trailing its mother – could now see the man they were talking to.

His face was round and flushed with a ruddy glow. His greying, receding hairline was still making a valiant attempt at concealing the bulk of his head, but it was waging a losing battle. He was in rolled-up shirtsleeves and open collar. On the living room couch Jerry spied a suit jacket and tie. The man was breathing a little heavily, as though he had been interrupted in the midst of exertion, and small patches of sweat dampened his shirt. It appeared that he had been searching the apartment.

"Yes, a terrible trag—" began the man, but Kat continued jabbering a mile a minute, bulldozing over his words.

"And when I heard about this unspeakable violation of personal space, well, let me tell you, I was heartbroken, to think about how horrible things have gotten, where we can't even feel safe in our own homes anymore…."

As Kat barged into the apartment, the man joined Jerry in the helpless baby duck routine, reduced to following her as she swept past.

"And I said to my fiancé here – oh, this is Trevor. Say hello Trevor." Without pausing to allow even so much as a peep from Jerry, she continued. "Where was I? Oh yes, I said to Trevor, 'Trevor, we really must go down to that poor man's apartment and say a cleansing prayer. His spirit may be trapped there, in that pit of murderous violence and mayhem.' "

"Well, I wouldn't exactly call it a pit of murd—" said the man, only to slip once again beneath the wheels of Kat's madly careening verbal bus.

"And here we are, ready to say our prayer, and what a beautiful space it is! I mean, look at that light! Those windows! Such an abundance of ethereal rays from blessed Father Sun!"

Jerry and the man turned their eyes to the far wall, where a shred of daylight anemically bled through a grimy pair of lucite windowpanes.

"Why, this whole space just cries out to me, 'Welcome! Welcome my children!'"

Kat spun in a circle, her face lifted to the ceiling, arms stretched out in glorious luxuriance.

"Yes. Well…" said the man, not quite sure how to proceed now that Kat had finally lapsed into silence.

"In fact," she said, relieving him of the burden of carrying the conversation, "I think I might enjoy living here myself. I assume the space is … shall we say… 'available' for new tenants?"

Kat blinked enticingly, then held him in her gaze, standing wide-eyed and smiling.

The penny dropped.

A look of comprehension came over the man's features. He rolled his eyes to heaven and said, "Oh, curse me for a fool! You're just looking to rent this place! And the previous tenant not yet even cold in his casket!

"I swear to all the planets and stars, you apartment vultures are going to drive me mad!

"I'm sorry," he said, turning to Jerry, whom he hoped to be the more reasonable – and sane – of this interloping couple, "but this place isn't available for rent yet. It hasn't even been cleaned!"

Jerry glanced around the apartment. Sure enough, everything looked as though the resident had just stepped out to get a jug of milk. There were a couple of dirty dishes in the sink, and a coffee cup on the counter. A cactus sat in quiet repose beside a small picture frame holding an ancient yellowed photograph of an equally ancient couple. Probably someone's parents. A small digital magnet on the refrigerator door beamed out an enthusiastic electronic message:

HELLO MONDAY! A BEAUTIFUL NEW WEEK HAS BEGUN

The only thing spoiling the illusion was the gigantic crimson blood stain on the carpet just beyond the couch. Bottles of cleaning fluids, a bucket and some scrub brushes betrayed the activity that Jerry and Kat's arrival had interrupted.

Not searching, thought Jerry. *Cleaning.*

"Oh, no, please don't turn us away so heartlessly! It simply *must* be available! This space was truly meant for us!" cried Kat. "Why, this glorious abode just cries out to me – *cries*, I swear! It *needs* us to be its new tenants. And I am here to answer its siren call."

"Look, lady," began the man, trying out a new, more assertive response to Kat's exhortations, "there's no way. You have to go to the Rental Office on the main floor and fill out the application just like everyone else. Then we can arrange an appointment for showing, once it's been properly cleaned and all the previous tenant's personal effects have been removed."

"Oh, dear friend," said Kat, "may I call you that?"

"Ah, really, I think 'Bob' might be better. That's my name, after all, and my clients—"

"Bob! Such a beautiful, melodic name," gushed Kat breathlessly. "But I won't hear of it. We have already passed so far beyond a cold, dry business relationship. We have shared this man's loss! We feel his pain and have both come to listen to his spirit's final farewell.

"'*Dear friend*' it must be! Because I truly believe that you and I will become such terribly close friends. I see such generosity of spirit in your eyes—" the man's beady eyes blinked furiously as he took a step backwards, shrinking away from Kat "—and you can't fool me – you're no small-minded rental agent who lives in slavish adherence to the rules – why, here you are, ready to scrub the evil out of this room yourself. Don't they have services to do this? But I can see you'll have none of that! No heartless strangers defiling the sanctum sanctorum of your beloved tenant – so much more than just a tenant, I can tell, you can't hide that from me."

As Kat paused to catch a breath the man's eyes flickered helplessly back and forth.

Hesitantly, he mumbled, "It's just that the cleaning services charge so much for this, and—"

"Shush!" cried Kat. "I won't hear another word of it."

"And now, sweet friend, dear Bob, I must confide in you."

She lowered her chin and surveyed him through raised eyebrows. Smiling conspiratorially, she dropped her voice to a whisper. The man leaned in to catch her words.

"Bob, I have a confession to make. This apartment, well, it has to be our little secret. I can't be making any rental applications. You see… Trevor and I… well, I need to tell you that we're not *precisely* engaged… it's, well, it's not something that our current spouses would approve of… if you get my meaning…." And she gave him the dirtiest, filthiest, most lustful leer that had ever crossed her face.

Once again, a look of comprehension washed over Bob's face.

"Ahhhh. I see…."

"Yes," susurrated Kat. "It's an age-old problem, but with the right kind of sympathetic soul, it's easily overcome. Can we count on you Bob? Can you be our Mata Hari? Will you help smuggle us over enemy lines, my dear friend? Will you play Julius Rosenberg to my Ethel?"

Jerry rolled his eyes. Not only was Kat laying it on too thick, none of her references made any sense. He regretted having shown her that documentary on famous spies of the 20th century.

Bob, however, was lapping it up like a Doberman with a bowl of beef stew. Kat obviously knew her audience better than Jerry. The man's legs wobbled as he withered under the unrelenting laser beams of Kat's eyes burning two heart-shaped holes into his psyche.

"W-Well," he stammered, "I imagine, if your friend here in the building vouches for you, we may be able to... ah, circumvent some of the procedure...."

"Wonderful!" breathed Kat heavily. "But Bob, would you mind if Trevor and I took just the teensiest little peek at the rest of the apartment? I am sure it's just as beautiful as this sumptuous space, but I'd hate to commit without seeing all of it, don't you agree?"

Kat blinked her eyes rapidly in expectation. She managed to transition seamlessly from smoking seductress to innocent waif as though God had flipped a channel with his remote.

"Ah, yes. Yes, of course. Would you like me to—"

"No, no, don't trouble yourself any further with us – we've disrupted your ceremony far too much. You must get back to what you were doing. We'll find our own way. Come on, Trevor."

Kat grabbed Jerry's arm and made a beeline for the bedroom before Bob could change his mind.

By the time they got to the bedroom Jerry was dizzy. It was hard to keep up with Kat when she got like this.

Kat noticed Jerry's expression and quickly glanced backwards to make sure they hadn't been followed into the bedroom.

"For God's sake, Jer! Get with the program! You're making me look bad here."

"When would that be? In between your Spirit World monologues or during the tales of espionage and adultery?"

"Just try to keep up, babe. Blink once for yes, OK?"

"Har de har. Look, he might follow us in here. Let's get searching."

"Absolutely. But don't worry about him making a sudden appearance. He'd be too terrified of interrupting us *in flagrante delicto*, although I doubt he'd phrase it that way."

They moved to opposite sides of the room and began searching, but soon realized there was nothing to be found here. The sock drawer held nothing but socks, and the closet boasted nothing more exotic than a herringbone seersucker jacket that elicited retching sounds from Kat. The bedside table offered only a small translucent time display floating in soothing aquamarine hues inches above the table's surface.

"We're wasting our time here, Kat. I saw another room on the other side of the living room. Probably a second bedroom."

"Right, let's go for it."

Sweeping back into the main room, they found Bob still standing where they had left him. He seemed unsure about scrubbing away the life blood of the previous tenant while a replacement bustled around measuring the place for drapes and evaluating closet space.

"Oh, Bob!" gushed Kat as they swept through the room on their way to the second bedroom. "Overwhelming. That's what this place is. Simply overwhelming. Can you feel it too?"

The question must have been rhetorical, because before Bob could open his mouth to respond Kat had disappeared through the opposite doorway.

She stopped dead when she entered the room. Converted into a small home office, the space might have been very cozy and welcoming in the past, but now it was a maelstrom of disarray. Papers, photographs, printouts of old news articles, countless file folders and their contents – all scattered throughout the room as though a mini-tornado had passed through.

"Whoever searched this place did a thorough job," grumbled Kat, frowning in annoyance. "The only question is, did they find what they were looking for?"

"That's the sixty-four-thousand-dollar question, Kat. Was our guy murdered because he refused to divulge the disk's location, or merely because he interrupted the search?"

"There were no signs of torture or prolonged physical contact, according to the police report. I'm going with an untimely interruption and a hasty – if ill-thought-out – response."

"Well, maybe his murderer missed something. Scan for electronic devices in this room, babe."

Kat pulled her glasses on and canceled the visual overlays. "Just show me electronics," she said to the Slimlines.

Immediately a small red dot appeared off to her right. But when she pulled a tumbled-over stack of journals off the indicated spot, all she found was a desktop picture display unit, still projecting a verdant landscape image. There were no other dots in the room.

"Nothing electronic in here, Sahib. The workstation has been removed, if that dust ring on the desk is any indication. But not by the cops. They didn't find any computer onsite."

A small corkboard mounted just above where the computer display would have been was peppered with business cards from local shops, along with some cartoons and an inspirational message torn out of a daily journal. Kat ran her eyes thoroughly over the remaining desk debris. There was no drawer in the stand and nothing meaningful in sight.

"We're done here, boss," she said. "Time to vamoose before Bob thinks up some tough questions we might not want to answer."

Taking a deep breath, Kat paused to compose herself, then abruptly strode forward into the main room.

"Bob!" she exclaimed in horror. "What in the world happened in that room? It's – it's – simply awful, my love! Such chaos! Such a clash of negative auras! It's so triggering! You should have warned me!"

"Ah, well, it didn't occur to me to mention – I mean you seemed so in tune with the—"

" 'In tune'? With that disruptive energy? You can't be serious! I'm sorry, Bob, my sweet, we simply can't stay in a place with such negative associations! That mess was simply devastating to my psyche! I may need to lie down now in peaceful prayer!

"Come, Trevor, I will need you to massage my temples! Let us be off, darling!"

Yanking Jerry by the arm, she swept off down the entrance passage and through the still-open doorway, disappearing into the corridor beyond.

Bob could still hear Kat talking as she moved down the corridor towards the elevators. It sounded like she was asking a question. All he could make out was the phrase, "sixty-four-thousand".

KAT SWUNG AROUND and stretched out full-length on the couch.

Her bare toes wiggled happily in the cool air from the ship's overhead vents. Arching her back like a spoiled housecat, she groaned happily as the couch molded itself to her form.

"Ohhh, such a day I've had, Jer! I've dodged marble hailstorms, cajoled and berated various and sundry personnel, and impersonated an adulterous floozy scouting an illicit love nest."

"And we still don't have much more than when we started the day," added Jerry, wobbling his way into the lounge, clutching two highball glasses. Handing one of the icy drinks to Kat he said, "Drink up, babe. It's good for what ails ya."

"Mmmm, you got that right, hon," said Kat, lolling back on the couch and running the bottom of the highball glass across her forehead. " *Vodka, orange juice, and thou'* — didn't one of your prehistoric poets once say something like that?"

"You're almost right – it was Omar Khayyam, and not so much OJ and vodka as bread and wine, but the sentiment is close enough."

Kat let out a loud "Oof!" as Batman divebombed onto her, seemingly out of nowhere. She swatted madly in his direction, but the cat evaded her wrath with a timely leap.

"Damn cat!" she cursed. "I swear to God, Jerry, he deliberately leaps onto my stomach when I'm least expecting it."

"He just wants your attention, that's all. You see him ambushing you, but I see a desperate cry for affection."

"I bow to your elevated powers of observation, my Lord and Master. Which of course makes me wonder what you gleaned from our little visit to the late, lamented Chester Belasky's apartment."

"Not a whole hell of a lot, I'm sorry to say. Our deceased friend played his cards close to the chest, I fear."

"Really, O Perceptive One?" asked Kat, rolling onto her side and peering at Jerry.

Jerry sighed morosely. "Okay, Kat. I'm ready to eat crow. What did you spot that I obviously missed?"

"Oh goody!" exclaimed Kat, rising to a sitting position and putting her feet on the floor. "I don't mind telling you, My Sun and Stars, that I absolutely live for these moments." She cackled contentedly.

Rising to her feet, she began pacing back and forth in front of the couch.

"So can anyone in this class tell me what they noticed about the furnishings in our poor homicide victim's dwelling?"

She looked up in mock concentration and said suddenly, "How about you there… in the front row. I'm sorry… I haven't learned all your names yet. Yes – you. With the empty expression in your eyes."

Jerry sighed again. "It was early modern boring, Professor. It looked like an AI interior designer had furnished the place."

"As it probably did. You're right, Freshman. Nothing special at all.

"So then, class, can anyone explain these business cards tacked onto the corkboard above the now-vacant workstation?"

Kat made a movement with her jaw, and a screen on the wall beside her displayed an image of a row of business cards.

"When I zoomed in on these a few minutes ago I noticed they're from local antiques stores. But why would our deceased archivist have sought out such a string of establishments?

I suspect he wouldn't know an antique headboard from a Louis XV settee. What do you suppose he was looking for in these shops?"

Kat had Jerry's attention now. He leaned forward excitedly and said, "It's a clue! But to what?"

"Do you think he was looking for something?"

"Or some*one*," said Jerry. "Maybe an expert who could help him find other old documents. Maybe something to support his claim?"

Kat frowned.

"I don't think so, Jer. According to our info, he already had everything he needed, and the disk needs no other supporting material. It's the piece that validates everything else."

"So what then?" asked Jerry.

"There's only one way to find out. We visit those shops ourselves. We might get lucky and find who – or what – our unlucky friend was searching for."

"Or selling."

"Whatever it is, I think our path is clear. We'd better turn in early tonight – we've got a big day tomorrow: we're going antiquing."

"**A** CHOO! ACHOO! ACHOO!"" Jerry stopped sneezing for a moment and leaned back against the transit seat.

Kat rolled her eyes. "Are we done yet?"

Peering at her through puffy pink eyes and wiping away a tear, Jerry moaned, "It's not like I'm having fun here, Kat," and then promptly sneezed in her face.

Some of the commuters across the aisle in the shuttle glanced over in annoyance, but soon ducked their chins back down to resume staring at their phones.

It was the end of a long afternoon of browsing through a series of virtually identical antiques stores scattered through the shopping district. Jerry and Kat were headed to the last one on their list, and were getting grumpier with each visit.

There had been no logical way to sort the stores. The business cards didn't appear to have been affixed to the corkboard in any particular order, but Kat had wanted to start with the last card in the row and then work their way backwards.

"It's just common sense," she had said. "When do you end a search? When you find what you're looking for, of course. He obviously came up blank in each of the earlier shops. Otherwise, why keep going?"

Jerry had objected, arguing that they might find important clues in the first shops that would help them determine what they were looking for. In the end they had compromised, and were searching based on geographical location, in an effort to make their journey to all eleven stores as efficient as possible.

It was depressing work, though. Jerry had been expecting collections of enticing items, or at least some old furniture, ornaments and various bric-a-brac, but the shops they had visited today were little more than low-end junk stores doubling as pawn shops. Most were jammed to the rafters with the detritus of broken lives. It was depressing as hell.

The items most people chose to pawn were obsolete trash, it turned out. Old, useless, and broken electronics filled each of the stores, along with cheap, ugly furniture that wouldn't even have been found in a homeless camp underneath a bridge.

And worse, everything was dirty, covered in layers of dust and grime. Some items on the stores' shelves hadn't been moved in years, until Kat and Jerry came along, poking and prodding, hoping to stumble onto some indication of what Belasky had been interested in.

In one shop, while desultorily examining an ancient home entertainment unit, Jerry had disturbed a stack of data cable adapters teetering on an upper shelf. When the units tumbled down around him they engulfed Jerry in several pounds of accumulated dust, initiating a fit of convulsive sneezing that had barely abated since then.

"I can't quite figure these places out," said Kat during an intermission between sneezing fits. "It's obvious they're barely selling any of their inventory, so why – and how – do they stay in business?"

"I've been wondering the same thing, babe. They have to be a front for something. Maybe they fence stolen items. There could be any one of a hundred different operations going on."

"No one's going to let us in on the secret anytime soon, though," said Kat. "I've never seen such a string of sullen, unhelpful shopkeepers. They make you feel like you're trespassing just by browsing their decrepit wares."

"I see that didn't deter you from buying something, though."

Kat chuckled, reaching into her pocket to pull out a little ceramic sculpture of just the back end of a black and white cat, tail lifted high, with the business end pointing directly out. A little word balloon said, "Talk to the butt."

"Batman will love it," she said.

" 'Batman'," said Jerry tonelessly. "You're sticking with that? As in, 'I bought my cat a souvenir of my trip to Pawn World'?"

"That's what I said."

"Well, it's probably the only authentic item we've seen today. It looks like early 21ˢᵗ century. I doubt if it's what Belasky was looking for, though. I think I might need to wave the white flag on this one, Kat. I'm still just as clueless as when we started this snipe hunt."

"You keep using expressions like that, Jer, and they'll stick you on one of these stores' shelves. At least then they'll finally have an authentic antique on the premises."

Jerry opened his mouth to voice a withering rejoinder, but it got lost beneath another explosive series of sneezes. Kat looked up at the commuters opposite and shrugged. They gave her commiserating looks of pity, and then lowered their chins once again.

 **AT HEFTED BATMAN** up to chest level and pointed his face at the cat butt magnet affixed to the fridge door.

"Look, baby, it's you!" she crooned. The cat looked unimpressed.

Jerry watched them with a look of disgust on his face.

"I'm not sure how appetizing a sight that is. Am I going to have to look at that every time I go get something to eat?"

"Shush," said Kat. "You'll hurt his feelings."

The cat suddenly remembered something he had to do, and frantically twisted around in an effort to free himself. Kat let him drop to the floor and he scampered off into the other room.

"Now look what you've done," she said accusingly.

"If only it were that easy. There's a reason a group of cats is called a 'pester', you know."

"What's the name for a group of ancient old men? A 'gesundheit'?"

"Ha ha. Watch out, I can turn it back on anytime, you know. Bring that cat back here for a moment and I'll show you."

Kat's eyes widened in horror. "Maybe I *should* have left you on a shelf," she said. "It's not too late to go back, you know."

"Speaking of which, I've been thinking about our little shopping trip today, and something occurs to me.

"That little row of business cards on the corkboard? It's a good clue, I'll grant you, but I think we read it all wrong. I think these were places our dear departed archivist visited and then eliminated. Why else would you keep a set of business cards tacked up, if not to keep track of where you've been?

"I think Belasky went from place to place with a specific idea in mind, and came up blank time after time. Except for the last place, where he may have asked the wrong questions or said the wrong things, and inadvertently revealed himself to the wrong kind of people.

"I suspect he was followed home and murdered, and then his place was searched. The killer probably thought he'd find the disk in his apartment."

"It seems a little short-sighted to kill someone before you have what you need," said Kat.

"Maybe our friend wasn't being cooperative. He might have tried to make a break for it, or grabbed for a weapon. According to the police report, he was fully dressed when they found him. The cops figure he came home and surprised the burglar, but I think it was the opposite: the bad guy followed him in."

"And why don't you think the murderer found what he was looking for?"

"Because the online chatter would have died down. But it's clear that people are still trying to locate the disk."

"Which leaves us back at square one."

"Not entirely, Kat. Call up that police report again. I want to go through the list of personal effects the cops found on the body."

Kat's eyes flickered rapidly behind her Slimlines.

"Okay, what do you want to hear?"

"Well, let's start with his wallet," suggested Jerry.

"Um, well, they found sixty paper credits, his ID card from the National Archives, a library card, a little sketch of a pigeon on a windowsill – it's not bad, either. Looks like our friend had hidden talents – um, there's a monthly transit card, and – oh my God, Jerry! There's a business card from an antiques store!"

"Bingo! There's where we should have started. That was the last place he visited. He never even had a chance to put it up on the corkboard. He must have been there right before he got murdered."

"I can't believe I missed that! I'm such an idiot! How stupid can I be?"

"Kat," said Jerry softly, "I like a good straight line as much as the next guy, but it's no fun fishing when the fish just jump right into the boat."

Kat looked at him sideways. She reached up and pulled the cat magnet off the fridge and pressed it into his hand.

"Talk to the butt, Jerry."

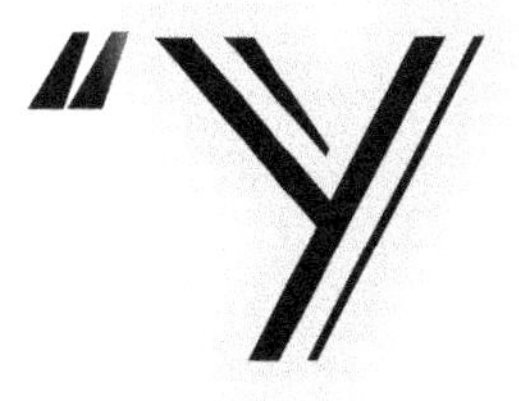**OU KNOW,** this could have waited until tomorrow," complained Kat, standing on the sidewalk next to the antiques store and looking up at the darkening sky. "You're starting to encroach on my 14 hours of sleep."

"Hey, you're the one who said the net is lighting up with all the online chatter about this disk -- tomorrow we'll probably have half the settlement competing with us. I never knew before that you were afraid of the dark."

"But do we even know what we're looking for? I'm not crazy about the idea of setting a murderous thug on our trail."

"I doubt there's much chance of that. I don't think we fit the profile of your typical interstellar claim jumper. But maybe we can pass for simple tourists looking for quaint souvenirs."

"I dunno, Jerry – I've never had much luck passing myself off as a 'simple tourist'."

"Maybe you won't need to. So far, no one in any of these shops has paid any attention to us. Just be discreet and keep your eyes open. We might stumble over something meaningful."

Looking skeptical, Kat took a deep breath, and then pulled open the shop door and stepped inside, with Jerry behind her.

There was nothing in sight to distinguish this place from the other shops they had browsed through. The same dusty collection of obsolete electronics, cheap costume jewelry and kitschy ornaments populated the shelves. In a back corner of the shop a man was reading a news foil, semi-reclining in a wooden armchair tilted up on its back legs. Behind the counter stood an older man with grey hair and eyeglasses, wearing a tweed jacket and plaid necktie.

As Kat drew near he shocked her by asking, "Is there anything I can help you with?"

It was the first time anyone in these stores had bothered to speak to either Jerry or Kat without being prompted. Kat was so surprised she goggled at the man, wordlessly, before Jerry came to her rescue.

"Don't mind my wife," he said, placing his hands on her shoulders. "She can't speak. An infection from eating spoiled seafood required radical surgery some years ago. Had to remove her vocal cords. Damaged her hearing pretty bad, too. Poor thing can only communicate with signs now, I'm afraid."

Moving around to face Kat, Jerry lifted her chin in his hands and said, very loudly and slowly, "DO YOU SEE ANYTHING YOU LIKE, HELEN? ANY CAT ORNAMENTS, MAYBE?" Nodding his head in a show of exaggerated enthusiasm, he added, "JUST LIKE KITTY AT HOME, DEAR. REMEMBER KITTY?" And he lifted his hand up, curling his fingers to perform a little scratching pantomime.

A variety of alternate hand gestures occurred to Kat, none of them appropriate for use in mixed company, but she settled for merely glaring fixedly at Jerry as he smiled broadly at her.

Jerry turned back to look at the merchant. "Maybe after she browses a bit more," he said.

Jerry and Kat almost jumped out of their shoes as the man behind the counter bellowed, "WE HAVE SOME NICE ORNAMENTS ALONG THAT WALL!", mouthing the words exaggeratedly as he pointed to the side and nodded at Kat.

Jerry turned away and bit his lip to avoid bursting into convulsive laughter, and he found himself face-to-face with a shelving unit filled with ancient computer workstations.

"Well hey!" he said. "Look at that! An old Chronus Flash Core 4000! I love these computers – this was a real workhorse. I ran my whole business off one of these until they discontinued the line. Couldn't find replacement parts anymore."

"You… used one of these until they discontinued the line?" said the man behind the counter suspiciously. Both men began studying him carefully. The fellow with the news foil had stopped tilting his chair and was sitting very still. Chronus Computers had gone belly-up over 130 years ago.

Jerry's mind raced. "Ah, I mean, I used one *after* they discontinued the line – I was able to pick one up for a real discount…." His lie sounded lame even to him.

Neither of the men appeared to swallow his story, but Chair Guy slowly lifted his news foil and went back to reading, and the counter man just pursed his lips and nodded.

Jerry glanced at Kat sheepishly and they drifted away to look at a different display, feigning interest in a collection of mid-22nd century sculptures produced by the colonists of the planet Callnus before a volcanic eruption buried the settlement in lava. Just as they turned into the next aisle, Jerry noticed Chair Guy pulling out his phone.

"I think we might have hit paydirt here, Jerry," murmured Kat quietly. "They both lit up when you mentioned that ancient computer."

"Well, in their defense, Kat, I suppose it *was* a pretty odd comment to make. I don't look old enough to even remember those machines."

"Not to mention having used one."

"Right. I guess I blew it. So much for sniffing around discreetly."

"So do they just think you're some kind of weirdo, or is something more going on here?"

"Only one way to find out, Kat. In for a penny, in for a pound, right? Might as well go for broke, now."

Casually strolling back toward the counter, Jerry looked up absentmindedly at the tweed jacket guy. Chair Guy had his nose buried once again in his news foil.

"Say," said Jerry, "I've been thinking... does that old computer still work? I may still have some of my old data disks from that Chronus. I can't find anything that will read those disks anymore. I might like to pick this one up to recover some old... photos... I have on them."

The counter man smiled and said, "Well, I'm not actually sure about that unit. I'd hate to sell you something that didn't work. People usually just want those things for the parts. Hobbyists, mostly.

"I'll tell you what, though. You bring your old disks to me and I can ask an associate of mine if he can read them. He's got a lot of old equipment that still runs fine. I'm sure he'd be happy to retrieve your data for a reasonable price. Less than that old dinosaur would cost you, I'd bet."

"Ah, right.... That's a good idea. I'll get my disks and bring them in. Thanks. Thanks a lot."

"My pleasure," said the counter man warmly. "Come back anytime. I'm always here."

"Great," said Jerry. Turning to Kat, who was back standing at his side, he hollered in her face, "LET'S GO NOW, HONEY. IT'S ALMOST TIME FOR YOUR MEDICATION."

Grabbing her hand, Jerry led Kat out of the shop and they escaped into the night. The broad avenue was almost deserted now, and all the shops were closed. There was no traffic passing by and no pedestrians in sight. Still trying to look like normal shoppers, they forced themselves to stroll at a leisurely pace, peering at all the shop window displays.

"Are your Slimlines scanning behind us?" Jerry whispered as they pretended to look in a store window.

"Always. So far, no movement behind us. No one followed us out of that place."

"That might change," said Jerry. "Let's see if we can throw them off the scent. Turn into this side street. Maybe we can duck into some other store before anyone spots us."

It turned out the side street wasn't much more than an alleyway. They hadn't made it more than a few dozen paces before Kat whispered, "Behind us. Just came into sight. Two guys. Not the ones in the shop, though. These are new players."

Jerry realized that he had made a critical error. There were no side exits, and the alley got darker the farther they went. And even if they could make it through before the men behind them caught up, there was no telling who might be waiting at the far end.

"What do your Slimlines see at the end of this alleyway, Kat? Are they picking up any additional lifeforms?"

"Well, there's no one in sight, and there aren't any heat signatures bleeding out from either side, but that doesn't mean there isn't a welcoming party moving into place. By time we get there, we could find ourselves surrounded."

"How do you think we should play this?"

"Jer, I think our best plan might be to split up. This little alley tees-off at its end into a cross street that should be well-lit. I'll go right, you go left, and we'll circle the block then meet up again on the far side of the buildings in front of us. The bad guys won't be expecting us to separate, and they might not be sure which of us to follow. They'll have to split up and their momentary confusion will give us a brief advantage."

"That's assuming they haven't already got people in place covering both ends of the next street. That's what I'd do."

"Which is an even better reason for us to split up. That way we can at least be sure there won't be a second string sneaking up on either of us from the rear. You clear your side, I'll clear mine. Easy-peasy."

Normally, Jerry would object to leaving Kat to fend for herself, but he knew that in this situation he was actually a handicap to her. In any ambush scenario her Slimlines gave her an advantage. Without Jerry to watch out for, she would be nimbler and more adaptable.

"Anything else up your sleeve, Kat?"

Kat smiled assuringly. "Of course, babe. My glasses have already jammed their communications, and as soon as we make our break, I'll activate their phones' alarms and strobe the flashlights. You'll be able to spot every threat from twenty meters away."

They had almost made it to the end of the alleyway. Jerry was relieved to note that the two men following them had stopped at the alley's entrance, until he realized they were probably there to prevent any retreat. That pretty-well guaranteed that the primary threat lay ahead.

"Okay, Kat," he said as they took cover in the shadows just short of the alley's exit. "Here's where we part ways. See you on the other side, baby."

"I wish you hadn't put it that way," said Kat, leaning over to give him a quick peck on the cheek before spinning off to the right and darting down the cross street.

THERE IS NO appreciable twilight on an airless asteroid, and night had descended on the settlement with little preamble. But even though the cross street was dark, it was still much brighter than the alleyway Jerry and Kat had just left; light bled out from storefronts and random windows on the buildings' upper storeys. There were also a few weak security lights above various shop doors, and a half-dozen decorative street lamps, which combined to create isolated pools of illumination.

Jerry tucked himself into a dim entryway a few feet past the alley, and considered how he might make his escape to the intersection about 100 meters away. He scanned the street but saw no movement. The scene looked as peaceful and deserted as a church parking lot on a Saturday morning.

They must be waiting for me to make my move, thought Jerry. *They might think I'm armed, and after the untimely death of Hector Belasky, wiser heads have probably concluded I'm better off captured alive. It's hard to interrogate a corpse.*

He picked out a spot beneath a leafy Maple beside a decorative fountain about twenty meters away, and readied himself for a mad dash. He was mulling over various strategies when suddenly the entire tableau was plunged into complete darkness. Every nearby light died in unison, and every window went black. Not even the glimmer of a reflected star could be seen, and if it weren't for the glow from the far-off intersection, Jerry would have had no idea which direction to run.

This has to be Kat's handiwork. She must be improvising. Well, it might be the opportunity I need to get out of here unscathed.

Jerry paused in the doorway for a moment, letting his eyes adjust. Thanks to the weak light bleeding out of the distant intersection, eventually he was able to discern a faint impression of the street before him. Gritting his teeth, he dashed off toward the dim splash of illumination far ahead.

Just when he thought his path might actually be clear, he noticed a shadowy shape whizzing up through the darkness on his left. The object turned out to be a hard-knuckled, meaty fist, and the ensuing blow to his temple knocked him to the ground.

**HEN KAT** dashed off and left Jerry behind, she immediately tried to activate the flashlights and alarms on all phones within fifty meters, but her glasses reported an unexpected problem.

"I'm getting microwave interference from somewhere around us, Kat," her Slimlines reported. "There may be a power transmission hub in one of these buildings. It's interfering with my access to local systems."

"Can you disable it?" whispered Kat as she crouched behind a sandwich board advertising lunch specials for a darkened restaurant beside her.

"Not without cutting off all the power on this street and in the buildings," replied her glasses. "And I'll have to disable the failsafes, too. It could take several minutes before this sector's grid completely shuts down."

"Do it!" hissed Kat, and hunkered down lower behind the sign. It didn't look like she'd been spotted yet, but that could change at any moment.

The street was deathly quiet. Kat could hear two voices whispering a few meters away. She cranked up the sound on her Slimlines and eavesdropped on the conversation.

"Dead or alive, that's what Sarkosian said. All he cares about is getting a disk they're carrying," whispered one of the voices.

"Do we know which one of them has it?"

"Not important. With comms down, we can't tell if they're even headed our way. We take out anyone we see. Both, if we can. But as long as we get the disk, everyone gets the bonus."

"Sweet."

Great, thought Kat. *I'll have to remember to thank Jerry for his big mouth. Hopefully before these goons pick through our corpses looking for something we don't have.*

Her thoughts were interrupted as the entire street and every building in sight abruptly plunged into complete and total darkness. Not even the faint starlight above the dome roof penetrated into the street.

Kat's glasses illuminated the view with a full-spectrum daylight image of the street, and she emerged from her hiding spot. She chuckled at the sight of several large men blindly stumbling around in the inky black surroundings.

After mapping out her escape route, she whispered, "Activate the phone lights and alarms!"

The blind men jumped in fright as their pockets sprang to life. She might have been better off disabling the phones' flashlights, but she had Jerry to think of; he didn't have her night vision advantage and needed his own way to spot his attackers. The shrill alarms would help Kat, though, by drowning out any sounds of her passage.

Not wanting to waste her momentary advantage, she jogged toward the closest man.

A short, brawny figure, he pawed the air while staggering along the pitch-black street, disoriented by the blinding flashes strobing out from his phone. In his right hand he clutched a plasma blaster, and she could see a small leather blackjack tucked into his pocket.

As Kat made her way toward him, she passed a collection of cement blocks, a few pipes, and several bags of potting soil piled against a storefront. She picked up one of the pipes, about five feet in length, then strolled over to the man and swung the pipe full force into his face.

A tiny blossom of teeth fragments, shattered jawbone, and various meaty debris erupted from the man's face. His head snapped back and he crumpled to the ground.

Pleased with the result, Kat jogged over to the next closest man and repeated the procedure, with identical results. But the third man whose face she crushed had the impertinence to tumble backwards into a shop window, shattering the glass and alerting the other assailants to her presence.

And sure enough, as she slipped past a boarded-up kiosk advertising the availability of news foils from across the galaxy, a hand shot out from the darkness. Its iron grip snagged a generous handful of her hair and tugged viciously, yanking her backwards.

Dropping her pipe, Kat reached up to grasp her attacker's hand and pull it down, relieving the pressure on her hair. She had practiced this specific move many times with Jerry in their daily jiu-jitsu sparring matches. She pivoted slightly to her left, raised her right leg, and drove her heel forcefully into the side of her assailant's knee, eliciting an ear-splitting shriek of pain.

The blow to his knee caused him to release his grip on her hair, but she kept hold of his hand. Pinning his arm under her own, she crouched and jerked his wrist up and backwards. His elbow snapped with an audible *crack!* and Kat released him. He sank to the ground, his screams doubling in volume, with knee and elbow joints bent in sickening, unnatural positions.

Kat bent over to retrieve her pipe as another thug, alerted by the screams from his confederate, raced toward her, his phone illuminating her in a series of stop-motion images. She grabbed the end of the pipe facing him and tilted it upward, leaving the other end firmly wedged into the pavement.

Kat heard the squish of bursting flesh as the thug impaled himself on the end of the metal shaft, coughing-up a thick mouthful of blood.

Alerted by the sound of an approaching alarm, she spun around just in time to avoid another attacker's fist, but he careened into her just the same. The impact knocked her Slimlines off her face and hurled her onto the sidewalk.

Her world was plunged into total darkness as her glasses spun away across the pavement. She rolled over onto her hands and knees and patted the ground, searching for them.

Her attacker, squinting down at her in the dark, kicked her hard in her solar plexus, knocking the wind out of her.

Kat gasped for air as the man kicked her again, this time in her shoulder. A lance of pain shot through her like a thunderbolt, galvanizing her into action. As she struggled to her feet, her gaze zeroed in on his brightly-pulsing pants pocket. Desperately, she reached out and clamped her fist around a squishy lump of flesh in his pants.

Squeezing with every ounce of strength she possessed, she straightened up while twisting her hand in a vicelike crushing grip.

Operatic in their intensity, the man's screams subsided only when Kat brought down her other hand in a powerful hammer smash to his nose. The shrieks turned to muffled gurgles and coughs, and his body writhed frantically as Kat continued to squeeze, twist and yank his anatomy. She finally released her grip and let the man fall. Raising her leg, she brought her boot down onto the spot where she figured his head would be. She was rewarded with a hearty crunch, and felt his body spasm and then go limp.

Dropping back to the ground, Kat patted around blindly, searching for her Slimlines. But an approaching cacophony of phone alarms warned her of several more attackers closing in on her position.

Abandoning her search, she crawled frantically in a lateral movement toward one side of the street, looking for some kind of hiding spot, then winced as her fingers jammed into the curb. Her head banged against a thick metal bar, nearly causing her to yelp in pain. Reaching out and patting it, she guessed it to be a wrought-iron bench. She vaguely recalled seeing one on the sidewalk beside a transit sign. Hearing the phone alarms rapidly drawing closer, accompanied by the ever-present psychedelic light show, she pulled herself under the bench and held her breath.

Several different sets of feet appeared in front of her.

"Did you see which way they went?" asked a voice.

"All I heard was someone screaming, so I came this way. They must have passed you."

"No way. I would have seen them. They've gotta be close."

"You wouldn't have seen them even if they'd been sitting on your lap. I can't see for shit, and these damn phones ain't helping, either."

"Screw the phones. Spread out. We'll cut them off, whichever way they went."

The footsteps thundered away but one pair of feet remained, inches from Kat's face. She curled up tighter under her bench. She wouldn't be safe for long, though. If she didn't find a way to escape in the next couple of minutes, Jerry would need to find a new partner.

THE HAM-SIZED FIST that smashed into Jerry's temple sent him tumbling into the middle of the street. As his assailant readied the knockout blow, all Jerry could make out was a large, nebulous mass. The shape shifted its posture, and then delivered a vicious kick as Jerry scrambled weakly to one knee.

To the big man's surprise, however, Jerry wasn't cowering on his knee, but was readying his counterattack. Neatly twisting back to avoid the oncoming foot, he grasped it by the ankle as it swept past his face. Lifting and twisting the big man's foot into the air, Jerry rose to his feet and yanked him off balance. He grunted in satisfaction as his attacker's other foot skidded on the damp pavement, flipping him backwards. Jerry grinned as the thug's head came crashing to the curb.

The big lug lay motionless on the pavement. As Jerry crouched over him, he could see the whites of the man's eyes sightlessly staring up. A dark circle of liquid seeping out from under his head glimmered in the darkness. Concluding that the man was no longer a threat, Jerry straightened up and ran once again for the faint splash of light at the end of the street.

He hadn't gone more than a few meters when two brightly flashing pants pockets burst to life just off to his right, coming from two men who had been silently crouching in the darkness, waiting for him to come closer. Shrill alarms filled the air along with the blinding lights.

The unexpected disturbances caught the men off-guard, freezing them in place for a moment as they as they tried to figure out what was happening. The one closest to Jerry straightened up and began fumbling at his pocket.

Seizing the opportunity, Jerry leapt and kicked him solidly in the groin, just to the side of the pulsing pants pocket. The man gasped in pain and buckled over.

The second man was unsure exactly how he should proceed. Crouching tensely, he considered jumping at Jerry to take him down.

Jerry stepped back one pace, then brought his foot up in a powerful arc, once again kicking the man who was still bent over in pain from the blow to his groin. This time Jerry's boot tore into the man's face, jerking him upright and sending him tumbling backwards into his partner. As both bodies fell back in a confused tumble of arms and legs, Jerry leapt forward, landing both knees onto the second man's chest with the sound of a sack of wet laundry hitting the ground. He felt the soft squish of ribs, then lifted his right fist and brought it down heavily on the man's throat.

The shape jerked violently and then went limp.

Breathing through a shattered nose while simultaneously vomiting from his groin injury, the first man clawed pathetically at the pavement. Ignoring him, Jerry took off once down the street. As he ran, he could still hear the shrill bleating of the men's phones in their pants pockets.

He was twenty meters short of the corner when a door to his right burst open. A man in a dark suit and tie stumbled out, holding his brightly flashing phone to guide himself out of the pitch-black building. The earsplitting alarm blaring out from the phone was painful to hear – it must have been damn near intolerable inside the building. In the blinding flashes Jerry saw confusion and panic on the man's face.

The goon was so disoriented it was effortless for Jerry to swiftly walk up and deliver a haymaker to his jaw. The blow sent the man spinning to his right, where his head collided soundly with a lamp post. His phone, along with a plasma blaster he held in his other hand, went clattering to the ground as he stumbled and fell.

Jerry picked up the blaster just as the man tried to stand back up.

"Uh-uh," said Jerry quietly, and pulled the trigger. A thick beam of light shot out, boring a four-inch-wide hole in the hoodlum's chest.

Just then, another stream of white-hot plasma burned through the air, slicing into the lamp post in front of Jerry and knocking him backwards with the reflected energy. Two more blasts followed, each barely missing him as he frantically crawled on his belly to take cover behind a decorative planter.

The shots were coming from behind him near the alleyway. A distant strobe light inching closer to the shooters meant that reinforcements were on the way. Jerry knew he couldn't hold out here – he needed to make his break before he was overwhelmed. He'd be silhouetted against the glow from the avenue ahead, but there was no way around that. Hopefully the strobing lights were messing with the shooters' night vision to even the odds a bit.

Firing blindly in their general direction (and gratified to hear a shriek of pain), Jerry made a mad, zig-zag dash for the corner. He kept firing behind himself as he ran, dodging a barrage of plasma blasts which lit up the air all around him. He dropped down to slide past the corner like a runner stealing second base.

There were no blinking pants or shrieking alarms ahead of him, but lights from storefronts and streetlamps still illuminated the avenue. Jerry balked at being so uncomfortably exposed. Intermittently reaching around the edge of the wall and firing unaimed blasts back into the street he had just escaped, he paused to gather his breath and his thoughts. Concluding that speed trumped stealth in this situation, he stood up and legged it down the avenue.

He ran full speed, expecting a plasma blast from behind at any second. If he could make the next corner before his pursuers could catch sight of him again, he might be able to lose them. In his haste, he slipped on a slick patch of pavement, skidding into a concrete planter box holding a large oak tree. The plasma blaster flew out of his hand and skittered away across the avenue. Desperate to reach the corner, Jerry abandoned it and resumed his sprint.

After what seemed like an eternity, he reached the corner, turned to his right again and raced ahead. As long as none of his attackers had anticipated his path, and had no way to transit through the buildings, he had time to pick a dark spot and wait for Kat to show up, as they had agreed. Keeping low, he darted toward the middle of the block while scanning the storefronts for a dim alcove where he could hide.

He was thinking he'd made a clean escape until, from the far end of the street, he spied a hoverbike skidding around the corner and heading straight for him. It slid to a stop a meter away. The rider was wearing a gaudy orange jacket with a full-face smoked helmet. Even in the dim light Jerry could make out two deadly-looking plasma blasters hugging each of the rider's hips.

Jerry looked to his left and to his right, but there was nowhere to go that the biker couldn't run him down. Neither could he afford to wait another second – by now the other thugs were surely on their way. He needed to deal with this problem quickly or he'd be sharing a drawer in the morgue with Hector Belasky before the night was over.

He clenched his fists and snarled, "Okay, asshole, I'm ready. Let's see what you got," and readied himself to leap at the bike as soon as the rider made a move for his pistols.

**AT COULD HEAR** feet pounding on pavement as the hoodlums ran back and forth past her, temporarily unable to locate her as she curled up under the bench.

A shout of excitement came from a few meters away, and the pair of feet that had remained by her bench turned and raced off. A few seconds later she heard cursing as the alert turned out to be a false alarm.

Combined with the ear-splitting shrieking alarms, the erratically strobing lights were disorienting and worse than no light at all. Most of her pursuers were shining their phones up into the air or jamming them into their pockets, vexed by the shadows and confusion of the beams coming from all directions and reflecting off the store windows. As one of the thugs ran past her, Kat looked up and was momentarily blinded by the piercing light pulsing from the phone he held at arm's length.

Little pinwheels danced in her vision, causing her to lose her orientation. She could no longer tell which direction she needed to go, and felt helpless in the oppressive darkness. Finally, during one brief moment when no one else was nearby, she dared to quietly hiss, "Find Slimlines!"

From about five feet away, lying askew at the base of a trash receptacle, her glasses shone out, glowing bright yellow against the ebony pavement. She scrambled out from under the bench, snatched them up and returned them to her face. The world sprang back to life.

"Damn!" she swore, alarmed that two men near the alley had also spotted the sudden yellow glow of her glasses.

Kat bolted toward the far end of the street, hoping to turn the corner before a shot from a blaster brought her down.

She ran past a decorative topiary in front of a florist and heard the yelping phone alarm a second too late. A hand reached out and grabbed her upper arm, spinning her around. Another hand grabbed her other arm and she found herself face to face with a muscular thug dressed in a dirty t-shirt and jeans. He was pulling her close enough that she could smell the foul odour of onions and beer on his breath along with stale perspiration soaked into his clothing.

"Got you!" crowed the man, squeezing Kat's arms so tight she could feel his thumbs poking deeply into her muscles.

"Me too!" grunted Kat, and drove her right heel heavily onto the man's left foot. He jerked in pain, which was all the opening Kat needed to bring her knee up forcefully into his crotch.

"Oof!" he grunted, and relaxed his grip enough for Kat to pull her right arm free, draw it back and ram her knuckles into his throat.

He staggered backwards, clutching his neck with both hands, as Kat spun back to run toward the intersection.

At least, she *tried* to run toward the intersection. Instead, she smacked directly into the chest of a towering man who stumbled into her in the dark.

As he blindly fumbled around for a handhold on her twisting body, she slithered out of his grasp and stepped backwards. He staggered toward her, arms reaching out both defensively and in search of her form. Kat lunged toward him, ducking under his arms to drive the heel of her right hand deep into his sternum, just below his breastbone.

She heard the man's breath burst out of him in a loud whoosh, and his eyes goggled backwards in his head. He clutched his chest and tried to breathe, but his lungs refused to respond. As he buckled forward, Kat grabbed hold of his hair in both hands and wrenched his face down. Savagely ramming her knee upwards, she felt his nose collapse under the impact, and he dropped to the ground like a sack of potatoes.

Kat could hear approaching phone alarms and spotted a pair of thugs racing toward her. A bright shaft of heat ripped through the air inches from her face as several pulses from two blasters fired madly in her direction. She ducked her head and bolted zig-zagging toward the corner, hoping she could make it before getting hit by a lucky shot.

Another shaft of plasma whizzed past her but this time she felt a sharp burning sensation in her hip. Looking down, she saw a charred, smoking gash in her pants. Cursing, Kat limped frantically towards the intersection and then froze as a blinding beam of light appeared at the corner.

A pizza delivery bike rider was stopped at the end of the street, with the face shield on his helmet up as he stared dumbfounded at the melee. His bike's headlight illuminated a series of broken bodies, a smashed shop window, and two large men madly firing plasma blasters at a terrified girl. A cacophonous din of blaring alarms filled the air, echoing off the buildings and seemingly coming from all directions at once.

"Hey!" he yelled, and then immediately regretted it, as the men swung their weapons in his direction.

The two thugs, eyes dazzled from the incessantly strobing lights they were shining before them, failed to comprehend the nature of this new player on the scene, and promptly directed several streams of fire into the hapless bystander.

The dying rider collapsed forward on his bike, pushing the throttle down in the process and sending it leaping forward with a tremendous burst of speed – directly at the two shooters.

The first man turned to dive out of the way, but succeeded only in slipping on the pavement and falling to the perfect height for the bike's hoverpad to slash into his forehead, neatly slicing off the top of his skull like an opened soft-boiled egg.

The second gunman, standing farther back and off to the side, fired desperately at the approaching headlight, but failed to anticipate the bike's change in trajectory created by the impact with his associate's cranium. The bike careened straight into his chest, picking him up and breaking his back as it rammed him into a wrought-iron drinking fountain on the sidewalk.

Kat stood momentarily frozen, staring dumbfounded at the scene of carnage before her. And then, coming to her senses, she trotted over to the bike, now motionless and quietly humming, pressed up against the fleshy cushion between it and the water fountain. The expired deliveryman lay upside down beside the idling bike, where he had been deposited by the sudden cessation of forward motion.

"Sorry, bud," muttered Kat grimly, as she pulled the helmet and jacket off the dead rider's limp form. "Talk about being in the wrong place at the wrong time."

She quickly donned the jacket and helmet, and then gingerly retrieved the blasters from each of the two dead men. Clipping the weapons onto her hips, she mounted the bike and backed it up, then sped to the end of the street and around the corner. It appeared there were no more assailants to attack her, but she didn't want to stick around and find out differently.

Kat zipped to the end of the block and neatly whipped the bike around to her left and raced along the street, almost running directly into Jerry, who backed away and snarled at her.

Oh, right! thought Kat. *Helmet and jacket. Makes sense.*

Slowly lifting her hands up so as not to alarm him, Kat raised the helmet's visor and grinned at him.

"Hiya, Sailor," she purred. "Wanna go for a ride?"

AS JERRY SLIPPED ONTO the seat behind Kat, a shaft of white-hot plasma burned past his head, narrowly missing him. Kat spun the bike around while Jerry crouched and fired back at the shooters with one of her blasters.

Two more blasts flared past them as Kat frantically wove the bike back the way she'd come.

"I thought you were going to take care of the ones on your side," she yelled back at Jerry, banking the bike violently to the left and heading full speed for the street corner.

"And hog all the fun?" he yelled back, firing once more and watching as a body flew backwards, with a gigantic hole cratered into its chest.

"Don't worry, Jer – I had plenty of fun all on my own. You're such a giving person."

"Never say I don't know how to show a girl a good time," he grunted, as Kat skidded the bike into a trash receptacle in an effort to dodge a rapid series of plasma blasts.

Kat leaned hard on the throttle and they rocketed out into the intersection, where she laid them down almost sideways as she turned the corner and bounced off a boarded-up news foil kiosk before accelerating off down the cross street.

"Where did you learn to ride this?" asked Jerry, as they sped along the avenue. "Or are your Slimlines doing the driving?"

"All me!" she laughed. "My first boyfriend was a biker."

"I don't know if I should be intimidated or turned-on."

"How is that different from always?" asked Kat with a wicked grin, juicing the throttle and slamming Jerry backwards in the seat.

They left the bike, helmet and jacket outside a transit station and boarded a shuttle to the industrial section of the settlement.

"With any luck, we'll hit a shift change from one of the factories and get lost in the crowd," said Kat, between bites from a steaming slice of pizza. "At the very least, they'll lead us to some of the finer drinking establishments on this godforsaken rock."

"That's an excellent idea, Kat," said Jerry enthusiastically, as he picked pineapple pieces from his slice and tossed them back into the box taken from the bike. "After the day I've had, hiding out in a bar with a bunch of worn-out miners sounds like the perfect way to decompress."

They got off at a stop located between two large refineries, and were immediately swarmed by a wave of blue-collar workers struggling to board the shuttle.

Stepping outside, they tagged along with a thick stream of refinery workers passing by the station and soon found themselves on a street boasting a strip of bars and little else.

Jerry looked skeptically at the row of establishments.

"I'm not sure how much 'hiding out' we can do here, Kat. We'll stick out like sore thumbs."

"All the better, Jerry. People will remember seeing us here. It'll make for a good alibi."

They were assessing their choices when Jerry froze and said, "Kat. Hold up. Can you recall anywhere you've been recently where you might have gotten some glitter spilled on you?"

"Glitter? You mean like the party stuff?"

"Yeah. Like that. Cause you've got several flecks on your left shoulder. Were you rubbing up against any strippers recently?"

Kat gave him a withering look. "No, and I haven't been to any 10-year-old girls' birthday parties, either. What do you think it means?"

"If I had to guess, I think it's a low-tech tracking device."

"For clowns?"

"For anyone. It's reflective and easy for cameras to spot. And you can't detect it electronically because it's just simple flecks of tin foil."

"What kind of lunatic carries a bag of glitter around with him?"

"The kind whose boss doesn't like a couple of off-world amateurs messing with him. One of the thugs you danced with must have tagged you – maybe they had it on their hands."

"Brush off my shoulder, Jerry." Kat got a steely look in her eyes. "Just wait 'till I get near one of their computers again. I'll show these small-town hoods who's an amateur."

Selecting the least-seedy of the available drinking establishments, Kat yanked the door open and stepped into a dark, crowded space filled with noisy, carousing miners. No one appeared in the least bit interested in them. They threaded their way toward a cluster of tables near the back and found a tiny space in a corner beside the kitchen doorway.

"I'm just guessing, Kat, but I don't think there's table service here. I'll go get us something from the bar. Don't go away."

When Jerry returned five minutes later with two glasses and a large pitcher of beer, he found Kat surrounded by a cluster of men.

"Oh good – here's the drinks. Fellas, meet my boyfriend, Rocco."

The assembled cluster of heads all turned and greeted Jerry warmly, then swiveled back toward Kat.

"Can't say it's a good idea leaving a lady alone in this place, buddy," said one of the men in a friendly tone. "Me and the guys was just debating which of us would get to carry her off."

"Then you should thank me for coming back in the nick of time," replied Jerry. "You'd be biting off more than you could chew with this one."

That elicited a roar of guffaws and several suggestive comments as the huddle parted slightly to allow Jerry room to squeeze through.

"Oh yum. Beer," said Kat unenthusiastically.

"It's not a big menu here. The only other choice was a boilermaker. Which, if I'm not mistaken, is just beer with a chaser."

"And you passed that up?" asked Kat, to a loud chorus of moans from her new friends. "Fellas, why don't we show Rocco how real men drink?"

A roar of approval erupted from the crowd around them, and within minutes the table was littered with empty beer and shot glasses. It seemed to Jerry that every time he or Kat put down an empty glass, two full ones magically appeared.

For the next hour Kat, Jerry and their newfound friends regaled one another with tales of the most fascinating misadventures from around the galaxy, liberally sprinkled with outrageous exaggerations and outright lies. A ribald drinking song broke out among the men, and to everyone's delight, Kat took over for one particularly obscene chorus, her high soprano floating above the miners' rough baritones.

"Haw! You've got a true miner's soul, Tiffany," gushed one smitten admirer.

"And hidden talents, as well," added Jerry. "I hesitate to ask where you might have learned that charming little ditty."

"I wasn't living in a convent before you met me, my love. A girl's gotta get out and have a bit of fun occasionally."

"I'm glad your liver survived the experience."

"Forget about my liver – can you imagine how many brain cells I must have wiped out? And lucky for you, too, considering how hard it is for you to keep up with me even now."

Jerry's response was lost in an excited roar, as two musclebound men at a table behind him struggled in an epic arm-wrestling match. As he turned to watch, his eyes happened upon an unlikely pair of men entering the bar.

Their clothing may have been off-the-rack suits but in this crowd it advertised them as foreign entities. Their casually buttoned jackets bulged suspiciously on one side, betraying the likely presence of plasma blasters.

Without being obvious, Jerry glanced at the bar's side door, and sighted two similar arrivals there. The men were peering into the dark room but neither team had spotted him and Kat.

As nonchalantly as he could manage, Jerry turned back around to face Kat, who was demonstrating to a rapt audience a paralytic wrist-hold that she had learned on the Wing Chun Planet in the Shaolin System. As she effortlessly twisted the hapless volunteer's arm, she would stop at times to point out the effects of a bit of added pressure here or a squinch more torque there, to the delighted grunts of approval from her audience and renewed yelps of pain from her "assistant".

"Um, Tiffany, when you have a sec, do you think we might have a word?" asked Jerry quietly.

"Sure, I'm done here anyways," she said, releasing her victim's wrist and high-fiving her disciples.

Collapsing back into her chair and drinking deep from her beer glass, she said, "Wow, instruction is thirsty work. But don't keep me on tenterhooks here, Rocco – spill."

"I think your glitter friends might have made an appearance. Check out the exits."

"Oy, Jerry. That was fast. What do we do now? Rush 'em?" Kat cracked her knuckles and flexed her arms.

"Probably a bad idea. They're carrying. There aren't any martial arts tricks that stop plasma blasts, are there?"

"Sad to say, I haven't learned them if there are."

"Maybe you could knock out the lights again. We'd have a better chance in the dark."

"No can do, babe. This place is old school – everything is manually controlled. Even the lights. There's no local network to access. Serves us right for hanging out in the low-rent district. Maybe we should have held on to those blasters I liberated earlier. Any other thoughts?"

"Just one."

Turning to one of Kat's fans, a largish fellow with faded tattoos decorating his neck and massive arms, Jerry said, "How would you like to do us a solid?"

The man gave Jerry a broad smile. "If Tiffany needs some help, I'm all in. Would it maybe have anything to do with cracking a few skulls?"

"You read my mind. See those wiseguys in suits by the doorways? We'd love it if you and a couple buddies could dance with them a bit while Tiff and I slip out the kitchen door."

"But be careful, Tony," said Kat. "They're packing heat."

Tony laughed and said, "So am I," and flexed his arms. "And these babies never need reloading."

After a quick glance over his shoulder, the big man leaned over and said, "Where are you headed?"

"Um, the Depot," said Jerry warily. "We have a ship there."

"Either of you ever ride a bike?"

Kat grinned and said, "I left my Katsumo downtown an hour ago."

"I should have guessed," he said, chuckling.

Pressing a fob into Kat's hand, he said, "Take this. I'm parked behind the bar. It's a black Patriot Flyer. Leave it at the Depot transit station with the fob under the seat."

"I owe you big for this, Tony," said Kat, leaning over to plant a kiss on the big man's cheek.

He blushed and said, "I guess I'm just a sucker for a pretty face, is all," then turned away and whispered briefly into a couple of his friends' ears.

As the men headed for the doorways, Kat and Jerry edged toward the kitchen with their heads down and their backs to the room. When the sounds of a commotion emerged from one of the bar's entrances, they slipped through the kitchen doorway, hustled past the startled cook and exited through the alleyway door.

A couple of men stood in the shadows smoking illegal tobacco cigarettes, but otherwise the alley was empty. A few feet away, a half-dozen hoverbikes were clustered against a cement wall. When Kat strode to the Patriot Flyer, it recognised the fob in her pocket. The lights illuminated and it started up with a quiet purr.

As they pulled out of the alley, they spied a large man in a dark suit flying out the bar's side door and landing face-first on a pile of broken beer bottles and jagged bits of rusted metal.

Kat winced sympathetically as she throttled down and sped away up the street, swerving around the mangled form on the ground. "Ouch. That's gonna leave a mark."

THE PAW PRESSED against Jerry's lips again, and again he feebly batted at his face and brushed it away.

The next time the paw returned, Jerry was close enough to consciousness to mumble, "G'waayyy," before burping and then snuffling uncomfortably.

His eyes momentarily flickered open, but couldn't make out any discernable shapes. A blurry black and white cloud hovered over his face and then vanished, followed immediately by an unpleasant pressure against his full bladder as the cat stood on his stomach.

"Aaaagh," he coughed, and raised himself up on his elbows.

His vision cleared sufficiently to discern a black and white butt and long black tail disappearing into the void past the mattress edge. Seconds later, accompanied by the sound of scrabbling claws skittering on smooth tile, a blurry monochrome shape raced across the room and out the bedroom doorway.

"Damn cat," mumbled Jerry, hunching into an upright sitting position and groggily rubbing at his face. "He's got a damn feeder – why can't he let me sleep in for ten minutes?"

Jerry looked to his left and saw Kat stretched out beside him, face-down and fully dressed.

"Good Lord, Kat. You didn't even take off your boots."

Kat forced open the eye that wasn't mashed into the pillow and hoarsely mumbled, "I was just being considerate. This way you won't have to dress me again before you bury me."

"Don't be such a drama queen," said Jerry, struggling to his feet. It was his third attempt and he was considering just crawling to the bathroom instead of daring to walk upright.

"What time is it, Jer?"

"Um… hold on, I'm looking… ah, I – I dunno. Sometime in the morning, I think."

"Okay, I can work with that," Kat answered, licking her lips and rubbing her face into the pillow.

Summoning a reserve of superhuman strength she hadn't known she possessed, she rolled onto her back and lay blinking at the ceiling. "What day?"

The only response was the distant sound of running water and long, hacking coughs issuing from the bathroom.

An hour later, they were both vertical and dressed (or, in Kat's case, re-dressed), hunched over the kitchen table, cradling steaming mugs of coffee. Batman sat off to the side on a cat perch, eyeballing them reproachfully while studiously chewing on one of his front paws. Kat glared back at him.

"I don't know what Batman's so pissed about – it's only 9:30am. That's two hours earlier than we usually wake up."

"Cats don't understand 27-hour days, baby. In his world, it's past noon. Even cats can't sleep as much as you."

"Hah," said Kat, sticking her tongue out at the beast. "Amateur."

"Speaking of which," said Jerry, attempting to segue into a more productive line of thought, "what do you think our next move should be? I'm sorta stuck here."

"I've actually been thinking about that, hon. I overheard a snippet of conversation last night that maybe we should follow-up on. One of those hired killers mentioned a man by the name of 'Sarkosian' – I think he might be the one who sent them.

"And if I'm not mistaken," she continued, flickering her eyes around behind her glasses, "that was the name on the—yes! There it is!"

Kat blinked, and the wall screen filled with an image of the monitor on Clara's desk. "Look there, Jerry. That's the access list for the storage box that held the disk. The last name is Belasky's, but look who the next previous party was: 'Sarkosian'."

"But over three months earlier," said Jerry. "If this Sarkosian fellow found the disk, why would he leave it there for three months?"

"I don't know about you, Jer, but I don't think I'd want to try to sneak any stolen disks past Clara – it would be easier to steal smoked salmon off Batman's plate."

"And safer. Clara probably hasn't had her shots."

"So you think maybe Sarkosian recruited Belasky to remove the disk for him? That would explain a lot."

"Only one way to find out, Kat – let's go have a little sit-down with the man himself. Can your glasses find where he hangs out?"

"Yup. He has an office in something called the 'Nebula Towers'. And – oh, damn – according to that building's security records, Sarkosian hasn't been on the premises in at least a week."

"All the better. Feel like a little covert break-and-enter, sugarbuns?"

"Is there any other kind? Just give me a minute to go find my black turtleneck, and we can be off."

JERRY GLANCED at the heads-up display hovering above the shuttle's exit door.

"This is our stop, baby," he said, taking Kat's hand as he stood up.

They stepped out of the bland, utilitarian transit station into a street scene bathed in sunlight and soft pastels. This was obviously the high-rent district in the settlement. Several multistorey buildings towered above them, while on the ground level various chic boutiques and specialty bodegas advertised hard-to-find luxury items and foodstuffs from distant corners of the galaxy.

Well-dressed pedestrians strolled the sidewalks, most of them either walking dogs or toting shopping bags. A couple of them were pushing baby carriages. Two children riding mini hoverboards flashed past, each trying to come closest to the unsuspecting adults they dodged along the way.

When the Nebula Towers came into sight, Jerry and Kat paused for a moment to admire the building. It was twenty stories of glass and titanium-chromium alloy, sculpted in graceful sweeping lines that reflected the sunlight into a million tiny glittering starbursts.

Jerry pursed his lips in a silent whistle of admiration.

"That's a mighty fine looking building there, Kat."

"State of the art, I'd say. My glasses are picking up an entire floor dedicated to nothing but maintenance systems: security, fire suppression, elevators, lights, door locks. They even have their very own environmental controls with independent life support – the entire building is sealed-off from the rest of the city. Although God only knows why they'd even want to do that. Maybe they're intending on turning it into a spaceship someday to fly off this backwoods hunk of rock."

Jerry chuckled. "I think the answer is much more mundane. It's all about Rich People anxiety. Back when I was ultra-rich and lived on Earth, we had our own private neighbourhoods with access restricted by locked gates and tall fences. Kept the po' folks at arm's length. The City of Palm Beach in Florida even had its own Resident ID cards for those who 'belonged'. It's the same thing here. Except now the Privileged Class doesn't even have to breathe the same air that all us unwashed masses are coughing and sneezing into and getting all smelly."

"Sounds like nothing but a way to stroke their egos. Which would explain what I'm seeing with this setup – it's just a joke, Jerry. All hat and no cattle, as my great-grandaddy back in Texas would say. This system looks like it was designed more with the goal of impressing the tenants than to actually provide real safety. The security protocols were so easy to bypass my Slimlines barely skipped a beat. I have full access to their entire system. We should be able to just stroll in like we own the place."

"Then why are we still standing out here with all the common people, getting all sweaty and greasy? Let's go, baby."

On the opposite corner across from the Nebula Towers was a small park with the requisite fountain, gravel paths, and scattered benches. On one of these benches sat two bored-looking men dressed in black suits. They both appeared to be in their early forties; one was large and solidly-built and the other was slimmer and looked slightly older, with greying hair at his temples. As Kat and Jerry crossed the street and approached the Nebula Towers, both men perked up and exchanged a brief glance.

"Now there's a surprise," said the larger man, digging his fist into his jacket and pulling out his phone.

"I can't tell for sure," said the other man, shading his eyes and squinting at the people across the street. "They're too far away, but yeah, I think it's them. Make the call. This is an unexpected bonus. They're obviously here to meet Sarkosian, so we get all three for the price of one. Are our guys in place?"

"They will be, in about ten minutes," said the other man. "Looks like we can put a bow on this thing right now."

Kat and Jerry walked up to the building's discreet, understated glass entrance doors. When they were within two meters, a small LED beside a keypad switched from red to green, and the doors silently slid open to admit them to a cool, softly-lit foyer furnished with tall flowering plants and a scattering of couches and armchairs that had never been sat on.

The elevator doors opened to admit them without the unpleasant necessity of pressing any buttons, and the elevator whooshed silently upwards.

"I'm assuming it knows where we want to go," said Jerry.

Kat nodded. "It recognizes us as tenants in Suite 1403."

"And you're sure there's no one inside?"

"Only if the building's own security system can be trusted. According to it, no one has been in 1403 in the last week. I don't know about before that – the records only show seven days' activity."

"It might be just a front."

"Well, we won't know until we get inside. But according to the city records, this is his only registered address. Maybe he's traveling. Or dead. Maybe he exists only on paper."

"Now there's a hopeful thought. You're a real ray of sunshine, you know that, Kat?"

"I'm just trying to give you another opportunity to exercise that cynical optimism of yours, Jer-bear."

On cue, the elevator hissed to a stop, and they stepped out into a carpeted foyer. Water trickling down a tiny waterfall in a small decorative fountain tinkled pleasantly.

A number of fat orange fish swam contentedly in a pool at the fountain's base. Several exotic jungle plants tastefully placed at intervals around the fountain shimmered in the discreet overhead lighting.

"I feel so warm and fuzzy, it makes me want to pitch a tent and camp here overnight."

Kat laughed. "I'm sure that would go over real well. Especially when we started melting smores over a campfire."

Kat turned down the hallway towards Suite 1403, with Jerry following, peering up at the ceiling.

"My what a lot of security cameras you have, Grandma," he said.

"The better to see you with, little girl."

They arrived at 1403 and Jerry looked at the door expectantly, waiting for it to pop open as all the other doors had. But nothing happened.

"Ah… 'Open Sesame'?" he ventured.

Still nothing.

"Um – 'Walt sent me' ?"

Nope.

"Don't get your panties all in a bunch, Jerry. I'm working on it. This guy must be super paranoid. He's running a separate quantum-safe cryptographic algorithm over the building's access protocol. And it's the first real security I've encountered.

"Fortunately, the software in my Slimlines includes a full database of all known quantum-safe algorithms, and I've already deciphered the one he's using. Now I just need to run a prime factorization on the encryption code, which looks to be 400 characters long."

"Wait, don't tell me – I know this one," said Jerry, who had been reading up on encryption technology. "Let's see… the number of seconds required to factorize a 400-digit code would be… um, 10 raised to the power of… something like 90, 92, maybe 94. More or less."

Kat looked at him coldly. "Yes. For a normal computer running a few million calculations per second. But considering that the age of the Universe in seconds is only about 10 raised to the power of 18, that would probably be longer than we want to wait."

"But you don't have a normal computer," Jerry pointed out.

"Right. And for a quantum computer like the one in my glasses, the calculation time should be reduced to—"

Kat paused, as a distinct *click!* sounded from the door. She checked the time display in the corner of her vision. "— 31 seconds. More or less."

"Show-off," said Jerry, and pushed the door open.

The room they stepped into was cool and dark, with a secretary's desk and a visitor's chair off to the side. As Kat silently closed the door behind her, Jerry moved to turn on the lights, but Kat pulled his hand back before he could hit the switch.

"Uh-uh, Jerry. I'm getting readouts that indicate this place is lathered in security systems. My glasses are handling them, but it's a safe bet that merely hitting the lights would activate a separate alarm protocol of its own. We'd better not touch anything electronic if we don't want to attract attention."

"That's all very well and good for you, baby, but I don't have my own personal set of see-in-the-dark goggles. It's pitch-black in here. What am I supposed to do? Follow the sound of your voice like a puppy?"

Kat giggled. "As much as I like that idea, it might not be necessary. There's a door in the opposite wall. I'm betting that's where we'll find the big man's actual office, and no doubt a wall of windows, as well. Take my hand and I'll lead you, my child."

Kat opened the connecting door to the next room, and gingerly poked her head inside.

"All clear. Follow me."

Dim, filtered light bled into the room from behind a tall stretch of venetian blinds. There was enough illumination to reveal a large desk, a filing cabinet, and a long leather couch and coffee table. Along the wall to the left was a wet bar and a door to a private bathroom.

Jerry moved over to the window and tugged on a cord hanging beside the venetian blinds, raising them to reveal a panoramic vista of other residential and office towers, and, far off in the distance, a racetrack and a lake. Sunlight filled the room, bathing the space in a soft golden glow.

"Pretty nice setup this guy has. I guess crime does pay, after all," said Kat.

"Let's find out how much. There's a terminal here. Think you can hack it without calling out the dogs?"

"I'll see. Hmm.... Well, there's security, but I can temporarily firewall my activities long enough to access the internal storage and clone his disk. When we're offsite I can take my time deciphering the data. As long as nothing here needs network access, I should be able to get all the information we need. If it's in here at all, that is."

"While you're doing that, I'm going to look around for an old-fashioned secret panel or hidey-hole. It's possible this guy is arrogant enough to actually keep the disk here, if he has it. I'll start by checking the bar."

Kat looked up at him sideways as he started opening cupboards and rooting around in a small refrigerator.

"Really, Jerry? The bar? It's only 10 am. Aren't you getting a bit of an early start on the day?"

"The clock may say 10am, Kat, but don't forget those extra three hours. That puts us at 1pm in normal time. And besides, hiding stuff in a freezer is a classic move. Can I help it if a few ice cubes fall into my drink while I'm searching the icebox?"

Kat sighed. "I don't know why I even bother. You're hopeless. But as long as you're there, make one for me, too, wouldja?"

Jerry chuckled and walked over to the desk, holding out a glass. "Way ahead of you, baby. And while I'm sad to report that the freezer holds no items related to our current quest, I am nonetheless extremely heartened to announce that the bottle of vodka I found therein hails all the way from Mother Russia. So the investigation wasn't a total failure."

Kat squinched up her face as she sipped the drink. "The orange juice could stand some improvement, though."

"Hey, beggars can't be choosers. Can you imagine how far away the nearest orange grove must be from here?"

"Not as far as you might think," replied a voice from the doorway. "As it happens, we have a small orchard right here in the settlement."

The voice belonged to a tall, well-dressed man who eased his way into the room. He was holding a small plasma blaster in his hand, and was pointing it in Kat and Jerry's general direction.

**F COURSE,** the oranges we produce aren't for just anyone, you know," said the man, closing the door behind himself. "We try to save such things for the worthiest members of our little community."

Jerry smiled at him warmly. "Then I hope you won't begrudge us our little portion for our drinks. It would be such a civilised gesture, and you look like a civilised man."

The man chuckled quietly. "Of course. It's the least I can do, considering this is most likely the last drink you'll ever have."

"In that case, I should have made myself a double," said Jerry. "Can I offer you one, Mr. …?"

"Sarkosian. As I suspect you already know. And no thank you. I never drink with anyone I'm about to kill."

"Now why did you have to go and say that?" asked Jerry. "Here we were, being all friendly and such, sharing drinks and getting cozy, and you go and ruin it by talking about killing. And we haven't even properly introduced ourselves yet."

"Oh, there's no need for that. I know exactly who you are: you're the two meddlers who caused all that trouble at the Archives. And then left a long trail of dead bodies downtown. Your names are unimportant, and you've caused me a great deal of bother. You took out several of my best men last night."

"*Those* were your best men?" asked Kat. "Wow. The labour pool must be really thin on this rock."

Sarkosian sighed. "I admit, pickings are quite slim when it comes to dependable killers for hire. And now I'm afraid they've gotten a good deal slimmer.

"Oh well," he said, "if you want a job done right…."

He left the thought unfinished and settled onto the leather couch facing the desk where Kat was sitting, doing her best to look innocent and unthreatening. Hidden behind her Slimlines, her eyes were flickering back and forth as she occasionally made little movements with her jaw.

Sarkosian laughed and said, "Don't bother trying to play any tricks with my system, my dear – you won't get very far. You're not the only one with a high-end computer, you know. How do you think I found out immediately that you'd entered the building?

"You probably used the same techniques at the Archives," he continued, "which would explain how you managed to leave no electronic trail. I don't know how you managed to track down my associates in the antiques store, but I suppose it was inevitable that your search would lead you to me."

"For all the good it did us. It's clear that you don't have the disk," said Jerry. "If you did, you'd be halfway to Earth by now."

"Oh, don't be so superficial. What would I do with a planetary system? Can you imagine the incredible headache it would be to run it all?"

"I can imagine the incredible riches it would bring."

"I'm already rich," replied Sarkosian, keeping a close eye on Jerry, who was casually edging across the room, ostensibly to put down his drink on the coffee table by the couch.

"Don't dismiss the virtues of an indolent life of luxury," he continued. "How could I enjoy being the richest man in the galaxy if I were spending all my time administering some backwater mining colony?

"And why would I? I can sell ownership of this airless turd for a king's ransom and live the rest of my life in splendour without ever lifting a finger again."

"Sounds like a great plan," said Jerry, casually sitting in an armchair across from Sarkosian, with his feet ready to kick the table up and into the other man's face. "As long as everyone plays by the rules, that is. But no interstellar corporation ever got to the top of the heap by playing nice. Have you ever thought that the big money might choose simply to eliminate you and either pluck the deed from your corpse, or count on it staying lost wherever you've hidden it?"

Sarkosian sighed heavily. "You bring up an excellent point. There's no denying that the mining consortium would prefer to maintain the status quo. Killing whoever has the disk would be the go-to strategy. But as long as my identity was unknown, that option was off the table. My anonymity was my life insurance policy.

"At first I thought your arrival at the antiques store was a godsend – you left the impression you had the disk, and I offered my 'associates' a juicy reward if they could retrieve it from your corpses. It didn't matter that they would find nothing. It was enough for word to get out that I was hunting for it, just like so many other parties."

"But now that you and your pretty partner have paid me a visit, that ship has sailed. No doubt your appearance here has been noticed. You're not as discreet as you'd like to believe. This is a very small settlement. Strangers tend to stand out.

"And now that you're here, the spotlight – and the cross hairs – will settle on me."

"I hardly think we deserve all the blame," said Kat. "You should have known that killing Hector Belasky would catch someone's attention."

"Belasky!" spat out Sarkosian. "If not for that little worm, none of this mess would have occurred.

"I spent three long years painstakingly pouring over bank

records and settlement data before I finally tracked-down that disk, forgotten in a dusty old box in the Archives. But I had to leave it in its storage bin. Even I can't remove anything from the Archives storage. I had to hope it would stay undiscovered until I could make arrangements to retrieve it. After all, it had already sat there for decades.

"And then, out of the blue, while performing some meaningless menial task, that pathetic civil servant stumbles upon it purely by accident.

"He only vaguely suspected the significance of what he had found. But he knew from the Archives records that I had accessed the storage box before him, so he reached out to me with some innocent questions, mistaking me for a fellow researcher. Unfortunately, I was on the other side of the galaxy, and by time I saw his message on the local net here, he had already made other cautious inquiries."

"So much for flying under the radar," said Jerry, discreetly shifting his weight and turning to face Sarkosian more directly.

"It turned out to be a blessing in disguise, actually," replied Sarkosian, moving over on the couch farther away from the coffee table. "Safety in numbers, right? Once the cockroaches came out of the woodwork, I simply joined their ranks and pretended I was hunting for the disk, too. That allowed me to put out feelers among my associates in case any nosy busybodies came along —" he glared meaningfully at them "— and started turning over rocks that should have been left undisturbed."

"Stop," said Kat. "You're making me feel bad."

"By time I reached him, Belasky had already used his privileged access at the Archives building to circumvent their security and spirit the disk out. I played down its importance, and offered to buy it from him purely as a curiosity from a bygone era. Academic interest, all that rot.

"I thought we had come to an agreement, but he must have gotten greedy or suspicious, because the next I knew, my friends at the antiques store were calling me about a little man who had an ancient disk he needed to access. They got suspicious when he balked at leaving them any contact information, so they followed him back to his home and then alerted me.

"It's sad, really – if he hadn't gotten greedy, I would have been content to just buy the damned thing from him, but in the end I was forced to take possession in a somewhat… less profitable… manner for him. Afterwards, I tripled the reward I was offering for the disk and pulled back to let the dust settle.

"I thought everything was back on track, but then you two showed up and started throwing wrenches. Now that my involvement is virtually public knowledge, my only hope is that the mining companies won't dare kill me if it means leaving the disk floating around somewhere just waiting to be found again. They need that disk to go bye-bye, once and for all."

"So why kill us?" asked Jerry, nonchalantly crossing his legs and bringing his right foot into position beneath the coffee table top. "Sounds like you have a lock on this thing. Call the cops, turn us in for the Archives mess, and you can go back to living your life of luxury."

"Call it tying up loose ends. As long as you two are alive, I'm not the only game in town. As far as the interested parties are concerned, maybe you brought me the disk today, maybe you didn't. Either way, they might believe it would be easier to extract its location from you than from me. But once you're both dead, I regain my exclusivity. Although, sadly, not my anonymity."

"I'm so sorry we've upset your applecart," said Jerry, tensing for a kick and a leap forward. "It wasn't our intention to shine a spotlight on you."

"Speaking of which— who opened those blinds?" said Sarkosian. He snapped his fingers and the lights in the room all came on, but the blinds that Jerry had raised stayed up.

"What did you do?" Sarkosian asked Kat sharply. "Why isn't the system lowering the blinds?"

"Because I didn't use your system to raise them," said Kat. "Jerry manually pulled the cord. They probably need to be lowered the same way before you can control them remotely again."

Sighing heavily, Sarkosian stood up warily and, keeping Jerry in his sight, carefully moved around behind the desk and grasped the cord to lower the blinds.

As he stepped in front of the window and began to pull the cord, a tiny hole appeared in the window glass, accompanied by a sharp *snap!* A blossom of blood and bone and brains burst out from the back of his skull and showered desk, rug, and Kat in a splash of red muck.

"**AT! DOWN!**" yelled Jerry, leaping over the desk and tackling her, knocking her sideways off her chair and sending them both tumbling into a heap beside Sarkosian's crumpled form.

The smell of fresh blood filled their nostrils as the carpet quickly became sodden with the bodily fluids pouring out of Sarkosian's shattered skull. One side of Kat's face was coated with his blood and brains, the thick scarlet muck dripping copiously from her hair. She twisted around beneath Jerry and tried to lift her head off the floor.

"Oof!" grunted Kat. "Was that really necessary? And get your elbow off my neck!"

"Not so fast, babe. Take another look at that window."

Kat squinted up at the window above them. Two more little holes had appeared in the glass, one significantly lower, as though the shooter had been aiming at someone sitting at the desk.

"Now that's just rude," said Kat quietly. "I'm only a visitor here."

Three more little holes punctured the window in quick succession, and little pieces of desk and computer erupted into the air.

Groaning, Kat and Jerry clawed themselves closer to the wall, and awkwardly disentangled themselves from each other. Staying on their hands and knees, they crouched beneath the low windowsill.

"Glad the building's designers passed on the floor-to-ceiling window design," murmured Kat.

Grasping the cord still gripped in the dead man's fist, Kat tugged it forcefully and the sheet of blinds dropped across the window.

"That might help a bit, but I think we have some other urgent concerns, Jerry. According to my Slimlines, there are several police cars pulling up to this building's front entrance, and the elevators just disgorged a number of large men into the hallway on this floor. Wanna bet they're not here to sell tickets to the Policeman's Ball?"

"The cops might be the least of our concerns. Can your glasses get a visual on those bodies in the hallway?"

Kat paused a moment then said, "Very prescient of you, my love. Not a uniform to be seen. Looks like the bad guys have decided to tie up some loose ends themselves."

"We need a distraction, and a way out of here that doesn't involve this suite's door to the hallway."

"Um, what about the window? Any ideas there?"

Jerry looked dubiously at the wall of blinds. "I don't think so. We're fourteen storeys up, and I doubt we'll find any climbing rope in here. Maybe there's something in the bathroom we can use."

"At least we can freshen-up before they kill us," said Kat grimly.

When they opened the connecting door they were surprised to find that it didn't lead to merely a bathroom, but to an entire suite, with bed and private bath, an efficiency kitchen, and a large jacuzzi tub by a fireplace.

"When this guy wanted to take a nap, he wasn't kidding around," said Jerry.

"And if my eyes don't deceive me," said Kat, peering at the far wall, "I do believe that would be the aforementioned second exit you were pining after."

At that moment, the sound of heavy footsteps thumped nearby in the hallway. A faint murmur of conversation suggested that a discussion was underway concerning the best method of proceeding.

"Kat, there's no way we'll be slipping past the crowd in the hallway without some kind of distraction. What can you whip up for us, baby?"

"I have just the thing, but first we need to get outfitted."

She ran over to the kitchen cabinets, and after a second returned with a tube of clear plastic wrap.

"Wrap this around your eyes. Try not to cover your nose and mouth."

Jerry gave her a withering look and pulled a long strip of plastic wrap off the roll, then began wrapping his upper face.

While he was doing that, Kat disappeared into the bathroom and returned a minute later with an armful of wet towels and thick terrycloth bathrobes, along with a bottle of toilet cleanser and a short chrome bar. She dumped it all on the bed, then proceeded to wrap her own face in cellophane, covering her glasses.

"Put on a wet bathrobe, then wrap a towel around your head and face, but leave a space to see through. The wet towel should filter out most of the gas."

"What gas?"

"Halon. According to my glasses, this building uses a condensed aerosol Halon mist as its fire suppression system. Normally, in a fire, the mist clears away pretty quickly, but I'm going to juice this floor's oxygen supply and mix it in.

"Adding in the chilled oxygen should produce a thick fog that will burn the eyes, skin and lungs of anyone who tries to breathe it, along with obscuring their vision."

"Um, Kat? Won't this kill a lot of the tenants? I'm not sure I want to commit mass murder just to save my own skin."

"Not to worry, my love. I'm sealing all this floor's tenants in their suites. Only the hallway's environmental systems will be affected. And this suite, too, just to mess with them. Anyone in the hallway or this suite will asphyxiate, suffer frostbite burns, become extremely dizzy, and pass out."

"Ouch. Are you sure a couple of wet towels and bathrobes are all we'll need? You didn't find any hazmat suits in that bathroom, did you?"

"Ha. If I had, I wouldn't be stopping at just Halon gas.

"But here, take this." She handed him a large knife she had retrieved from a kitchen drawer, and carefully passed him the bottle of toilet cleanser after breaking off the cap. "I'm going to kill the lights on this entire floor. It won't be pitch-black in the hallway, though – there are little light strips along the floor that should turn on automatically. But it should add to the general disorientation.

"When we leave this room, turn left and run as hard as you can. There are service elevators at the far end. Unfortunately, our playmates are also to the left, but if anyone gets in your way, I'm sure you know what to do with that knife. Or splash their face with the stuff in that bottle. It's basically just coloured bleach. Aim for their eyes."

"And you?"

"I'll be right with you the whole time, and I'll be able to see in the dark, so I figure these are all I'll need." She hefted the chrome towel bar in one hand and a knife in the other. "Hopefully you won't get splashed with too much blood."

They finished wrapping their heads in the towels, then moved over to the door. Various muffled sounds were coming from the hallway. Kat nodded at Jerry and they both took a long, deep breath, then all the lights went out.

Immediately, loud klaxons wailed from all around them, and streams of thick mist poured out of vents in the ceiling. After waiting a few seconds, Kat yanked opened the door and she and Jerry leaped into the hallway and bolted to their left.

Two long yellow strips along the floor ran off into the distance, and faint circles of light shone from emergency lights above them. The illumination from the emergency lights was almost completely smothered by the icy white cascade of mist pouring from the ceiling. In the middle of the fog bank, Jerry could just make out a group of staggering bodies, stumbling around confusedly, hands raised to their eyes, as the sound of wracking coughs punctuated the deafening klaxons.

Silhouetted against one of the emergency lights, Kat was visible in front of Jerry. He watched as she raised her arm high in the air, then swung her chrome billy club into the face of one of the staggering shapes. The body crumpled to the ground, and Kat disappeared into the darkness.

Trying to keep up with her, Jerry bounced straight into one of the thugs. Before the fellow could react, Jerry squirted a stream from his bottle and was rewarded with a hideous scream of agony as the bleach mixture splashed into the man's already-burning eyes.

Another mountain of muscle barreled into him. A large meaty paw grabbed Jerry by the throat, pushing him backwards. The hand tightened and lifted Jerry up onto his toes, before suddenly going limp as Jerry drove his knife into the man's neck. A thick stream of scarlet liquid erupted from under Jerry's hand as he twisted the knife viciously.

The gurgling brute collapsed to the floor in front of Jerry, who casually stepped over him and back into the crowd.

Anxious to avoid any more close calls, he dodged through the mass of gasping bodies, randomly slashing with one hand

and spraying toilet bowl cleanser with the other. One by one, the field of assailants fell before him. Confused and disorganized, the hired muscle had expected to find two civilians cowering in an office, and were unprepared for hand-to-hand combat in a dark hallway during a gas attack.

Good Lord, thought Jerry. *There must be at least two dozen thugs here. Whoever wanted Sarkosian out of the picture is pulling out all the stops.*

Stumbling among the blindly careening goons, Jerry barely managed to stay upright after tripping on a crumpled form on the floor. Far ahead, he thought he could make out a figure with a long protrusion extending from an arm, and he pushed through the melee more vigourously to catch up with Kat.

He lost his knife, slippery with blood and wedged in the chest of one of their attackers. Splashing his bleach mixture with abandon, he chuckled at the angry cursing and yelps of pain that accompanied the wracking coughs and shrieking klaxons. Finally, he was free of the crowd, and raced down the hallway. Kat was nowhere in sight.

Along with the icy toxic fog filling the air, the towel and cellophane were badly restricting his vision. Squinting at the floor, he tried to follow the light strips, but suddenly they came to an end, and Jerry ran forward a few more steps before he tried to skid to a stop.

He was too late. As he halted his mad forward dash, he planted his front foot into nothingness, and pitched forward into the black abyss of an empty elevator shaft.

"**G**OTCHA!" **GRUNTED KAT,** yanking Jerry back with a firm grip on the back of his robe.

"Yow. I just barely caught you there!" she yelled into his ear, trying to be heard over the deafening klaxons. "I didn't open these elevator doors just for you to ruin all my fun. Lucky I was ready and waiting for you."

"How about a heads-up, next time?" yelled Jerry.

"What, you want maybe I should plant hazard flares in the hallway?"

Kat dragged him off to the side. They were at the end of the hallway, where it opened into a small foyer in front of three elevators. Jerry couldn't make out anything in the space, but Kat could see clearly.

They cowered there, just around the corner of the hallway, and were starting to have trouble breathing, even through their wet towel masks, when a large shape barreled past them and disappeared into the blackness of the elevator shaft. His scream of surprise could be heard for a second before the klaxons drowned it out.

Two more shapes followed him in quick succession, and then no more of their pursuers appeared.

Kat clicked her teeth together twice and the klaxons went silent. The Halon gas mist stopped pouring from the ceiling vents. She and Jerry pulled themselves to their feet and took a couple of tentative breaths as the last wisps of the gas sank to the floor.

"I'm leaving the lights off for a minute while I scope out the hallway behind us," whispered Kat.

Craning her neck around the corner, she peered down the hallway. A tumble of still bodies lay in a shallow mound halfway down the hallway, but one hardy soul was still staggering around, coughing viciously and scratching at his face.

"Be right back," she whispered, and trotted off down the hallway. A few seconds later Jerry heard a hollow metallic thump and a moment after that, Kat reappeared. The lights came back on.

"All clear, babe."

Jerry had already removed the towel from around his head and was pulling the cellophane off from over his eyes.

"Good work, Kat. Now how do you propose we exit the building? No doubt the other tenants are pouring out like rats fleeing a sinking ship, but those cops outside might be a wee bit curious to see us emerge covered in blood."

"Well," said Kat, "if we take a service elevator we can go directly to the loading docks at the service entrance. They probably won't be looking there because none of the elevators work during fire events. They'll be using the emergency stairwells at the front of the building."

Jerry looked at her skeptically. "They'd have to be pretty stupid not to have the service entrance covered."

"Precisely. Or have you somehow developed newfound respect for our local constabulary's brain power?"

Jerry sighed. "Okay, it's still our best shot. Where's that elevator?"

As they stood in front of the open shaft, an elevator hissed into place in front of them. They spotted three crumpled bodies tangled on the roof before it came to a stop.

"I hope they don't drip on us," muttered Kat as she gingerly stepped into the unit.

"Yeah, I'd hate to see you with even more blood on you,"

Having been wrapped in plastic and towels, Jerry's head and neck were relatively clean, but Kat was drenched from head to toe in splattered fluids. Her red hair was slick and nearly black on the side of her head that had been pressed into the carpet as Sarkosian's life drained out of him.

When the elevator settled into place and opened onto the service bay, Jerry cautiously peeked out at the loading dock and the access ramps.

"Kat, take off that robe and put it back on inside-out. I've got an idea."

They hustled over to the entrance ramp leading into the service bay, and Jerry pressed against the wall, craning his neck around the corner.

"Damn near every cop in the settlement is outside. Along with several hundred pissed-off rich people. Despite your precautions, it looks like most got a good lungful of your special brew – there's people everywhere on their hands and knees, retching uncontrollably."

"Yeah, I think I might have accidentally flooded the emergency stairwells, too. Oops."

Jerry stepped back as a large red and white vehicle screeched to a stop on the access road beside them. A light bar on its roof strobed while two men in white coats leaped from its cab, carrying canisters of oxygen and several face masks, and ran towards the crowd of choking residents still pouring out of the building's main entrance.

"Now," hissed Jerry, and he and Kat slipped into the ambulance's cab. Kat turned her back to the side window and lowered her head while Jerry eased them past a knot of police cars and then accelerated down the block.

"I see now why you wanted to keep the white robes," said Kat as they turned a corner and disappeared into a side street.

"Not only that, but I think they're Egyptian cotton, Kat. These blood stains should rinse right out. Score!"

THEY LEFT the ambulance idling behind a grocery store, then stuffed their robes into a trashcan down the street, with Kat overruling Jerry's protestations. A nearby transit station provided a quick escape, and within minutes they were sipping cold drinks while bringing Howard and Suzie up to speed.

"What do you mean he's dead?" asked Howard. "How could you kill our last remaining lead on the disk?"

"*We* didn't kill him. We just happened to be there when he left to meet his maker," objected Jerry.

"Same difference. Whenever you and Kat are in the area, people die, artwork explodes, and all Hell breaks loose. You two are like hand grenades with the pins pulled."

"That's unfair, Howard. Jerry and I barely escaped with our lives. If you think this job is so easy, maybe you should have done it yourself."

Howard sighed, and brushed his hand through his thinning hair. "Okay, fair point. I guess I'm just frustrated. And disappointed. It looks like that disk is lost forever now."

"Not necessarily," said Kat. "We haven't had a chance to go through Sarkosian's computer data yet. There's bound to be some kind of clue as to where he hid the disk. I can have my glasses cross-reference every byte of his data. Jerry and I have worked with a lot less, I can tell you that. Don't lose hope."

"I'll make some coffee," said Suzie brightly, "and then we can break the data down into manageable blocks and look for patterns. Your glasses might be good at crunching the numbers, but a little bit of human intuition can work wonders, too."

Kat's Slimlines had retrieved a mountainous volume of data from Sarkosian's computer. The man had fingers in dozens of pies, including several interstellar corporations and investments that spanned the galaxy.

As well, he had been studiously assembling a timeline of the disk's movements over the last century and a half since it was first placed in the bank vault. Along with the disk's history, there was an exhaustive list of the involved parties and their descendants, and their current whereabouts. DNA, retinal scans, and holograms of hundreds of the original founders' relatives filled an entire subdirectory.

Kat was scanning this list when one particular entry caught her eye. She opened the folder, and a picture popped up. Kat gasped and dropped her coffee cup.

"Kat! What the hell?" asked Jerry.

Speechless, Kat just looked up at Suzie. The other girl stared back, and her face grew pale.

"What is it, Kat?" asked Jerry. "Come on – spill."

"Maybe you should ask Suzie," said Kat quietly.

All eyes turned to the young blonde girl sitting quietly at her workstation. She licked her lips and coughed, then said, "Okay. I should have known it would come out eventually. I might as well come clean."

"What are you talking about, Sue?" asked Howard.

"I have a small confession to make, Howie. You see, when we met, well, it wasn't purely by accident."

"Go on," said Howard quietly.

"Well, I suppose I should start at the beginning. I'm not a conference organizer, like you thought, Howard. My real name is Susana Colemann Barossia de Acevedo y Aréizaga, and my father is the great-grandson of New Terra's original founders.

"My family is the rightful owner of this system, and my father has spent the last thirty years of his life trying to reclaim our property."

"So he sent you here to spy on us?" asked Kat.

"*No!* In fact, he has no idea I'm here at all. I came here on my own, to see if I could find what he couldn't.

"It was that man, Sarkosian, who got my attention, although I didn't know it was him at the time.

"I was studying philosophy at the Sillestrian Institute when I was alerted to an inquiry about me, accessing my personal data. Anywhere else, the probe would have gone unnoticed, but the Sillestrians are unusually protective of their data.

"I backtracked the query but all I could determine was that it had originated from this settlement. That piqued my curiosity, and I decided to follow-up and do some digging of my own."

"But you needed administrative access to the settlement's computer network," said Howard, in a steely tone.

"Yes," admitted Suzie, blushing. "And I had intended to merely get you to take me on as an unpaid intern, Howie. I didn't expect I would actually end up… liking you…."

"Mm-hm," grunted Howard, obviously not convinced.

"And I certainly never expected that anyone who actually had the disk would be reaching out to you. I almost had a stroke when that happened. And when we discovered he had been murdered, I panicked. Then, when you mentioned your friend Jerry, well, that gave me hope again that we might actually recover the disk."

"And what were you going to do when we found it?" asked Jerry.

"I hadn't thought it through that far. The concept of actually finding the deed was just a fantasy. I never seriously expected it would happen.

"I will tell you this, though," she continued, and when she spoke a small catch in her throat betrayed her emotion.

"My father has devoted his life to recovering our family's birthright. He has driven us into bankruptcy and ruined his health. He spends his days obsessing over it, and it has destroyed him. I would never try to steal the disk from you if you ever recovered it, but I would beg you to consider the injustice of losing an entire family's heritage, all because of a careless trustee of records over a century ago.

"If you ever did retrieve the disk, I can guarantee that my family would be excessively generous to you. There's enough wealth involved to buy dozens of planetary systems, if that's what you want.

"And to you, it might be only money, but to my father, and to my family, it is our legacy. It is who we are. It is our past. It is our future."

THE ROOM WAS QUIET as each of the four reflected on Suzie's revelations. Howard was the first to break the silence.

"Well, I can't say I'm not disappointed, Suzie. I understand what you did, but I have to be honest, my feelings are hurt."

"They shouldn't be, Howie," said Suzie. "There's nothing false about how I feel about you. You're a very sweet, loving person."

"That sounds like qualities you look for in a dog," said Howard. "I thought our relationship went a bit deeper."

Suzie said nothing, and the silence hung heavy again until Kat spoke up.

"Well, hey, this still doesn't solve our problem. Has anybody found anything in the data that might point us to where that disk is hidden?"

"I think I might have something here," said Jerry. "I've been examining Sarkosian's finances, since I have something of a corporate background."

"To say the least," said Kat.

"And I've found what may be a promising connection.

"For the most part," he continued, "Sarkosian restricted his investments to large interstellar concerns – companies that would be virtually immune to fluctuations in local economies. And I noticed something possibly significant about one of these companies, a privately-owned operation headquartered in a system quite far away.

"This company specializes in warehouses and storage facilities. They own and operate literally thousands of them across the galaxy. And, as it happens, one of their sites is in this very settlement.

"It's the high-security storage and quarantine facility at the port of entry. It doubles as a secure Customs facility and a bonded warehouse. But it's also available to the public, like when valuable goods need to wait in transit for logistical reasons."

"I see where you're going with this, Jerry, but wouldn't a storage facility be the most obvious place to hide something like our missing disk? And if anyone found out, it wouldn't take more than a few well-greased palms to 'disappear' the package. I wouldn't want to trust something this valuable to any public storage facility."

"I'm going to disagree with you here, Kat," said Howard. "I know this operation. The city uses it to store sensitive materials, and it's a tight-run ship. Once something enters the warehouse, only the person who originally checked it in can remove it – in person – using a DNA-coded authorization and a retina scan. Along with a security passcode set at the time of entry."

"That's hardly encouraging news either, Howard. If the facility is that secure, how are we supposed to find one tiny package hidden somewhere in the entire warehouse, and then remove it without the correct passcode, DNA, or retinas? Jerry and I aren't magicians, you know."

"That sounds like a challenge," said Jerry, grinning.

"Oh, good Lord," said Kat, rolling her eyes. "Save me from neanderthals and their constant need to prove themselves. What did I ever do to deserve this? Why can't you just brag about your penis, like normal men?"

"Silly Kat," chuckled Jerry, leaning over to plant a kiss on her lips. "You know that comes *after* the heist."

**AT STRETCHED OUT** her leg and wiggled her sock-covered toes enticingly. She giggled as the little black and white cat leapt on her foot and wrestled it into submission.

"Owww, oh, oh, ha, aaowwwww!" she cackled.

Jerry watched her with a grimace on his face.

"I wish you wouldn't encourage him like that. You're giving him bad habits. The other night I unconsciously flexed my foot in bed, and got stabbed with razor-sharp needles in three toes."

"Don't talk nonsense, Jerry. There's no such thing as 'razor-sharp needles' – needles are plenty sharp all on their own."

He scowled at her in exasperation, then whooped in delight as Batman gave Kat an impromptu rendition of a wolverine on the attack. She yanked back her foot with a howl of pain, and the startled cat flung itself to the ground and skittered away into the rear of their ship.

"Yeah, you better run, buster," growled Kat, rubbing at her wounded foot while Jerry guffawed.

"Do you really think," said Kat, once Jerry's laughter had subsided, "that we can pull this off?"

"Won't know for sure until Howard downloads the specs on that building. I'm not sure exactly what we're facing."

"I already expect the worst. Even their technical blueprints are kept in a secure vault offworld. I hope Howard's right about a copy in storage in City Planning."

"It sounds plausible. The settlement wouldn't jeopardize its safety by allowing any major construction to occur without vetting its structural soundness. And in a tiny enclosed bubble like this, anything your neighbours do can have a significant cascade effect on the whole community."

"In the meantime, Jerry-baby, I suggest we get a full night's sleep tonight—"

"By which you mean your new standard allotment of eleven hours—"

"*A full night's sleep*," continued Kat doggedly, "and brainstorm it out tomorrow mor— afternoon. Howard should have had a chance by then to digest whatever information he can glean about that facility. We can all put our heads together and come up with something workable."

"I'm down with that. I can hardly think right now, as it is – there's so much new information to digest."

"Are you referring, perhaps, to Little Miss Heiress?"

"Yes, that, among other things. Do you think she's for real?"

"What – you think she's some kind of Trojan Horse secret agent inserted into our little gang to spy on us? Maybe. I dunno. I'm no longer the trusting soul that I was before I met you. You've turned me into a jaded woman."

"Much as I'd love to take credit for that—"

"Says the man who carries around 'Boris & Natasha' business cards."

"Would you prefer, maybe, a 'McLovin' driver's license?"

Kat looked blankly at him, and Jerry sighed.

"I can see you still have a long way to go in your education, Kat. I've really dropped the ball on this one."

Kat punched him in the arm, then leaned over and pecked him on the cheek. "I hope Suzie is exactly who and what she claims to be. I like her."

"I like her, too, but appearances can be deceiving. In fact, something you just said has given me an idea. 'Out of the mouths of babes', I suppose."

"Care to share, Ensign?"

"Not enough information yet to make that determination, Admiral. Request permission to perform undercover work."

"WHAT?" howled Kat. "What kind of 'undercover' work? And with whom, might I ask?"

"No need to ask, baby, I'll show you."

Picking her up in his arms, he swung around in a circle and tottered off to the bedroom.

**AT, HOW MUCH** do you weigh?"

Kat's head snapped around and she fixed a withering glare on Jerry.

"How about you go f—"

"Hey hey, relax baby, I just need to know how to calibrate your weight allowance into this plan."

Howard and Jerry had been brainstorming for the last hour, muttering quietly, heads bent together, scribbling away on a paper pad, then swearing softly and ripping the pages off and crumpling them up. The floor around their feet was populated with a generous helping of these discarded ideas.

"How much room for error do you have in your calculations?" asked Kat.

"Um, I guess maybe 50 pounds or so."

Kat looked confused and Jerry immediately caught himself. "Oh, sorry babe – Howard and I have been working in non-metric measurements. They don't use metric on the station."

"Are you serious? And do they still do their computing on an abacus, too?"

"Whatever. Different cultures, right babe? Anyhow, it's 25 kilos."

"What is?"

Jerry sighed. He was sure that Kat was being purposely obtuse, but he needed the data. He soldiered on.

"The room. For error," he added. "About 25 kilos – or 50 pounds."

He looked at her expectantly.

"Well, I weigh more than…." She did a quick mental calculation. "Um, more than 100 pounds, and less than 200, so put me down for 150. The margin of error should take care of the rest."

"Really, Kat? This is what you're giving me to work with?"

"I wouldn't advise going any further with this, Jer. Just sayin'. Cause I love you." Kat's voice carried a subtone of menace, and Jerry knew when to cut and run.

"Okay, Kat, point taken. As long as you promise never to ask me if a piece of clothing makes you look fat."

"ARE YOU SAYING I'M FAT?" Kat barked.

Jerry paled. He could actually feel the blood draining from his face. He quickly glanced at Howard, who looked even paler than normal.

"Buh, buh, buh," he sputtered.

Kat broke into convulsive laughter. "Oh, calm down, Samson, I'm just messing with you. Geez, you're no challenge at all." She turned on her heel and walked off toward the coffee machine.

"Now I know why death-defying adventures don't scare you," whispered Howard. "I don't mind telling you that was a terrifying experience."

"You said it, Howard. I have stared into the abyss and emerged unscathed. Everything else is child's play compared with navigating that woman."

"She certainly is a formidable creature, I'll give you that."

" 'Formidable' is a good word. I'd hate to be that storage facility – it has no idea what it's up against, once we sic Kat on it."

"**OKAY, KAT,** front and center! Come listen to this plan. I think we've got something here."

Kat was dozing in a reclining chair on the other side of the room. At the sound of Jerry's voice her eyelids flickered to life and she gave a quick jerk. The little black and white cat that had been sleeping on her tummy grumbled an unhappy mew at the disruption, then jumped down. He slunk over to a structurally-unstable stack of wide paper printouts sitting on the floor, leapt up onto it, and flopped back to sleep.

Kat unwound her legs from around the arm of the chair she was curled up in. With a deep breath, she roused herself and tentatively stood up.

"Yow," she said, stretching her arms up above her head, then dropping them to look groggily at Jerry and Howard.

"How long have you two been at it?"

Jerry glanced down at his computer display. "Um, I dunno. Three or four hours, looks like."

"That's a long time for you. This must have been a tough nut to crack. Hit me with the deets, boss. I'm all ears."

The prospect of laying out their plan galvanized Howard to such an extent that he lifted himself out of his chair and ponderously wended his way through the obstacle course of various machines filling the office. As he began to speak he became more animated; his eyes gleamed and his words spilled out in a torrent.

"I'll sketch it out for you in broad strokes, and Jerry can fill in the details. If you think we've overlooked something, please point it out. One can lose focus on the big picture sometimes by concentrating on the minutiae. You know – a 'forest for the trees'-type scenario. This is where your perspective will really help us.

"This is a map of the facility," he said, tapping a large electronic whiteboard that sprang to life, displaying a detailed architectural drawing. "We'll get into this in much more detail later, but for now it should serve as a good introduction to what we're facing.

"The building is essentially a one-storey warehouse. It is a standalone, self-contained construction. There are no lower levels, no plumbing and no sewage lines. All electricity is generated onsite. With a big enough crane you could pick it up and drop it back down in the middle of the desert and it would continue to function exactly the same.

"If any of the humans onsite need to use a bathroom or get a drink of water, they have to exit the building and walk over to a service facility about 500 meters away. There are no pizza deliveries or any other service people allowed into the main building. I'm not even sure if the guards can bring a coffee with them when they report for work.

"Aside from the main entry portal, the entire building is wrapped in an electronic field that restricts the passage of anything bigger than a few molecules in size, along with any and all electronic transmissions. It's a giant Faraday cage on steroids. Even your magic glasses would draw a blank. The only thing that passes through the field is air. Even rainwater would bounce off, if it ever rained here."

He pointed at the upper left corner of the drawing.

"Here's the main entrance. All new arrivals come in here. Everything is thoroughly scanned, of course, for explosives or electronics. That's the limit of the scan, though – the clients do expect some measure of privacy.

"But then everything is also vetted by real humans, who perform a cursory visual examination of the item or packaging coming in. And then everything entering is weighed, down to the last gram."

"Why weigh the stuff? Are they charging by the kilo?"

"No, it's much more practical than that: any items being withdrawn from storage must weigh precisely what they weighed when they were checked in. The same security you encountered at the Archives. Even one gram difference will prevent the system from releasing the object or package. There's no tucking anything away into some larger object to get it out of the facility, or swapping any item for another.

"And finally, there's a 3-D scan to ensure the departing item precisely matches the size and shape of the item checked in."

"Alright, I get it. Deposit and withdrawal must match," said Kat.

"In every possible way," agreed Howard. "And that covers only the exterior and the entrance gates. The inside of the facility is where security really kicks into high gear, mostly via state-of-the-art electronics and robotic surveillance. If a fly ever got in there it would probably be detected and removed – or killed – within minutes of its entry.

"You, know, Howard, I'm not hearing a lot to cheer about here," said Kat. "You're saying we have to break into a 10,000-square-meter facility that's sealed up tighter than the Royal Treasury of Ob, find a wallet-sized data disk, and smuggle it out past a team of highly-trained guards and state-of-the-art electronic security safeguards."

"In a nutshell. Yes."

"I'm just dying to hear this plan. Are we going to nuke the place and then vacuum up the debris? Because that seems to me the only way we can pull off an operation like this."

Howard chuckled softly.

"No, Miss Kat, there are other ways. At least one that we can think of, and it's considerably quieter and infinitely more discreet than your suggestion, I assure you."

"Okay then, bub. Go on. Colour me intrigued."

"Right. Next we get to the facility's interior. Jerry can handle this part better, I think. This is his skill set."

Jerry moved over to the floor plan and cleared his throat.

"The crucial flaw in their security system is that there are no humans inside the actual storage area. All items are handled exclusively by robots. And for security, they rely entirely on electronics and mobile robotic patrols."

"I hardly think that's a flaw," objected Kat. "Humans are notoriously unreliable. Electronics never sleep or lose focus, and robots never need to take a bathroom break. And they're especially hard to bribe."

"Noted, but for our purposes, the lack of human observation will be this facility's undoing.

"But we're jumping ahead – let me lay out the details.

"Items are accepted or released from storage only between 8am and 5pm. Then, at precisely 5:05pm, the entire storage area goes into lockdown, and four mobile robot sensors begin a centimeter-by-centimeter 360° scan of the interior, moving rapidly through the facility down four straight aisles.

"This way, every evening a new 'map' of the space and its contents is created. It takes approximately four minutes for the robots to map their four individual 'zones' which they will then continuously patrol for the rest of the night. Any variation in their 'map' – any addition or subtraction, along with any motion aside from the robots themselves – will trigger a system-wide alert that will lock down the exits until the conflict is resolved.

"Has that ever happened?" asked Kat

"Only once," said Howard. "About two years ago one of the birds from the animal section popped-out a faulty screen and the robots picked it up immediately."

"Wait. There are animals there, too?"

"Of course," said Jerry. "We're talking housecats, show

dogs, thoroughbred stallions – you name it. Every animal coming onto the asteroid has to pass a fourteen-day quarantine. This is where they keep them."

"Sounds like overkill to keep Whiskers locked in a high-security facility just to clear quarantine."

"Except," said Howard, "before this place was built, animal kidnappings were a major criminal enterprise. Old ladies love their cats and dogs, and nothing says 'I love you' like paying a juicy ransom."

Jerry cleared his throat and resumed talking.

"The animal section is physically separated from the rest of the interior and has its own secure loading dock, with the same safeguards as the main entrance. But there'll be no smuggling inside Bowser's tummy – Bowser and the items in storage never cross paths. An interior force-field separates the two sections, and it's never turned off. If it ever were, alarms would lock down the whole facility, so I recommend keeping clear."

"Are there cameras monitoring the facility, as well?"

"In the entrance area and outside in the compound, but not inside the storage area, because the interior was designed to prevent access from anywhere outside the storage space. Cameras need transmission lines or wireless communications, either of which could be used to hack into the security systems. The interior robots and electronics are shielded from all exterior access. They need to be programmed offsite by the facility's own techs. There is no remote or wireless access to the robots' systems, only a single physical access port that needs to be manually connected to a service technician's diagnostic station. Offsite."

"The techs can't come into the facility during down-time to run diagnostics on the robots?"

"No, Kat. You're not listening: no human *ever* steps foot inside the storage area. There'll be no impersonating a maintenance tech to access the site."

"How about air ducts? We've used those in the past," said Kat, thinking back to how she first met Jerry.

"Nothing larger than 15 centimeters in diameter. You could stick your arm into one, maybe, but not much more than that unless you lose a considerable amount of weight."

"Aside from the animals, why does the site need air at all? Why isn't it filled with argon gas or something similar?"

"There are other items that require atmosphere, Kat. Exotic plants, food items, certain kinds of artworks, even some specific fabrics. It would be too difficult to separate each special-needs item. It's more efficient to keep a normal environment in place. But it's irrelevant, because humans simply never get inside."

Kat stared at the blueprint in silence, then exhaled deeply.

"So far, guys, I'm just not seeing it. Tightly-controlled access combined with impenetrable security and continuous surveillance doesn't exactly sound like a walk in the park. I can't think of any way to extract our disk except for using some kind of remote device, and that's clearly off the table."

"You're not thinking laterally, Kat," said Jerry. "We're going to use their own security system against them, turning their strengths into weaknesses.

"You should be proud – you were actually the one who gave me the idea. We're going to smuggle something into that facility which will allow us to locate and retrieve the disk, and then to remove it from the building."

Kat snorted.

"Right. And what might this miraculous device be, pray tell?"

"It's you, Kat. We're going to smuggle you inside and then smuggle you back out again. With the disk."

PART III:

THE SET-UP

Luck is when preparation and opportunity meet.
— Pierre Elliot Trudeau

JERRY TURNED HIS HEAD yet again and scanned the street behind them. Kat glanced over at him with a look of exasperation.

"Maybe it would be easier on you if you just walked backwards, Jer. Either that, or you might consider growing flexible eye stalks."

"Oh sure, it's alright for you, Kat, what with your fancy see-behind-you x-ray specs and all, but us normal folks have to go Old School if we don't want to be jumped from behind."

"It would be better if you just left the surveillance to me, then, Jerry. We might actually eke out some small advantage if anyone tailing us thinks we're unaware. But as long as you keep pulling a Linda Blair every thirty seconds, we look like fugitives on the run."

"Where did you get that Linda Blair reference?" asked Jerry, casually glancing at a store window that reflected an image of the street behind them.

"I've been exploring your collection of ancient horror movies while you work. You don't think I've been *reading*, do you?" she asked, shuddering slightly at the thought.

"Certainly not," replied Jerry, grinning. "I would have noticed. You mumble while you read. And your lips move."

He ducked to avoid her swat, and slipped off the curb, almost stumbling into a trash receptacle.

"Very graceful," said Kat. "Should I call the Flying Wallendas and see if they're hiring?"

Jerry opened his mouth to deliver a juicy rejoinder, then closed it again abruptly as they turned a corner and came face-to-face with the address they were searching for.

The building façade was covered in fantastical shapes in a nightmarish mix of colours. There were towering centaurs, galloping unicorns and shrieking griffins, as well as an entire tableau of fire-breathing dragons swooping down on winsome maidens cowering behind knights brandishing swords and shields in heroic poses.

The sculptures looked to be pounded out of several different metal alloys and were in various states of ageing, with fine green patinas on several bronze creations and a rainbow of pastel-colours on the silver forms. The shapes looked like they had been randomly hung over whichever empty spots on the wall were most convenient.

An empty lot sat beside the building, at the end of the block. It was surrounded by a chain link fence that had already started to accumulate its own collection of metallic hallucinations. Inside the lot were heaps of twisted raw metal, loosely grouped into piles according to the metals' composition.

Kat looked dubiously at Jerry. "If you tell me we're here to pick up a suit of armour, I'm bailing."

Jerry chuckled quietly. "Patience, grasshopper. You'll figure it out soon enough. Embrace the unknown.

"And speaking of which, do you see a door buzzer? Or should we just walk in?"

"No buzzer, I'm going with independent entry," said Kat, tugging a bar welded onto a metal door that had been hammered into an imitation sarcophagus, featuring a life-size disinterred corpse writing in agony. Two bulging eyes goggled at her from over a gaping, toothless mouth as the door swung open under her grasp.

Kat took a tentative step forward into a cavernous warehouse illuminated by a row of gigantic skylights stretching from one end of the space to the other. Random towering shapes in various stages of completion loomed throughout the building, encompassing a wide range of real and mythical creatures, not only of Earth but also from several other planets.

Stepping between the legs of a 15-meter-tall nickel and iron giant horned Rodassian Canyon Lizard, Jerry ducked his head beneath the skeletal framework of its spiked tail and called out, "Helloooo! Mr. Petrovsky? Are you here?"

His voice echoed eerily off the surrounding metallic forms, resonating in deep bass tones as the sound waves bounced around within each sculpture before exiting as vaguely musical vibrations.

Near the back wall of the warehouse, a shiny bald head appeared, poking up from between the shoulder blades of a larger-than-life Silverback Mountain Gorilla frozen in mid-leap, arms stretched out high in the air and jaws wide open.

"On my way," the man called, sliding face-down along the gorilla's back and gracefully landing behind the beast.

"Viktor Petrovsky at your service," he said, walking over and wiping his hands on the front of his coveralls. "You are Mr. Wayne, I take it? Bruce Wayne?"

"In person," said Jerry, shaking the man's hand. "And this is my apprentice, Ms. Prince."

"Please, call me Diana," said Kat, flashing a friendly smile.

"I can't tell you what a pleasure it is to meet you both," said Petrovsky, leading them over to some chairs clustered around a desk buried in layers of sketches and technical drawings. "I'm a big fan of your work. Do you have much chance to get out of Gotham these days?"

Jerry looked alarmed, then embarrassed. Kat burst out laughing.

Petrovsky chuckled. "You should know better than to cull your aliases from comic books when dealing with a sculptor of fantastic beasts, 'Mr. Wayne'. Where do you think I get my inspiration? From encyclopedias?"

"I – I'm sorry," stuttered Jerry. "It's just that we're trying to fly under the radar on this job. Please don't take it the wrong way. I hope you're not offended."

Petrovsky laughed and clapped Jerry on the back.

"Not at all, not at all! It's a welcome change from the usual stuffed shirts who hire me. If I have to do even one more cat sculpture portrait for some doting dowager, I might turn to dipping the little beasts in molten bronze and be done with it."

"We're not letting this guy anywhere near Batman," murmured Kat.

Scanning the gigantic sculptures around them, Jerry said, "These pieces don't look all that stuffy to me."

"Oh, these are what I do for myself. Can't let the inner artist suffocate, you know. Fortunately, there's a market for them, as well. Several collectors throughout the galaxy are quite enamoured of my work. I just hate to see some of them go. I think of many of them as my children. I'm sure that sounds silly to you."

"Not at all," said Jerry, craning his head back to admire a flock of pterodactyls suspended from the rafters.

"Can I twist your arms and convince you to join me in a refreshment?" said Petrovsky, rooting through a small fridge. "Let's see, I've got some tonic water, gin, rum, lime juice, a bottle of tomato juice smuggled off a cargo ship from Benson's World, no celery or Worcestershire sauce, I'm afraid, so Bloody Marys are off the table, and no vodka either, for that matter… looks like we're fresh out of Scotch, too, that's a pity, I'll have to look for some next Market Day… oh! I didn't know I had this bottle of Peppermint Schnapps, that's a nice surprise… or I could make you a coffee, I suppose, if you don't feel like a cocktail so early in the day…."

"Bite your tongue," said Kat. "You had me at gin and tonic. And since you have lime juice, too, it's almost like a sign from above."

"Well, I wasn't sure if superheroes drank," he said, eyes twinkling.

"We're off duty," said Kat, with a grin. "And since we're bonding over alcohol, I suppose you should know our real names."

"Oh, please, no. I so much prefer 'Bruce' and 'Diana'. They suit you. Maybe you can think of one for me, too?"

"How about 'Mister Mxyzptlk'," suggested Jerry.

"I love it!" said Petrovsky. "The trickster is my favourite villain. But just 'Myx' should do for short."

"Deal," said Jerry, clinking glasses with him.

"Well, I suppose we should get down to business," said Petrovsky. "I'm sure you didn't drag yourselves all the way over to the bad side of town just to swig rotgut gin."

"The gin's not that bad, but you're right about the business, Myx," said Jerry. "We need a special custom job, and I'm afraid time is of the essence."

Petrovsky shrugged. "I'll be happy to oblige. My panorama of *Fluffy and Her Kittens Cavorting in the Garden* will just have to wait.

"Besides," he added in a conspiratorial tone, leaning closer to Kat and winking, "I can usually charge more if I delay a job. Makes the clients think I'm a real artist."

"It took Michaelangelo five years to paint the Sistine Chapel," said Kat.

"Exactly!" laughed Petrovsky. "Maybe I should add in the hand of God scratching Fluffy behind her ears. I could double the price.

"But we digress – tell me more about this custom job."

"We're not particular, Myx" said Jerry. "You can probably just adapt something you've already got lying around. We need a large animal – a cow, a horse, camel—"

"Or a griffin, maybe, or a dragon—" added Kat in a hopeful tone, still not sure exactly what Jerry had in mind.

"And it has to be hollow, of course, with a secret latch inside that will allow one occupant to emerge from a hidden exit at a time of their choosing. It has to be airtight and the interior needs to be lined with a copper fiber mesh over sheets of carbon nanotubes."

"I'm starting to get the idea," said Petrovsky.

"You and me both, Myx," said Kat.

Jerry turned to look at Kat and pretended to size her up, and while staring directly at her, added, with a meaningful emphasis, "The space inside should be, oh, at least four – no, five feet long and two feet high."

Petrovsky looked at Kat, who had gotten very quiet. "Perhaps we should be calling you 'Helen' instead of 'Diana', my dear."

Kat grimaced and said, "I wish. In all the versions I've read, Helen was never actually *inside* the horse."

"**OW I KNOW** why you didn't want to let me in on the specifics last night, Jerry. It won't work."

"Howard and I went over every last detail. It will work just fine."

"Not if what you told me is correct. You said everything is weighed and scanned when coming in and going out. Okay, let's say you can smuggle me in. But how do you keep my weight from changing by even one gram while I'm inside? Are you expecting me to stop perspiring? Not to mention the added weight of the disk I'll supposedly be carrying on the way out. It's not possible."

"We thought of that, Kat, and we think we have a solution."

"You *think*? Would you like to rephrase that, Jerry?"

"Okay – we *know*. All will be made clear once we have a chance to sit down and go through it with you step by step. Last night was just the broad strokes."

"And even if you can somehow get me in and back out again, how am I supposed to wander freely through an enclosed space with four surveillance robots that will lose their little silicon minds the minute I set foot in the warehouse?"

Jerry sighed.

"Kat, relax. I would never put you in danger."

Immediately rethinking his statement, he said, "I mean, never intentionally—"

"Keep trying, Jerry," said Kat.

"Never delibera— ah, well, you know what I mean, Kat.

I'll only *allow* you to do this if you are as convinced as I am that it's perfectly safe. We're all going to sit down tonight and hash this operation out, minute by minute, and when we're done you'll have a newfound respect for my intellect. Just you wait and see."

"Humph. I'm not sure if my respect for your intellect will ever match my joy at seeing this lifeless chunk of space rock shrinking in my rear-view mirror."

"That will come, too. In the meantime, our next activity should do absolute wonders to improve your mood."

"What, are we going to get drunk and forget we ever heard of this place?"

"Even better, Kat – we're going shopping."

TRY AS SHE MIGHT, Kat couldn't contain her happiness as they strolled down the street. Jerry grunted in consternation to look at her.

"A city full of thugs trying to bump us off, the authorities looking to lock us up and throw away the key, even our friends concealing their real identities from us, and all it takes to make you whistle a happy tune is an afternoon of shopping."

"Oh, don't be so paranoid, Jerry. *One*: no one is looking for us – anyone who could identify us is either dead or in a coma, and thanks to my glasses, even the city's video surveillance system has no record of our existence."

"And 'two'?"

"*Two*, when else do I ever get to go on a shopping spree? I'm going to enjoy every last minute of this."

"Even though we're not going to keep any of it?"

"That's irrelevant. The fun part is the *buying*. If you'd ever been a girl you'd understand that."

"I'll have to remember to make that switch the next time I get regenerated. Maybe life will be more interesting on the other side of the street."

Kat wrinkled her nose. "Don't forget to send me a postcard if you ever do that. I'd love to know how that works out for you."

They paused for a moment to look in the window of a furniture store selling faux leather couches and armchairs.

"Whaddaya think, Jer? Worth a look?"

"I don't think so. This stuff looks kind of cheap. Don't

forget, the furniture we're shipping needs to look like something a dealer in rare antiques would have in his own home. These pieces would be more suitable for furnishing a budget hotel lobby."

"Are these people even going to look at the furniture? I think you're stressing over something unnecessary."

"The devil is in the details, Kat. The whole picture needs to be in sync. You wouldn't spend thousands of credits shipping junk like this. It has to be special. Let's move on."

The next block didn't hold any better prospects, and they were about to turn around and try a different area of town when Jerry spotted a discreet sign on a shop door.

ABERFOYLE & POLLARD
FINE HOUSEHOLD GOODS
BY APPOINTMENT ONLY

"This looks like what we want, Kat."

"But we don't have an appointment."

"We've got something better," said Jerry. "Money."

He pressed his thumb to the bell and kept leaning on it until the door was yanked open by an officious looking man in a neat grey suit.

"What do you think you're doing?" screeched the man.

"We need to buy some furnishings," said Jerry, nonplussed.

"Do you have an appointment? Can't you read the sign? Make an appointment and we can discuss it." The man moved to close the door in Jerry's face.

"We need furniture right away," replied Jerry calmly, moving his foot to block the door from closing. "We don't intend to sit on the floor while you pencil us in on your calendar."

The man goggled at him with a look of pure wonder. It was obviously not within his recent experience to be pushed around by a member of the public.

"Move your foot," he said. "And then go away."

"I will do neither," said Jerry. He extracted a thick sheaf of credit notes from his jacket and said, "I'm not here to haggle over prices. I'm here to buy whatever you have onsite today. You can take my money right now or I can go elsewhere. Make your mind up quickly, though. I don't have all day."

Jerry had learned long ago the distinct psychological effect the sight of real money had on people. Even the most haughty and arrogant sellers were moved by a wad of thick banknotes waved in their face. Numbers on a piece of paper or computer screen had nowhere near the same power.

The gentleman standing before Jerry was no exception to the rule. His eyes bulged to see the stack of thousand-credit notes that Jerry casually brandished in front of him, and his attitude adjusted accordingly.

"Well," he said, "if you're not special-ordering anything and are content with display models or what we already have in stock, I suppose we could accommodate you right now…."

"Excellent," said Jerry, striding past the man. "My name is Carter, John Carter, and this is my associate, Dejah Thoris. We are the executive assistants for a well-known industrialist who does not want his commercial interest in this system to become common knowledge."

"Discretion and confidentiality are our byword," said the man, trotting to keep up. "I can personally assure you that our transaction today will never be known to any but we three."

"Personal assurances are worthless," said Kat dismissively. "Yet we have no choice but to trust you. I will make my selections. If you have anything halfway acceptable, that is."

Kat swept off into the interior of the salon, which boasted several mock living room arrangements. Sumptuous, overstuffed leather armchairs and couches surrounded coffee tables adorned with gold and platinum filigrees on their legs and edges, as well as a generous sampling of side tables, bookshelves, and ornate lamps.

"Those will do," said Kat, waving her hand in the direction of a Louis XVI tableau. "Barely. But we'll need another settee, if you have one, and that sideboard is absolutely hideous. Take it out."

"Over here," she continued, "this lamp. That couch and the armchair. And that wonderful tapestry, over there. The one with the foxes and hounds."

The merchant tapped frantically on his tablet as he noted her choices.

"That wine rack. And those hangings. Oh – those statues – what are they? Are they originals or copies?"

The man followed her eyes over to a series of tabletop-sized bronze statuary and exclaimed, "Those? Those are Remingtons – he was quite well-known on Earth, once, you know. And of course, those aren't originals. The original pieces are scattered among several different museums on Earth, I believe."

"Copies, eh?" Kat sniffed in disdain. "Well, I suppose if it's all you have…."

She moved deeper into the salon. Jerry watched the merchant scurry after her, tapping all the while on his tablet as she gestured left and right. He leaned against a high-backed armchair and smiled, amused that this was all it had taken to completely change her mind about the job.

Eventually, Kat swept off back toward the salon's entrance, and the shopkeeper made his way over to Jerry.

"It looks like we're done here," said Jerry, glancing at the numbers on the tablet. "I'll send some people by to pick up the pieces in a day or two. And I'll need complete documentation on everything, in case we need to ship it offworld."

The man nodded and swallowed thickly as Jerry peeled off several credit notes. "Ah, I'm sorry, but I don't think I can make change for you," he said. "We don't keep currency on the premises. So few people choose—"

"No change needed," said Jerry, cutting him off. "Consider it our way of thanking you for ensuring that everything goes smoothly when my people come by later."

The merchant pumped their hands enthusiastically before showing them to the door, and when Kat and Jerry were once again on the sidewalk, Kat couldn't help but laugh.

"I hope you don't mind I took the lead, there, Jer."

"Wouldn't have it any other way, hon. When it comes to emasculating and dominating men, I defer to the experts."

AT NIBBLED IDLY on her tongue while running her pencil down the list, noting each check mark beside the entries.

Batman perched on his cat tree beside the small desk where Kat was working. He lolled over onto his back and desultorily batted at a small fluffy ball dangling above his head on a thin elastic cord. His heart wasn't in it, though, and he rolled over again, then leapt down onto the paper in front of Kat, riding it across the desk like a mini hoverboard. He slid off the desk and thudded into Kat's chest, deftly clinging onto her t-shirt with a decidedly injudicious deployment of claws.

"*Yow-wow-wow!*" screeched Kat, lurching backwards in her chair. She and Batman tumbled to the floor, but before she could deliver any punishment, the cat tore off in the direction of the bedroom.

Jerry looked up from the news foil he was reading and tsk-tsked.

"Kat, stop fooling around with the cat and finish looking over that list, wouldja."

She shot Jerry an evil look, then stood up and righted the chair. She pressed her fingertips against her temples and moaned.

"This is giving me a headache, Jer. Why couldn't you and Howard make your checklists on the computer, like normal humans?"

"So you say, but nothing works as well as pen and paper – or, in your case, pencil and paper. There's no scrolling back and forth between screens, no lost data, no distracting graphics or popup notes...."

"You used to manage several multinational corporations employing hundreds of thousands of people. Please tell me you used computers *then*."

"Of course we did. But the real value in computers is in performing repetitive tasks or managing large data sets. And I had people who did that for me. Then they summarized their findings and gave me a written report. On paper. It must have been a good system – I was very successful."

"So was the guy who invented the wheel – but I wouldn't want to have to work with a stone hammer and chisel today."

"Then you're lucky we've got plenty of pencils and paper. Now please tell me if we've covered all the bases. I'm way too tired to run any more errands."

"It looks complete to me."

"You got ahold of your engineer friend to send you more oxygen masks?"

"Yep. Did it while you were in the shower."

"Should I be jealous that you talk to this guy only when I'm not around? Seems a tad suspicious to me."

Kat laughed. "Brian? Oh, God, no. I love him to death, but have you ever met a real, living, breathing engineer?"

"I don't believe in stereotypes."

"You would if you ever met Brian. You know he designs prototypes for new EV suits, right? His company is actually the inventor of my snugsuit."

"Yeah, so?"

"Well, you don't just design a new suit then send someone into vacuum wearing it – it has to be tested.

"So, to stress-test his new suits, Brian built a bunch of life-size animatronic robots – all of whom just happen to look like tall, blond, Scandinavian women. He refers to them as his 'girlfriends'."

Jerry laughed. "Okay, Kat, say no more. You've made your case."

"He's sending me a box of masks overnight. So I can keep a bunch of them on hand for my next urgent situation. Which I assured him would never occur."

"Pollyanna, I salute thee."

"Har de har. Wait and see. Next time, *you're* the one who'll be wearing a mask or swimming through vacuum."

"Only if there's a bevy of Scandinavian supermodels waiting for me at my destination. And not the imaginary kind."

Kat peered down at her t-shirt and cursed softly to see two tiny red spots where Batman had been clinging on to her.

"Dammit. One of my favourite shirts, too."

Peeling it off, she tossed it aside and pounced on Jerry, knocking his news foil to the side.

"Meow," she said.

"My thoughts exactly," said Jerry, gripping her around her waist while she straddled his lap and nuzzled up into his neck. "Let's just keep those claws sheathed, though, okay, baby?"

**AT LAY ON HER BACK** and stared up at the cabin ceiling. Beside her, Jerry was snoozing on his side, curled up and breathing deeply.

"I'm bored, Jerry. And not just bored. I'm jumpy, too. The waiting is getting to me."

Jerry snuffled, then rolled onto his back. He blinked slowly two or three times, and finally turned his head to look at Kat.

"Not much we can do about that, baby. Until Myx finishes the horse, we're treading water. Nothing left to do but wait. All boxes ticked, remember? Why don't you go play with Batman or meditate or something?"

He rolled back onto his side and closed his eyes again. Kat continued to fidget.

After a few minutes she said, "Can't we at least get out of here and go hang with Howard and Suzie? I could use a change of scenery. We haven't even left this ship for two days. I'm getting cabin fever here, Jerry."

Jerry sighed and rolled onto his back again.

"Honey, you know we can't chance being spotted. The last thing we want is to lead anyone back to Howard and Suzie."

" 'Anyone' like who? There's no one left who can recognise us."

"You know that's not true – what about those two guys in the antiques store, or that rental agent from Belasky's apartment? Or Clara – she can probably accurately describe us right down to our shoe sizes. And what makes you think none of our admirers ever thought to snap our picture?

"I might be less paranoid, Kat, if the online chatter about the disk had died down, but ever since Sarkosian's death it's ramped-up into high speed. And we've been elected as Most Likely to Possess, putting us directly in the crosshairs."

"Look, Jerry, either Belasky or Sarkosian must have spilled the beans about what's on the disk, judging by some of these messages, but everyone seems clueless about who we might be."

"Because we came late to the party. But that doesn't mean we can just stroll around town without a care in the world. We were lucky to get all our shopping done without being spotted. I don't want to tempt Fate."

"And I'm not suggesting that we do. We can avoid the back alleys and opium dens. There's a discreet little jazz club here that offers dining in a romantic setting with a live band. It's a nice opportunity to dress up and recharge our batteries.

"Just dinner and some good music, Jer. Two hours. Three, tops. We'll go directly there and come back with no detours or sightseeing. Whaddaya say, hon?"

Jerry sighed. Kat knew every button to push, and she was hammering on them mercilessly. He loved good jazz, and after two days of eating nothing but Kat's culinary creations he was starting to look longingly at Batman's food dish.

"Fine," he said, regretting it as the words escaped his lips. "Two hours. There and back. Then we're done."

"Oh baby, you're the best," squealed Kat excitedly, pouncing onto him and peppering him with kisses. "You'll see, you'll love it. You may be grumpy now, but you'll thank me later."

"Maybe," he said. "Miracles do happen."

*　　　　*　　　　*

Kat's most distinctive feature was her long red hair, so she tied it back into a severe bun. She and Jerry both dressed in the most nondescript manner they could, Kat wearing a simple black knee-length dress, and Jerry sporting a black suit jacket and dark shirt and pants.

The jazz club was one short block away from a transit stop, and since they saw no one on the street during their walk over, they arrived feeling confident and relaxed.

"See, honey?" cooed Kat, pecking Jerry on the cheek. "What did I tell you?"

"Hmmph. I'll defer judgment till we're back home, okay?"

The club was hopping. A fifteen-piece jazz band was playing on a raised stage at the far side of the room. There was a small dance floor in front of the stage, and around that a dozen round tables for dining. The dance floor was crowded with couples trying their best not to step on their partners' toes, and well-dressed diners occupied all the tables.

"Good evening," said a striking brunette just inside the entrance. She was wearing a tight, eye-catching emerald dress with a low scoop neckline that perfectly complemented her large green eyes. The tasteful string of pearls she wore around her neck competed for attention with the revealing swell of her breasts; as far as Jerry was concerned, the pearls were losing the match.

"Do you have a reservation?" asked the woman.

"I confess, we don't," said Jerry. "This was sort of a spur-of-the-moment decision."

"Oh, I'm sorr—" began the young woman, but before she could proceed any further, Jerry caught her attention with a 500-credit note, which he gently placed on the tablet she held.

"What I mean to say," she continued, barely missing a beat, "is that I'm sorry that the kitchen will be closing in thirty minutes. If you intend to eat, you'll have to order right away.

"Please follow me," she said, turning and leading them to a table that had just been cleaned.

On either side of the dining area was a slightly elevated section behind a short chrome railing. In this section there were only comfortable armchairs and tiny tables for holding drinks. A number of patrons sat in this area, drinking and tapping their feet to the music. The darkest alcoves farthest from the stage were populated with individuals interested more in quiet conversation than in the music, and in one of these corners two gentlemen sat intently watching Kat and Jerry as they were ushered to their table.

"I must be dreaming," said one of the men. His name was Frenetti, and he was solidly built, with thick cords of muscles in his neck, arms and back that filled-out his custom-tailored suit. The highball glass he toyed with almost disappeared into his meaty paw, and he gently swirled the ice cubes around in the Scotch with an imperceptible motion of his hand.

"I can't believe it myself," said his companion, an older individual with greying hair at his temples. "What are the odds?"

"Mebbe it's a setup," said Frenetti. "This sort of thing doesn't just fall into your lap. I say we get more info before we make any moves. Mebbe ask 'em a few careful questions."

"Well don't look at me – I don't want to join the body count they've been racking up. I don't care what the finder's fee is."

"I agree entirely," said Frenetti. "Norman should take care of this. Bout time he did something to earn his protection."

"I thought that's what the cash and the free drinks was for," said the other man, and they both chuckled.

*   *   *

Jerry was swallowing the last bite of his steak just as the band concluded a particularly energetic rendition of "Two O'clock Jump", and he put down his fork to join the rest of the patrons in enthusiastic applause.

"Likin' it, are you, Jer?" asked Kat, smiling.

"Okay, you got me baby. This was a good idea. I feel like a new man."

The band put down their instruments and filtered off the stage for a break, and the trumpet player wandered into the dining area, glad-handing various patrons. Eventually his path led him to Kat and Jerry's table.

"How do you like the show?" he asked, standing between their chairs and putting a hand on each of their backs as he leaned over to talk. "I'm Norman Herd. I own this place."

Jerry glanced up at the big bass drum emblazoned with the name, "The Thundering Herd".

Norman followed his eyes and said, "As in."

Jerry beamed up at him with a broad smile.

"Best music I've heard outside of Regis Prime, Mr. Herd."

"Please. Call me Norman. And thank you – that's a great compliment. I played in a couple clubs on Regis before settling here. They know their jazz on that rock."

"You played on Regis?" asked Jerry, raising his eyebrows. "Then what in the world brought you here? That's like leaving Broadway to play the Catskills."

Norman laughed and said, "Maybe not quite as bad as all that. And I have other interests. Several thoroughbreds at the track belong to me. My plate is full here, and I've got no complaints."

"It's our good fortune, then, Mr— Norman. Wish I'd found this place sooner. We would have come every night."

"You're too kind. Stick around and take in the second half. We do a version of 'I'm Beginning to See the Light' that'll knock your socks off. Nice meeting you both."

Norman straightened up, and as he did a tiny charcoal-grey worm twisted slightly on the place where he'd rested his hand on Jerry's back. The worm nuzzled into the cashmere, bored a little hole, slithered into the material and disappeared.

As Norman wandered away and engaged another couple in conversation, Kat glanced at her watch and said, "I'm afraid we'll have to miss that performance. We're way past our two-hour allotment already, and I don't think it's such a good idea to be on the street too late."

Jerry grimaced.

"Now who's being the wet blanket, Kat?"

He sighed.

"But you're right. Again. We'd better be shoving off."

He waved meaningfully at their waiter, and laid a small stack of credit notes on the bill when it arrived.

As they slipped out of the club, Jerry noticed Norman joining two men drinking at one of the tables off to one side. He was happy the man was occupied elsewhere and wouldn't notice Kat and Jerry leaving. He didn't want to seem rude.

Their departure did not go unnoticed, of course. All three men watched them from the corners of their eyes, and only once the pair had left the club did they speak.

"What did you say to them?" asked Frenetti. "They sure ran out in a hurry after you left. I told you to get them to stick around until our boys could get here."

"I tried," said Norman. "I was friendly, just like you said."

Norman licked his lips nervously. He didn't like dealing with these gangsters, and especially didn't like paying them off each month and then having to watch them guzzle his liquor for free every night.

But what choice did he have? Everything he owned was tied up in this club and his horses. Between the mining consortium and the local syndicates, this settlement was nothing but a ruthless fiefdom that bled honest businessmen for every penny they could pay.

"Tell us you planted the tracker," said the man with the greying temples.

"Of course I did. I'm not an idiot. But you'd better hope they don't have electronic countermeasures in place – they didn't seem like stupid people to me."

"That won't be a problem. We already know about these two and their little tricks. The tracker's not electronic – it's organic."

Norman was horrified.

"Organic? You mean I just infected them with a parasite? Have you lost your mind? I'm happy to let you have the run of my club, but I draw the line at breaking Interstellar Law. I don't care how powerful you think you are on this god-forsaken pebble – disseminating parasitical organisms will land us all in a penal colony for the rest of our lives."

"Lower your voice, you little shit," said Frenetti. "It's not a parasite. It's just a mindless lump of cells goosed-up with a unique strontium isotope. Our scanners can locate it anywhere in the settlement. And it won't be detected because strontium is already in all of us. Just not this particular isotope, is all. But it won't set off any alarm bells. It'll just sit in their clothing and do nothing."

"I still don't like it," said Norman, and stood up to leave. "Next time you need an errand boy, get someone else. And not in my club, either."

Watching him walk away, the man with greying temples said quietly, "That's going to be a problem."

"Who? That little *impiegato*? Not for a second."

"Which is exactly how long he'll hold up under interrogation."

"You worry too much. There won't be any interrogation. The boss isn't so stupid. Anything happens to those two, it'll be a tragic accident, nothing more. You'd be surprised how many different ways there are to die on a mining settlement."

Frenetti downed the last of his Scotch, stood up and straightened his suit jacket. There was no bill, of course. There never was. But the buxom young waitress knew him well and made sure to cross his path when he was on his way out.

"Thanks for the service, honey," he said, grabbing a healthy handful of her ass while he stuffed a 100-credit-note down the front of her dress, making sure to fondle and squeeze her breast before withdrawing his hand. The waitress giggled and batted her eyes at him, but he paid no further attention to her as he made for the door.

Frenetti's partner watched him and gritted his teeth at the thought of the 100-credit note wedged in her cleavage.

"You're a little too free and easy with our dough, Frenetti. That's our stake you're throwing away on empty-headed bimbos. We come up short at the track, tomorrow, it's on you. *You* can explain why we couldn't grease the palms the boss told us to."

"Calm down. I already told you, you worry too much. In less than an hour the boss is gonna be kissing our feet, when I tell him how I pasted a tracker on them two."

"You mean how Norman did that."

"I mean exactly what I say. Norman was just the means. The tracker was all me. Us. Whatever. Doesn't matter, because the finder's fee on these two is so big it'll set us both up for a year."

"Maybe we should have played it safe then, and just rubbed them out when they left."

"Don't be stupid. The boss said no more heat. Wants it to look like an accident. How's it gonna go over if you whack them right outside the club? What kinda accident is that?"

"Okay, you're right, Frenetti. So how do you suppose he's going to take them out?"

"Depends where they're holed-up, I figure. If it's a high-end hotel suite, maybe a drunken fall from a balcony. Or could be an airlock malfunction – they wouldn't be the first clueless tourists to lock themselves out of the dome. The possibilities are endless."

"Well, we'd better deliver the tracking info right away. The sooner we hand this over, the less likely it'll go sideways."

"That's the first smart thing you've said tonight," said Frenetti with a grin. "Feel like a twofer? I'll let you guess which time tonight those two offworlders get their bells rung. If you're within an hour, I'll buy the drinks at the track tomorrow."

"You're on," said the greying temples. "But if we're gonna split that finder's fee, I might skip the track and come back here for that little waitress. If she lets you feel-up her tits for a hundred, just imagine what she'll do for a cool grand."

Frenetti guffawed and slapped the other man on the back, then waved down a cab, and they both got in and disappeared down the street.

IT WAS A short cab ride. In a settlement only fifteen kilometers wide, space was at a premium, with an orderly, logical arrangement of neighbourhoods according to usage.

The two men stepped out onto a quiet residential street. They were near the edge of the city, and the stars were clearly visible through the crystal-clear dome.

"It gives me the creeps to see stars like that," said Frenetti. "They shouldn't have made the roof so clear. Who needs to be always reminded that we're sitting on an empty rock in the middle of space?"

"You mean like on every other planet in the universe?" said his partner, smirking.

"I mean like not stuck on an airless chunk of stone that could spin away and take all of us with it."

The greying temples just shrugged. "So let's get inside. I don't want you having a panic attack on me."

Frenetti glared briefly at the other man, then turned to the mansion in front of them.

The property was set back from the street, in a deliberate display of wasted resources. Green, well-tended lawns surrounded the main house, and a wide driveway sweeping around the building indicated the presence of servants' quarters in the rear.

A butler answered their ring at the door, and ushered them into a wood-paneled room deep in the house where two men sat holding highball glasses. They looked up as the two guests arrived, but did not offer them a seat or drinks of their own.

Only once the butler had left the room and closed the door behind himself did one of the seated men speak.

"Leo," he said, barely nodding to Frenetti. He ignored the Frenetti's partner. "You have good news, you say."

"Yessir, Mr. Carvallo," said Frenetti. "I – we – Tony and me, we spotted those two offworlders you're looking for. They came into the club tonight – Norman's place, right? It was just the two of them."

"Are you sure it was them? Why would they be at Norman's? Is he making a play for this too, now?"

"I don't think he was involved, Mr. Carvallo, I swear. And I know it was them for sure. I snapped a picture of them when they came in, and I sent it to Little Joe, you know, from our numbers drop on Sixth. He used to work for Sarkosian, before his head developed that big hole in it." Frenetti paused to chuckle at his own joke, but when he saw the other man wasn't smiling, he quickly got back to his story.

"Little Joe was sitting less than five feet away from them when he first saw them, and he says it's them alright, no question."

"And you put a tracker on them?"

"Yessir. Well, not me, personally. Didn't want to queer the deal or nothing, getting too close to them. We had Norman do it. With one of those worms you gave us. Watched him do it. Smooth as silk, they had no clue."

Carvallo stood up and stepped over to a wall screen and tapped it. It came to life showing a map of the settlement. Frenetti tapped his phone and a small red dot appeared on the wall display.

"They're in the Port Depot hangar," said Carvallo. "Must have their own ship. Explains how there's no record of them on the regular transports.

"Did they meet with anyone in the club?" he asked Frenetti.

"Not a soul. Well, except for Norman, of course. They came in and ate, then hit the road in a hurry."

"Do you think something spooked them?"

"I don't think so, Mr. Carvallo, sir," said the man with the greying temples, speaking for the first time. "They might have been there to meet with someone who didn't show, maybe someone who spotted me and Fre— Leo."

"Which would mean they still have the disk," said Carvallo thoughtfully.

"Ben," he said, turning to his drinking companion who was watching the three men, "this could be a blessing in disguise. Which of the mining companies down there owes you a big favour?"

The seated man snorted and said, "Hell. All of them. What do you need?"

"Something that will not only remove these two loose cannons once and for all, but will ensure that the disk they're holding doesn't get away from us again. And thanks to their chosen sleeping venue tonight, I think I know just how to handle that...."

"When all this is over, I intend to have that disk in my hands, and if you think the companies sit up and jump at your commands now, just wait till you see how they act once we've got them by the short and curlies. Time to make a call, my friend – I want those two on ice before the night is done."

Carvallo stared at the glowing red dot on the map and smiled greedily as the man in the corner tapped a number on his phone.

Seemingly forgotten and left standing in the middle of the room, Frenetti and the man with the greying temples looked at each other nervously, wondering which of them should pipe up and ask for their finder's fee.

THE PAW PRESSED against Jerry's nose once again, and once more he batted it away without fully waking up.

This happened twice more, until finally Jerry forced his eyes open and snarled, "Go away, Batman! What's gotten into you, anyways?"

The cat didn't leave, but rowled unpleasantly and scratched Jerry's cheek, drawing blood.

"Ow! What's your problem, you little—"

Jerry froze in place. The cat sat motionless, watching him intently.

Jerry got it. A low, subsonic thrum, so soft it was inaudible, but powerful enough to be felt. A rumble he had never heard before while sleeping here.

"Kat!" he hissed.

Kat woke up immediately. The tone in Jerry's voice was unmistakably urgent.

"Can you scan outside the ship and see what's going on?"

She shook her head. "No can do. Remember, all our sensors were stripped by that asteroid cloud. And the ship walls prevent me from getting a decent LIDAR image."

"Back to basics then, I guess. We'll have to look out a window."

Jerry padded away soundlessly into the corridor leading to the main salon's viewports. Batman scampered back and forth unhappily, jumped up onto the bed, then back down onto the floor, then put his two front paws up on the edge of the mattress and stared at Kat.

"You want me to get up, too?" she asked.

The cat said nothing, but continued to stare. A creepy sensation running up her spine, Kat slid out of bed and grabbed her glasses from the night stand.

"Okay, Bats, you win, let's go see—"

Jerry ran back into the bedroom so fast he barreled into her, almost stepping on the cat.

"Out! Now! Let's go!"

Grabbing her hand, he fairly pulled her through the ship. He slapped his hand down on the pad to release the ship's access hatch and cursed impatiently as the hydraulics hissed and slowly started to move the door aside.

Kat turned and looked across into their ship's main salon. She paled when she saw what was outside.

A gigantic ore carrier, several storeys high and loaded to the brim with huge chunks of unrefined rock, was right outside their ship, no more than five meters away, and moving closer. The entire wall of viewscreen was filled with its bulk, and when Kat looked up she could see another fifteen meters of it through the overhead screen as it towered over them.

The mountain of ore it carried start to tilt. Mouth agape, Kat watched the first small rocks the size of bowling balls tumble off. Long spiderwebs of fractured glass burst across the overhead screen as the rocks thundered down onto it.

Kat saw the hatch was now open far enough to squeeze through. Batman had already dashed out, and was scampering away as the jagged hail of rocks bounced off their ship and cratered into the pavement outside the door.

The impacts became more forceful, pouring down now in a deafening cascade. One large chunk smashed through the viewscreen, plunging into the main control panel.

An explosion of sparks erupted from the panel and the ship's emergency lights snuffed out. The access hatch, still only about forty percent open, froze in place.

The ceiling over the corridor leading to their bedroom caved in as a particularly forceful impact shook the ship. Seconds later, the entire front cabin was smashed into oblivion beneath a dozen refrigerator-sized boulders.

The waterfall of rocks continued to rain down on the ship, buffeting it violently as the boulders bounced off and onto the pavement all around it.

"Jerry!" Kat screeched. "There's a storm of rocks coming down outside the hatch! We're dead if we try to leave, but we're dead if we stay—"

"Hold on, Kat, just wait a moment."

"'*Wait*'?! Have you lost your mind? That whole load of ore is about to bury us alive! What are we going to do?"

"Look," said Jerry, pointing at the mountain of boulders towering above them.

Peering through the shattered glass, Kat noticed the barrage was gradually lessening. Fewer smaller rocks were left on the mountain of boulders, most having rolled off during the initial onslaught. But one gigantic boulder started to shift, and was poised to tumble off in the next second or two, followed by several dozen more house-sized chunks of raw ore.

"Now, Kat! Get out and run like hell! In a straight line, and don't even bother putting your head down – *move!*"

Jerry forcefully pushed her out of the ship and she tumbled onto the pavement, then scrambled to her feet and fled for her life. Twice she jammed her bare toes into rocks on the ground that she was unable to avoid, and a chunk the size of a garbage can missed her by inches and smashed a crater into the pavement beside her, but she kept running.

She still hadn't slowed or turned to look behind her when she heard the world's loudest explosion, and knew immediately that the gigantic boulder she had seen teetering on the pile had come down onto the ship.

Jerry! she thought, briefly faltering in her headlong dash, but before she could react further, she heard, "Run faster, Kat! We're not in the clear yet!"

As if to add emphasis to his warning, a sudden flood of massive boulders roiled across the hangar decking, threatening to overtake them in a granite tsunami.

The smaller boulders were less plentiful here, and Kat was able to scamper through them more quickly. She spotted Batman off to the side in a narrow passageway leading into another section of the hangar. She made a hard right, hurled herself at the alcove and stumbled several meters into it before skidding to a halt.

Kat spun around and looked back, hoping to spot Jerry, but he didn't appear. *Oh good Lord,* she thought, *I hope he didn't get caught in that last wave.*

The roar of falling rocks died as quickly as it had begun, and within seconds Kat saw no more boulders tumbling past the alcove where she and Batman were huddled.

She craned her neck around the corner of the passageway and scanned the scene. Their ship was no more. In its place stood a large mound of boulders atop a wide field of scattered rock. The tremendous weight of the ore had flattened the ship like a pancake.

The ore carrier was still hovering in place but slowly starting to turn. It was fully automated, of course, and was following its programming to return to base once its cargo had been delivered.

There was no one in sight. There was no possibility anyone could have survived that assault, so there was no reason for their would-be assassins to risk being spotted at the scene of the crime.

She took a few steps toward the sea of boulders and looked around. Jerry was nowhere to be seen. But Kat had definitely heard his voice – *I couldn't have imagined it, could I?* – so he must be out here somewhere. *Or could someone have been waiting and grabbed him? But then where would they be? I see no exits.*

"Batman!" called Kat. There was no reason to be quiet – after the deafening cacophony of several thousand metric tons of ore crashing down on their ship, anyone on this level would already be on their way to investigate.

The cat tentatively peeked his head out around the passageway entrance.

"Batman, come here!" called Kat.

The cat scampered over toward her, but before he reached her she said, "Batman! Find Jerry! *Jerry*, Bats. Where is he?"

Well that's got to be one of the more pointless things I've ever done.

Might as well ask my Spirit Animal for help. Which is also a cat, she thought morosely.

Kat suddenly remembered her Slimlines, which she was still unconsciously clutching in her hand since she had left the bedroom. Jamming them on her face, she scanned for life signs among the piles of boulders around her, but the abundance of exotic minerals in the scattered ore so overwhelmed the scanners in her glasses that she gave up and took them off.

"JERRY! *JERRY!*" she wailed. Fear was giving way to dread, and dread in turn to grief. She was trying to sort out her next moves when a strange, unearthly sound keened through the air. It sounded like something that might come from a cat.

Kat spun her head around frantically, trying to place the source of the sound, but the ghostly wail slithered through the air and bounced off all the jagged surfaces. It came from everywhere; it came from nowhere. Then it stopped, and a second later a small black and white shape appeared atop a boulder about fifteen meters distant, in a section where many of the largest rocks were clustered.

Kat clambered over a string of large boulders, fighting her way through to the rock where the cat was sitting, chewing on one of its paws.

She climbed over to the boulder and peered down. Jerry was lying face-down at the base, a gigantic red stain drenching the left shoulder and upper back of his t-shirt. The side of his head looked wet and dark red, too, and he wasn't moving.

"Jer!" cried Kat, but the form on the ground didn't stir.

Kat couldn't reach him – another large boulder had come to rest beside the rock he was lying against. The upper edges of the boulders almost touched, but at the base there was just enough room to accommodate his body.

Kat examined the position of the boulders, then carefully slid to the ground a few feet away, and squeezed her way through to a spot by Jerry's head.

"Jer! Wake up!" she said, and slapped him lightly on his cheek. After a second, she slapped him again, a bit harder. She was about to slap him a third time when he groaned and moved slightly,

"Jerry! Can you hear me? Are you hurt bad?"

"Ohhhhh, oh, oh my God," he moaned. "Did anyone get the number of that truck?"

Kat almost punched him. "*Making jokes?* Now? You must be okay. Or at least close to the way you always were."

Jerry tried to turn his head but winced and stopped moving.

"Where am I? The last I remember I was running for my life, and then the lights went out."

"We're in the middle of a couple dozen boulders the size of railway cars, and you're wedged between two of them. And judging by the cantaloupe-sized rock I see over there – one with a nice red paint job – I'd have to guess it had an argument with your head, and your head lost."

"My shoulder hurts, too."

"Maybe it glanced into your shoulder after knocking some sense into you. I hope it's not broken. Your shoulder, that is, not your head – I'd be surprised if anything could get through that thick skull of yours."

"You're a real Florence Nightingale, you know that, Kat?"

"If she was a devastatingly attractive genius with a killer right hook, then I'll accept that comparison. In the meantime, we need to focus on getting you out of there. Can you move your legs?"

"Yes. It doesn't feel like anything is pinning me down, but it's such a tight fit between these boulders, I don't think I can crawl out. We may have to wait for help."

"I don't think that's a good idea. Our best chance is to disappear before the authorities arrive. There's enough rock covering our ship that it'll take them a day or two before they can search for our bodies. Assuming they can get into it at all — it's probably squashed flat. But that gives us two days' advantage. Are you sure you can't wiggle out on your own?"

"Maybe with some help. You don't have a winch on you, do you?"

"Fresh out. But how about I just tug your good arm? It would be easier grabbing you under your shoulders, but that's probably not an option if you have a busted wing."

"Let's start with the arm, babe. We can move on to Plan B if that doesn't work."

Kat twisted around to where she could find some leverage, took hold of Jerry by his upper arm, and gave a mighty pull. Jerry slid forward so swiftly she tumbled back on her heels and smacked her head on the rock behind her.

"Owwwww," she moaned, rubbing the back of her head. "You did that on purpose, didn't you?"

"Not guilty, Your Honour. You just don't know your own strength.

"And the good news," he said, "is that I can move my left arm. Not broken, probably just a bruised shoulder. Now get off your ass and lead me out of this lithic labyrinth."

Kat rolled her eyes heavenward. "Don't make me regret pulling you out of there, Sahib."

Kat helped Jerry clamber up onto the boulder. He whistled in awe as he surveyed the mass of scattered rock.

"How did you find me in all this? Slimlines?"

"Nope. Went Old School. Used a tracker."

"A track—?" began Jerry, but then he spotted the black and white cat curled up on the boulder.

"Batman! My buddy! Saved me twice in the span of one hour. Extra smoked salmon for you tonight, fella!"

"Don't make promises you can't keep. That salmon Batman prizes so highly is now quite out of reach, buried beneath a mountain of rock."

"Ooh, you're right." Glancing down at his ripped and bloody t-shirt, he added, "Along with our clothes."

"But thanks to your inexhaustible paranoia, Jer, at least we wore sweat pants and t-shirts to bed. For which I am eternally grateful. The only thing which would have made this night worse is if we'd had to go through all this naked."

"Oh, I don't know about that, Kitty-Kat," said Jerry, wrapping her up in a tight hug. "It's pretty private down there under the boulders. Feel like a little after-near-death-experience nookie?"

Laughing, Kat twisted free of his embrace and scampered across several boulders.

"Only if you can catch me, old man."

"Now there's a challenge I will happily accept," said Jerry, painfully inching his way after her. "Ouch! If I don't cripple myself first on these damned jagged rocks, that is."

The little black and white cat lifted his head off his paws and watched them work their way across the stony obstacle course, then stood up, yawned, stretched, and silently padded after them.

J ERRY STILL INSISTED on avoiding Howard's apartment, but he let Kat ask Suzie to deliver a sack of clothes to the transit stop by the Port Depot hangar.

When she arrived, Suzie crept into the deserted alley behind the transit station and looked around. The alley was silent and empty, and once she was confident there were no unwanted occupants, she carefully placed a bulging garbage bag onto a pile of flattened cardboard boxes stacked against the building's rear wall.

"Yeah, that doesn't look suspicious at all," said Kat loudly, stepping out from behind a tall retaining wall jutting out from the building.

Suzie jumped a full six inches into the air at the sound of Kat's voice.

"Oh my God, don't do that!" she howled. "You told me you wouldn't be here."

"I couldn't be sure you wouldn't be followed. But I can see now that you weren't. So it's okay."

Emerging from the shadow of a tall steel tank of used cooking oil behind the donut shop, Jerry looked around warily.

The two girls hugged each other and Suzie said, "What an awful mess Howard and I have gotten you two into. We were simply devastated when we heard about last night.

"The local news foil says it was a malfunctioning ore carrier. There's people out there digging but they're afraid to move the rock too quickly because the pile that's left on your ship is too unstable. They say it might take several days to clear the site."

"What kind of rescue mission is that?" said Kat.

"No, they're calling it a salvage operation – they say the ship was in storage and unoccupied. One of the mining companies is going to cart it away after all the ore has been removed."

"So they can go through it with a fine-tooth comb, looking for that disk," said Jerry. "Well, that's good news, anyways. It will take the heat off long enough for us to do the job."

"You're still going through with it?" asked Suzie. "Even though they tried to kill you guys?"

"*Especially* because they tried to kill us," said Kat. "We take this sort of thing very personally, you know."

"Glad you came when you did, Suzie," said Jerry, getting down on one knee to root through the garbage bag she'd brought. "All I've been able to think about for the last thirty minutes is deep-fried donuts and hot coffee."

Jerry was no longer wearing his t-shirt, Kat having torn it into strips to make bandages which she had wrapped around his head. He grunted in satisfaction and pulled out of the bag two large bottles and a small box.

"Good. Disinfectant and actual bandages. And a clean t-shirt. Life is beautiful."

Suzie laughed.

"Glad you're so easy to please, Jerry. Now I'm afraid you'll pass out from joy if I offer to go get some donuts and coffee for you."

Jerry looked up at her and frowned.

"Don't toy with me, Suzie. I've had a long night."

Kat chuckled and said, "We take our coffee with lots of cream, Suzie. The donut choices I'll leave up to you."

Just before Suzie disappeared round the corner on her errand, Kat called her back and said, "Good grief, I can't believe I almost forgot – I think they also have chicken fritters there. Get an order of those, too."

"Um, Okay," said Suzie. "Do you want ketchup or any dip with them?"

Kat turned her head to look at Batman, who was reclining on a cardboard box in the sun while studiously licking his left leg.

"No," she said to Suzie. "Just the chicken. He doesn't like ketchup."

Half an hour later, Jerry put down his coffee cup with a sigh and stretched out more fully on the strip of cardboard he had propped up against a stack of "Modern Mining" magazines recently discarded by the donut shop. The cat on his lap stirred slightly as Jerry adjusted his position, then went back to sleep.

"You're a man of simple tastes, Jerry. A box of donuts and a coffee, and you look like you've just eaten a royal banquet."

"I guess staring Death in the face teaches you to appreciate the little things in life. Especially the little things that have fur." He ran his hand along the cat's back and the creature flexed his paw, gently gripping Jerry's sweat pants with his claws.

Kat tsk-tsked.

"Nothing good will come of this. That beast was already supremely spoiled. I shudder to think how you'll pamper him now."

"Which reminds me, Kat. We absolutely can't forget to stop in at the pet store before we visit Myx."

"Noted, boss. I looked one up right after he called to tell us the horse is done. There's a specialty pet bodega in his neighbourhood. We can drop in on the way."

"When should we leave?"

Kat checked the display in her glasses. "Well, we said 10am, and it's already 9:15. I guess right now would be good."

Jerry sighed, then said, "And just when Batman and I got comfortable! I swear, Kat, you have the worst timing."

Kat rolled her eyes. "Normally, I'd be insulted. But I suppose I should be grateful that you two even took the time to save me last night. I'm sure for Batman it was a close choice between me and the smoked salmon."

When they walked into Petrovsky's warehouse studio, the eerie sensation of creeping through a primeval forest overcame them once again. Outside, the sun was still low on the horizon, and the small amount of light filtering in through the skylights threw long shadows beneath the towering statuary.

Kat placed Batman's new cat carrier on the floor and unlatched its door. The cat stuck his head out and sniffed the air, then tentatively stepped over to the base of a life-size chrome mermaid lolling on an emerald-coloured tangle of seaweed. He sniffed carefully at the glittering scales on her thick tail, and once he was assured of her inanimate nature, lost interest and wandered away deeper into the forest of metallic artworks.

A discordant series of tones rang out from the far end of the warehouse, where they found Petrovsky laying on his back beneath the carapace of a gigantic cockroach, cursing loudly while he hammered at the metal.

"Myx!' called Jerry, getting the sculptor's attention. "You can stop now. I think it's dead."

"Oh, that's so funny, Bruce. I've never heard that one before."

Groaning, he pulled himself out from under the insect and brushed off the front of his coveralls with his hands.

"You two have perfect timing. That one is killing me – I'm so ready for a break. Hello Diana, nice to see you again."

"You too, Myx. Can't wait to see my new tomb."

"I'd prefer you didn't refer to it like that – tempting Fate, and all."

He led them through the maze of quiescent beasts and stopped before a life-size bronze horse. Its head was held high and the front-right leg was bent at the knee, lifting its hoof off the ground. It wore an ornate bridle and saddle with a jewel-encrusted pommel that sparkled even in this dim light.

Jerry pointed at a small flap that poked out from under the saddle's edge. "What's that?"

"That," said Petrovsky, "is just a scrap of leather laid over the latch to keep the saddle from locking closed. You forbade me from including any exterior latches, so if you should accidentally close the saddle without anyone inside the horse, the only way to release it again is by cutting it open.

"It goes against my principles. If anyone were locked inside –" he glanced quickly at Kat – "and then to become incapacitated, no one could rescue them. It's airtight, as you requested. And soundproof, too.

"The head and neck are mostly solid, to balance the weight once the stallion is… loaded. The hollow interior chamber is lined with the materials you specified."

"Did you have any trouble obtaining the materials?" asked Jerry.

"That's the advantage of living in a mining settlement, and in fact the reason I originally set up shop here. Countless raw metals and alloys are plentiful. I can always find anything I need in only one or two stops."

A few meters past the horse and halfway to the ceiling, Batman stepped into view, silhouetted against the skylights as he picked his way up a staircase of dorsal ridges on a half-finished dragon.

"I take it that's the cat you told me about. He already looks at home here."

"Don't get any ideas, Myx," said Kat. "We just need a safe place to leave him while we're… busy. We brought enough food with us to keep him out of your hair, but he's coming back with us when we're done."

"Calm down, Diana, I have no intention of kidnapping your cat. And I'm not sure you needed to bring any food for him – he'll probably stuff himself on mice while he's here."

Kat was horrified. "Good God, I hope not! He's not some kind of wild beast, you know."

"Come on, you two," said Jerry. "Focus on the task at hand. I want to field-test this thing before the movers show up. They're already loading up the furniture – we've probably got only about thirty minutes before they get here."

Petrovsky showed Kat the latching mechanism on the inside of the saddle, then he and Jerry helped her climb in and watched as she pulled on the interior grab-bar and sealed the hatch shut.

"Wow," said Jerry. "That's nice work. You'd never guess in a million years that thing opens up."

"Well, let's hope it does," said Petrovsky, with a frown. "I've never actually operated the release lever – couldn't very well test it on myself, you know. Why isn't she opening it back up?"

"Give it a sec," said Jerry with more confidence than he felt. "She's probably just taking a minute to get the feel of it."

A soft click and a hiss came from the horse, and the saddle moved slightly as one edge almost imperceptibly lifted up from the horse's back, and then the piece swung on its interior hinge all the way up and fully open.

Kat sat up and her head and chest came into view above the horse's back. She looked for all the world like a boater in a huge bronze kayak. Jerry and Petrovsky helped her climb out, and once she was back on the ground she paused to twist her waist and flex her back.

"That's a mighty tight fit in there," she said, squinting at Petrovsky. "You should design coffins."

"As long as this one doesn't become yours," he said. "Did the release mechanism feel smooth? Give you any trouble?"

"No, that worked perfectly. And you were right – I couldn't hear a thing. Totally soundproof. Could you hear me yelling at you?"

Jerry and Petrovsky shook their heads.

"Which means there'll be no calling for the cavalry if something goes wrong," said Petrovsky.

"You're a glum one, aren't you?" said Kat, laughing. "You must be Russian."

"Don't remind me," he said. "I moved away from my homeland to improve my surroundings, and I end up spending my days in a dark, drafty warehouse at the far edge of the galaxy. I guess you really can't escape your heritage, after all."

"This place isn't Hawaii, but it's hardly the Gulag, either," said Jerry. "You must be worth quite a bit by now, too. I'm sure you could afford to move somewhere bright and sunny."

"And give all this up?" asked Petrovsky, lifting up his arms and turning in a circle.

"My ancestors would haunt me mercilessly. No, Mr. Wayne, this is where my travels end."

Batman was curled up in Petrovsky's armchair beside a glowing cast iron wood stove. It was heated by an internal electric element, of course, but the sculptor enjoyed the anachronism.

"So you're the magic cat," said Petrovsky, settling into a much less comfortable chair. "Saved two people's lives today, I hear."

The cat did not look up.

The sculptor reached over to a can sitting on the small table where he ate his meals. As he pulled the tab, the cat looked up with sudden interest at the click and hiss, and within a heartbeat was sitting on Petrovsky's lap.

"Oh ho, there's no shame in you at all, is there?" he laughed. "Well, I like that. Real honesty is so rare to find these days."

The cat craned his neck slightly to lick a dollop of smelly wet cat food off the proffered spoon, and then waited patiently while another gobbet was retrieved.

"I really do hope your caretakers make it back safely, but I have to admit I wouldn't be saddened at all by the prospect of becoming your new owner."

The cat turned his head ever so slightly to look at Petrovsky with one eye, and then returned his full attention to the glop of food. It wasn't smoked salmon, but it would do for now.

THE CARGO TRANSPORT Jerry and Kat were riding in was basic, but not intolerable. The ship offered meals and a sparsely-furnished cabin, but little else.

There were no other passengers, and indeed no other cargo. Menos II had little to recommend it, being primarily a scientific research planet with 972-day-years and unpleasant weather, orbiting an uninteresting red giant. And considering that each of those days was sixty hours long, the planet's residents stayed indoors in underground buildings and conducted their business without regard to the local season or time of day.

Jerry had no interest in the planet's features, or lack thereof, and had chosen their destination purely for its proximity to the asteroid settlement. Once on Menos II with all their supplies in one place, he and Kat would assemble the final shipment for transport to the asteroid settlement.

"It's better if our cargo arrives from off-asteroid," Jerry had explained to Kat. "The personnel at the secure storage facility don't care where it's coming from, but being offloaded from an interstellar transport just looks more natural. To deliver it from a local source might draw attention."

"I hope Batman will be okay with Myx," said Kat, fidgeting in the stiff seat in the ship's passenger section. "We've never actually left him with a stranger before. What if he runs away?"

"Stop fretting, baby. You know full-well as long as there's fresh cat food served three times a day, Batman isn't setting foot outside that warehouse."

"But what if one of those sculptures falls on him? Or another cat gets in and attacks him? Or—"

"Oh *please*, Kat. Besides, I know that's not what's really bothering you. You're stressed about the job, and you're projecting. Let it go. Everything will be fine. We've been over it and over it. Easy-peasy, lemon squeezie, remember?"

Kat gave him a weak smile.

"Can't help it. I hate these jobs that take days of planning. I'm much better thinking on my feet."

"You just think you are. But a carefully thought-out plan beats panicked action every day of the week."

"Jerry, everyone has a plan until they get punched in the mouth."

"You've got some nerve, young lady, throwing 20th century quotes at me. We've made it through every scrape so far, and mostly by outwitting the bad guys. This is no different."

"We've never robbed a bank before."

"Just as well. This is much harder than a bank job. I wouldn't want you to have a false sense of self-confidence.

"Look, Kat, we're in the home stretch. Once this cargo ship drops us off at Menos II, we're just coasting downhill. And I'll be with you the whole time."

"Until you hand me over to the world's most secure vault and abandon me in enemy territory for 18 hours."

"Actually, it's 21 hours. You're forgetting the extra three they tack-on after midnight.

Kat rolled her eyes. "Even better. How could I have overlooked that?"

"Would you rather I go instead?" asked Jerry.

Don't be silly," laughed Kat. "You probably couldn't even figure out how to operate the release lever. We'd end up having to bury the whole horse at your funeral."

Jerry leaned over and planted a kiss on her lips.

"I hope those oxygen masks from Brian will be waiting when we arrive," he said for the thirtieth time. "Good thing we didn't have him ship them directly to us on the asteroid – they'd have been lost with our ship."

"Now who's stressing, Jerry? You know the package is there. You're projecting, too."

"If only there were something we could do to take our minds off it…" he said thoughtfully.

Kat punched him in the arm. "Oh no you don't, you one-track monster! There'll be none of that until that disk is safely in our hands and we're a few million parsecs away from that dirty asteroid."

"You wound me, honey. I'm only thinking of you – I just don't want to send you off feeling unloved."

Kat laughed and gave him a hug.

"Oh, Jerry, what are we doing? Why aren't we on a beach somewhere with an icy pitcher of Margaritas beside us?"

"Because we both know you'd prefer suffocating quickly inside that horse over the slow suffocation of mindless boredom on a beach."

"Aaaaaand there we have it, folks – is it any mystery I'm stressed out when I have a partner like this to calm my nerves?"

The package from Brian was indeed waiting for them when they arrived at Menos II, along with several other items Jerry had ordered from various sources. They wasted no time offloading their cargo into a short-term storage unit in the transport hangar. The moving company was happy to sell them four high-end antigrav pallets, onto which they carefully arranged their cargo.

"Whatever you do," he said for the umpteenth time, as he tightened the bolts on the clamps around the horse's feet, "don't forget about these when you're done, or the whole operation is shot."

"Good grief, Jerry, I got it. Would you like me to tie a red string on my finger to remind me, too?"

"Don't be a wiseass – you'll have a lot on your mind, but everything depends on this detail. And there's no do-overs."

"Okay, okay, I got it, boss. And you said *I'm* stressing. Sheesh."

Straightening up, Jerry took a step backwards to admire his work, then checked the time and said, "Okay, Kat, they'll be arriving in a few minutes to load up our shipment. Time to get dressed," and he tossed her a small white package.

Kat wrinkled her nose and sighed. "A year ago, I would never have predicted that diapers would become one of my primary clothing accessories. The next job we do, you're the one in the Pampers."

"But it's such a sexy look for you, sweetie."

Kat shot him a withering glare, then morosely trudged off to the bathroom to change.

When she returned a few minutes later, wearing a comfortable black jumpsuit and snug black booties, Kat was amused to see that Jerry had also changed his clothing.

"I love that pink suit. Very fetching."

"Just more window dressing, honey. Gotta play the part, right?"

He helped Kat climb into the belly of the horse, then leaned over to give her a kiss as she settled in. "See you in 36 hours, babe."

She grunted in assent, then fastened an oxygen mask around her face. Grabbing the pull bar on the underside of the saddle, she lowered the lid and with a soft *click!* disappeared from view.

PART IV:
THE HEIST

OK, boys; let's go make a withdrawal.

– John Dillinger

ANOTHER WASTED DAY *gone forever from my life*, thought Tomás, watching the second-hand sweep around the clock dial. *Minute by minute, day by day, this damned job is eating up my life and shitting it out. Before I know it, I'll be old, grey and feeble, like Ahmed over there. Waiting for retirement and a sad, lonely death.*

Ahmed sat on the other side of the wide room, at the far side of the x-ray scanner, eyes closed and chest gently moving. Probably sleeping.

Tomás had managed to beat out a wide field of competitors for this job only after completing several psychological tests, enduring three exhaustive interviews, and producing a stack of glowing recommendations from former employers.

It was true the position paid extremely well, but Tomás had been drawn to the opportunity primarily in the hope of exciting assignments. The prospect of putting his life on the line as personal bodyguard to some powerful business magnate, or maybe performing dangerous espionage in an interstellar intrigue, had teased his imagination.

Instead, however, he was crushed to discover that his valuable skills were left to atrophy as he sat in this windowless foyer, acting as a glorified clerk. The agency that had recruited him was known for finding personnel unafraid to embrace death-defying assignments. Tomás ground his teeth in anger. Ticking-off boxes in security checklists was hardly the death-defying duties that he craved.

Another month, he thought. *One more month of this living hell, and then I'm chucking it all and heading off to the farthest frontier in this galaxy. Some place where men are scrabbling to forge a home in the face of incredible odds. Somewhere—*

Tomás's reverie was cut short by the arrival of this morning's shipment by an interstellar transport company. The gate over the loading platform clanked to life, rising to reveal four large pallets of goods.

A prissy, fidgeting man in an expensive pink suit rose from the guest couch near the door. Pacing back and forth, wringing his hands and sweating profusely, he anxiously supervised the delivery.

One of the movers handed the nervous man a tablet to sign, and then left once the confirmation was noted.

Tomás's tablet also displayed the bill of lading the man had just signed, and he tapped the screen to summon the autobots that would move the pallets into the main warehouse storage area.

"I'm showing four pallets for delivery," said Tomás in a bored monotone. "That correct?"

"Yes, yes, that sounds perfect," said the nervous man.

"Which would make you… Bartholomew Carrington-Smythe. Is that right?"

"Quite right," said Carrington-Smythe.

"Okay, Mr. Carrington-Smythe, since you're the one checking in these goods, only you can retrieve them, is that understood?"

"Yes, yes," said the other man, watching with great unease as a second set of anti-grav pallets moved into place underneath the original pallets holding the shipment.

"And for that, we'll need a DNA sample," said the guard, extracting a swab from a small hardshell case. "And a retina scan, too, which you'll provide by looking into that eyepiece over there.

"And, finally, we'll need you to enter an alphanumeric passcode onto that tablet beside it. Sixteen characters, at least, please.

"You'll need to match all three requirements when you return. If you are unable to remember the passcode, there is a mandatory 180-day waiting period before you can retrieve your goods. And you'll be charged for that storage time."

"What if I'm dead or otherwise unavailable?"

"Then we'll need your corpse. In the absence of that, the goods stay with us for a period of seven years. The courts have upheld this requirement, so even if your heirs petition for the items in storage, without your actual body to accompany their request, not a single gram of it will be released."

"For seven years," said Carrington-Smythe.

"Exactly."

"Well, let's go ahead. This is only a short-term storage until our local mover can pick it up tomorrow, anyways. I'm not expecting to die overnight."

"Who is?" said the guard, with a chuckle.

Carrington-Smythe watched nervously as the last of the four storage facility pallets slipped into place.

"Why do you need extra pallets underneath my own?"

"There's a number of reasons for that, sir. First, our pallets are dedicated autobots which will stay with your goods until the day you remove them. They will confirm that the entry and exit weights of your shipment are identical, down to one gram. Which is why we disable the antigrav function on your own pallets until they have been cleared for release.

"Second, no one will ever physically touch your goods while they are here. They stay on your own pallets exactly as they arrived, without even the most fractional adjustment in position. We record a 3D scan of the pallet and verify it upon withdrawal. This assures you that no one has tampered with your belongings in any way since the moment you entrusted them to our care."

Ahmed was monitoring the passage of the pallets as they slowly moved through the scanners, and paused them when he came to the second-last in the row. On that pallet were four large plasti-mold crates, a large bronze horse statue, several more smaller statues stacked in a display case, and three cases of wine.

"This wine isn't on this list of contents," he said, frowning at his tablet.

"It's a late addition," said Carrington-Smythe.

"You'll have to initial here, then," said Ahmed, scribbling quickly on the tablet before handing it over.

Once the documentation was complete, the two guards checked the scans on their monitors, then grunted, and, with a little jerk, the pallets continued on their way. A wide door slid open, and the pallets moved forward into a large holding area. The door slid closed once again behind them.

"What happens now?" asked Carrington-Smythe.

"The system will find a place for them," said Tomás. "The pallets can't go any farther until the door on our side closes and a door on the far side opens. No one is allowed in the actual storage area. Even I have never been inside the warehouse, and I've been here for almost a year."

"Well, that makes me feel a lot safer."

"As you should, sir. Nothing has ever gone missing from any shipment since this facility was first opened."

"I'll hold you to that, young fellow," said Carrington-Smythe. "If there's anything amiss when I retrieve my goods, I promise that you and your co-worker here will both be held personally responsible. These items were checked-in on your watch, and I won't hear any excuses later. Bartholomew Carrington-Smythe is not someone to be trifled with."

With a curt nod, he turned and strode out of the building, slamming the door behind him.

You snotty little shit, thought Tomás. *You think you're so much better than me, talking down to me like I'm a child.*

I have got to get a better job....

**AT DID HER BEST** to pay attention to all the little shakes and bumps as the horse made its journey, but eventually she gave up trying to figure out what each little twist and turn meant.

To help pass the time, she watched some videos on her glasses, or tried to sleep, but her mind was racing too hard.

She was confident their shipment would make it into the facility on time, and contented herself with watching the countdown timer in the corner of her vision.

When the time had decreased to under thirty minutes, each minute seemed to drag longer than the previous one. By the time only sixty seconds remained, she was ready to scream.

An eternity later, the countdown flipped to 0:00 and the display turned green. Unclipping the inner latch, Kat gently released the vacuum seal on the saddle. A brief hiss of escaping air accompanied a subtle change in air pressure, followed by a gentle breeze filtering through the widening crack as she lifted the saddle up and over. Internal hinges held the saddle in place once it was fully opened, leaning back like the lid of an open suitcase.

Painfully unwrapping herself from the pretzel-shaped ball she'd curled into, Kat grasped the lip of her hidey-hole and sat upright. She unclipped the oxygen mask, took a deep breath, and quietly moaned in pleasure as the fresh air filled her lungs.

The storage bay sat in absolute stillness and total darkness. Kat didn't notice the lack of illumination, as her glasses had already been set to full-spectrum display mode, but without the hum and clatter of the ubiquitous machines that filled the settlement, the space was unnervingly quiet. Her own breathing seemed to fill the warehouse with a deafening roar.

No time for relaxation, she thought. *I can relax when I'm dead.* She chuckled inwardly at the statement, a phrase she'd stolen from Jerry. He had already spent more time dead than many people had spent alive, so his perspective on the matter was unique, to say the least.

She checked the four little units clipped to a belt around her waist. She hoped to hell the interface was accurate, otherwise this was going to be a very short adventure.

Grunting, Kat stood up, unsteadily getting her bearings, and then with great care lifted a leg over the edge of the opening and lowered it down into the stirrup hanging from the horse's side. She pulled her other leg free and extended it down onto the platform, then pulled her foot out of the stirrup and stepped away from the horse.

Their shipment had been placed in an open slot about five meters wide, midway down a seemingly endless stretch of unsorted items. A wide aisle separated her from another similar row of pallets and various cargo. There was little definable separation between the storage spaces in each row; the autobot pallets were all that was needed to locate each client's belongings.

She checked the time display in the corner of her Slimlines: 4:58:06. The facility would have gone into lockdown at 4:55, at which point the surveillance bots were set to disconnect from their charging base and move into place to begin their nightly survey at 5:05.

She had just under seven minutes to get to the head of the far aisle. Even though feeling hadn't yet fully returned to her cramped leg muscles, Kat gritted her teeth and limped across the platform, then sprinted off as best she could towards the warehouse entrance.

The space was immaculate. The floors were unscuffed and perfectly clean. Kat was happy she'd worn runners with extra-grippy soles – she'd need all the extra traction she could get.

At least my glasses take the guesswork out of finding my way around. Thanks to the architectural drawings and floor plans that Howard had downloaded, her Slimlines painted her path with a bright yellow line stretching away in her display.

Kat reached the end of her aisle and made a right turn into a broad corridor fronting the wall. Moving a bit more smoothly now that her legs had regained their full mobility, she raced down the corridor. She passed one of the surveillance bots that was arriving in position at the foot of its own aisle, but she paid it no heed. If she didn't do the bots in precise order, she would run out of time before she reached #4.

She and Bot #1 arrived at the foot of the first aisle at the same time. Without pausing, she leapt onto the little platform at its base and fumbled at her waist for one of the interface units. The bot took no notice of her presence. *I guess watching for hitchhikers was never a programming concern.*

Kat checked her time and smiled in satisfaction. She had made it with 52 seconds to spare. Grinning, she made a mental note to rub this one in Jerry's face later.

The bot looked a lot like a giant upright vacuum cleaner, with a wide base and a skinny tower. Various sensors and lenses peppered the upright shaft. Kat was careful not to cover any of these with her hand as she gripped the tower and crouched down.

Three days ago, Howard had ordered four surveillance bots from the manufacturer, specifying the exact model number he wanted and explaining that he was evaluating several different systems for a security contract on Corona Majoris. As the bots' manufacturer had no other Coronan clients, they were only too happy to oblige. And luckily, because they were older units, the company had a number of the bots in stock, ready for immediate delivery.

Once the bots were in transit to Corona Majoris, Howard had rerouted the shipment to his own lab. The units came complete with programmable control interfaces, of course, and it had taken less than a couple of hours to install wireless access and write a piggyback protocol that told the bot to ignore any leggy, redhaired women it might come across during its surveillance duties.

Kat gripped her bot tightly as she perched on its base and moved the interface unit into position. Powerful magnetic clips fastened it to the bot with a little *snick!* Immediately, a green light illuminated in the corner of Kat's glasses.

"Interface complete. Running program… complete," said her Slimlines.

Kat leapt off the bot and spun back the way she had come. As long as a bot hadn't completed its initial scan, nothing it came across would set off its alarms, so Kat could approach them freely. But she had to make it to all four before the last one reached the end of its aisle.

Running full speed, Kat rocketed up Bot #1's aisle until she came to a break in the storage spaces, where she leapt into the next aisle.

Bot #2 was about two meters behind her, as its passage wasn't quite as fast as Kat's. And they weren't quite halfway down the aisle yet, which meant she should easily be able to catch up to the last one before it completed its trip.

She repeated the procedure she had followed with Bot #1, leapt off without waiting for confirmation, and raced away up the aisle in search of #3.

There was another break in the row of spaces between her and the next aisle, and she grinned excitedly to spot Bot #3 just ahead as she crossed over. She reached down to grab the third interface, but her hands were slippery and she fumbled it, watching with horror as it skittered away and disappeared beneath a loaded pallet to her right.

"Oh my God!"

Kat's blood froze in her veins. If the interface unit had skidded out of her reach beneath the pallet, this entire operation was ruined. She had no spares – a critical oversight, she realized – and no time to spend laboriously fishing it out.

Kat threw herself onto her face and peered under the pallet. When she spotted the unit, her heart sank. It was well and truly out of reach.

And then she realized she could probably reach it if she tried from the other side. It was relatively close to the far edge, having skidded almost all the way beneath the length of the pallet.

She had to be careful, she knew. This pallet and its contents had already been mapped by Bots #3 and #4 – anything she moved out of place would set off the facility alarms as soon as either bot passed by again on its rounds.

Stepping carefully around the items sitting on the pallet, she made it to the other side and dropped down to feel around blindly beneath the platform. The interface unit was just barely within reach. She felt her fingertips brush against it, gritted her teeth, and stretched her arm and fingers out as far as she could.

She got two fingers on it, carefully eased it a bit closer, then managed to grasp it with her whole hand. She yanked her arm back out, and without pausing to take a breath, she leapt to her feet, picked her way back across the pallet, and turned up the aisle to chase after Bot #3.

The bot was farther away down the aisle than she had expected. Kat pushed down hard as she ran at maximum speed up the aisle. She caught up to the bot and leapt onto its platform, bent down and smacked the interface unit into place.

She fairly fell off the bot as she let go, but threw herself back to her feet and resumed running up the aisle.

Based on Bot #3's position, Kat suspected Bot #4 was now only seconds away from completing its scan. She flung herself down the aisle and skidded to the right as she came to the broad corridor at this end of the warehouse.

She looked ahead and was horrified to see Bot #4 emerging from its aisle. As Kat thundered across she could see there would simply not be enough time left to mount the bot and then place the interface unit.

But spending long hours with Jerry watching replays of old baseball games had taught her that there was something a bit faster than merely running and jumping into place. She raced straight at the bot and just as it arrived at the end of its route, Kat dropped down onto her butt and slid past, reaching out and smacking the interface unit into place as she skidded by.

She held her breath in terror, then exhaled in a loud burst as the light on the unit turned from red to green and her glasses announced, "Program complete."

"SAFE!" screamed Kat in her mind, and lay panting on the floor as she listened to the ecstatic cheers of the crowds in the bleachers.

KAT WATCHED THE BOTS trundle away on their rounds, disappearing down their respective aisles. Once her breathing had returned to normal, she stood up and collected her wits.

When they had been planning the job, one of the thorniest issues had concerned how Kat might locate the disk once inside the facility.

Jerry had come upon a solution, explaining that disks from the late 21st century had included a feature designed to overcome a persistent problem with data storage: magnetic degradation.

Information on disks was stored as binary data in magnetic patterns. After a decade or more, however, those magnetic fields weakened to the point where data was lost and the disks became unreadable.

The remedy for this degradation was remarkably simple: a battery or other small power source was built into the disk, and at regular intervals refreshed the magnetic impulses.

Jerry suggested that Kat's glasses simply scan the items in storage and flag any small power sources.

"That could be an overwhelming task," Kat had objected. "There must be hundreds of disks in that place – I might as well check every pallet individually."

"Not when you consider that for the last hundred years or so we've done away with magnetic storage," explained Jerry. "As you well know, modern data storage uses lasers to write the data into glass cubes. The only disk with a power source in that facility is the one we want."

Kat looked at the aisle stretching away in front of her, and shrugged. Maybe this would be easy, after all. She started walking down the aisle, humming quietly to herself as her Slimlines scanned each pallet she passed.

After an hour, she had walked through the entire facility, up and down each aisle, and still hadn't come across any power sources.

Could we have gotten it wrong? Maybe Sarkosian didn't *hide his disk here after all?* she wondered, leaning against a large crate at the end of the last aisle. *No, I don't think so – this is definitely where I would have put the disk, if I were him....*

Kat chewed her lip for a moment while pondering the solution. Why couldn't she locate any power sources among the items stored in this unit...?

"Got it!" she exclaimed out loud, and jumped at the sound of her voice echoing through the space.

The answer had come in a flash: *of course I can't detect the disk – Sarkosian wouldn't have left it just sitting out on a shelf. Nor would he just drop something like that into his pocket. He'd want to keep it clean, safe, and secure. He's almost certainly put it in a shielded case, both for concealment and for protection.*

But that hardly helped her – if she couldn't scan for it, she was back at square one. There was nothing to differentiate the case from any other item in this place.

No. Wait. That's not right.

Every other item in this facility could be scanned – whether it was wood, or metal, or any other compound. But if the disk was secured in a shielded case, then that would set it apart.

It will be the only item my glasses can't *scan.*

Reinvigorated, Kat set out at a brisk pace, striding down the aisles again as her glasses searched for any object that they couldn't analyse. She no longer felt the creeps whenever she passed one of the surveillance bots. They simply didn't see her, rolling by without paying her any mind.

Kat was three-quarters of the way up Aisle 3 when her glasses announced, "Unknown object in this unit, Kat. Two meters in, third shelf from the bottom."

When Kat looked at the storage unit, a glowing rectangle in her glasses identified the unreadable object. Before stepping in to retrieve the package, however, Kat stopped to assess the space it was in, wary that this storage area may have been boobytrapped.

This collection of items was laid out in an unusual manner. Instead of multiple pallets holding various goods, there were actual shelves to either side, behind hinged metal grills. There was also a second level of boxes above everything, separated from the lower items by a steel mesh roof.

This is interesting. It looks like a permanent long-term storage space, with items stored individually. Almost like a personal safe deposit box, but without the prying eyes of bank personnel. Maybe that 'No Humans Allowed' rule doesn't apply if you own the joint.

Kat nervously looked to her right and her left, as though she were expecting a troop of armed guards drawing a bead on her. But the only other occupant in sight was Bot #3, quietly rolling up the aisle as it scanned the storage spaces.

Shrugging, Kat stepped into the little enclosed storage space and walked up to the spot her glasses had indicated. The cage door was unlocked. Kat swung it open and saw a small grey carry-case on the third shelf from the bottom. She spun it around and flipped a latch by the handle, popping open the cover.

There was nothing inside the case except for an unmarked rectangular silver slab the size of a playing card, with a primitive interface port on one end. She picked it up and turned it over in her hand. A holographic label pasted on the other side advised that this item was the property of the settlement's Official Archives.

"I'm reading a faint power source, Kat," her glasses announced.

Kat held her breath for a moment, pausing just to stare at the disk. Untold riches in the palm of her hand.

A subtle movement in her peripheral vision caught Kat's attention. She turned to see Bot #3 stopped outside the unit, with its entire scanning array flashing wildly and focused directly on her.

What the f— and then she realized she was standing here in the unit with a cage door ajar, and the disk case laying open on a shelf while she waved the disk around. There was no part of this scene that even remotely matched the previously-stored image in the bot's memory bank.

Kat gritted her teeth in anticipation of a din of alarms and security alerts, but after a few seconds, noticed that the bot was still standing in place, still scanning this storage unit.

It's confused, she thought. *It can't see me, so there's a hole in its vision. I'm blocking the open cage door and it can't figure out why it can't scan this part of the space.*

Kat jammed the disk into a pocket on her jumpsuit and snapped the empty case closed, then spun it back around and did her best to match its exact placement on the shelf before she had moved it. She swung the cage door shut and turned to face the bot.

It stayed in place, still scanning, sensors still flashing just as wildly as before.

I need to get out of the way. It's going to melt down soon if it can't reconcile this irregularity. But it's blocking my exit! I can't get past it.

Kat looked to her left and right helplessly. She was trapped in this space, between caged-in shelving units that met a metal grill roof above her head.

She looked up carefully at the wire roof. It was about seven feet off the ground. She gritted her teeth, then jumped up and grabbed the grill, but was unable to find a grip, and came tumbling back down to the ground. The bot didn't seem perturbed by her acrobatics, but stayed in place, still trying to scan the area that Kat's body was blocking.

Steeling herself for another leap, Kat flexed her fingers, crouched, then launched herself as hard as she could at the wire roof.

This time, her fingers found purchase and she held on tightly. Then, drawing on a reservoir of strength she hadn't known she possessed, she brought her knees up and curled into them, and pressed her feet into the cage roof.

Gripping with her toes through her booties, Kat jammed her feet against the wire grill and straightened her legs, then pulled her chest up to press against the roof.

The pain was almost unbearable. The wire bit into her fingers and she could feel blood dripping down her hands. The muscles in her arms screamed in protest, and within ten seconds she was forced to let go. She barely avoided a face-first landing, dropping in a twisting heap, smashing her knees and elbows onto the hard floor.

She knew she didn't have the strength to repeat the maneuver, but when she turned to look at the bot at the entrance, it was gone.

She jumped to her feet and saw that it was once again rolling along the aisle, contentedly scanning to the left and right, as though nothing whatsoever were amiss.

Anxious to exit the cage before the bot returned, Kat was about to race out and back to her horse when she noticed a little jewel box sitting alone on a different shelf. There was a logo on the box superimposed over an image of a solar system.

I know that logo, thought Kat, and opened the box. Inside was a small wedge of silver-coloured metal.

Laughing, Kat grabbed the silver wedge and stuffed it into another of her pockets.

This is turning out to be a very good day after all, she thought happily.

"**O**H WHAT A beautiful morrrrrning, oh what a beautiful dayyyyyyyy…" hummed Tomás as he leaned back in his chair, skimming over the schedule of the day's arrivals and departures that glowed on his tablet.

What a difference a day makes, he thought. *When I see that arrogant son of a bitch today, I should thank him. He really gave me the push I needed.*

The previous evening had seen Tomás in a foul mood, still smarting from the way he had been spoken to by that officious twerp in the pink suit. After sulking at home and guzzling half a dozen beers, he had grumpily checked his email, a nightly endeavour that usually consisted of sifting through a list of job offers that were even more depressing than the one he currently held, if that were even possible.

But there it was, from an exclusive employment agency that had never so much as given him the time of day: his dream job, smack in the middle of one of the most vibrant sectors of the galaxy, the Tinseltown system.

There were three habitable planets in the Tinseltown system, so named because each of the planets was a virtual paradise. All the most desirable properties had been snapped up by the rich and famous, many of whom were celebrities in the sports and entertainment fields.

There was considerable travel among the three planets as the residents shuttled back and forth on their various publicity junkets or performance tours. And where there is travel, there is opportunity for kidnapping.

The bodyguard job offered in the email called for someone with exactly his qualifications and skill set. He'd replied immediately, and within minutes received an enthusiastic response from the employment AI. confirming that the position was still available. All he needed to do to seal the deal was provide a letter of recommendation from his current employer.

Tomás grinned broadly. His performance at this job had been flawless, without a single negative comment. Management loved him, and the customers all praised his efficiency and courtesy. The new job was as good as his.

Looking up as the client entry door swung open, he admitted the dickhead from the previous day, looking just as arrogant but dressed in a pale lilac-coloured suit today instead of pink.

"Right on time," said Tomás cheerily. *Even this annoying pustule can't spoil this day*, he thought.

Carrington-Smythe did his best to prove Tomás wrong, sneering at him down the length of his nose and replying, "Of course I'm on time. That's how professional people conduct themselves. I don't know what kind of lax behaviour you engage in, but I have no patience for persons who can't at least adhere to a simple schedule."

Tomás gritted his teeth and forced himself to smile.

"Absolutely, sir. And you're here to retrieve your shipment, as arranged. Are your local movers here yet?"

"They're on their way. I wanted to make sure there were no delays. You may retrieve my items now."

"Of course, Mr. Carrington-Smythe. Right away. Would you be so kind as to step over to the scanners so we can verify your DNA and retina scans? And the passcode, of course."

Carrington-Smythe did not dignify the request with a response, but merely strode over to the machines and began the verification procedure.

Tomás sighed and swallowed hard, thinking to himself, *Just a few more days. Once I have the letter of recommendation, I'll deliver it in person. And if I never see this miserable rock again it'll be too soon.*

When Kat returned to the horse after retrieving the disk, the only thing on her mind was to curl up in her hidey-hole and let her torn fingers and sore muscles recover. But she remembered the task Jerry had been obsessing over, and she forced herself to deal with it right away.

Ferreting around inside the horse, she located a small wrench. She dropped to her hands and knees and began working the bolts that secured the clamps holding the horse's three hooves in place on the pallet. She loosened the two rear bolts to the point where they were almost falling out, but left a bit more tension on the bolt on the horse's front-left hoof.

She stood up and grabbed the horse's neck, tugging the beast from side to side. It rocked alarmingly easily, and Kat furrowed her brow in concern. She still needed to climb inside the thing, and wasn't sure she could do so without tipping it over onto its side.

She very gingerly placed a foot in the stirrup and tried to lean forward over the horse's back while lifting herself up and into the hiding space. The horse tilted perilously to its right, but the final bolt was enough to keep it from tipping too far. Kat settled into her spot and the statue stood upright once again.

She was about to pull the saddle down over the opening to seal herself inside again, but suddenly remembered that the bots had scanned this space while the saddle was ajar. She couldn't close it up again until the facility reopened in the morning.

Oh well, she thought, *at least I'll get lots of fresh air.* And settling back, she promptly fell asleep.

Kat awoke several hours later to the sensation of gentle rocking, as though she were curled up in a boat on a peaceful lake. She dreamily opened her eyes, not quite conscious, when she realized with a start that her pallet was moving.

Oh my God, I must have slept right through the pickup!

She lifted her head up and peered over the lip of the horse's back. Her pallet was gently gliding down the aisle toward the main cross corridor. Two other pallets preceded her own, and she could see the fourth one taking up the rear.

Kat grabbed the bar on the inside of the saddle and swung it up and over, but stopped just before she latched it shut. *Might as well wait until I'm at the exit – it will take the guesswork out of the timing.*

Her pallet made a slow turn and then continued on its path, coming to a gentle stop a few minutes later. Kat dared a quick peek out through the crack beneath the edge of the saddle and saw she had arrived at the main access door, which was just now starting to slide open. She lay back and pulled down firmly on the bar, and the saddle snapped shut with a satisfying *click!*

Carrington-Smythe was pacing back and forth in the foyer, running his hands through his hair and tugging on his clothing.

"Is there some kind of problem with my belongings?" he shrieked at the hapless guards. "What's taking so long? Have you lost track of them? I swear, if you've lost—"

"Nothing has been lost, Mr. Carrington-Smythe," said Tomás. "Your pallets may have been placed in a far corner of the facility. It's probably just taking longer than normal to retrieve them."

"*'Probably'*? 'PROBABLY'?" screeched the man. "Do you mean you don't know exactly where they are? Just how incompetent are you two morons, anyway?"

"There's no need for personal insults, sir. I assure you that all your items will arrive very shortly, in exactly the same condition as when you entrusted them to us," said Tomás in an even, measured tone. He pressed his fingernails into his palms in a concerted attempt to keep his cool.

"Well, they had *better* be in exactly the same condition, or I guarantee that I will become your worst nightmare."

Too late, thought Tomás.

Their attention was redirected to the warehouse door as it began sliding open, revealing the four pallets waiting in the inner area.

With a gentle movement, the pallets started to glide forward, but before they reached the threshold, Carrington-Smythe leapt forward and screamed, "Stop! Oh God, stop the pallets!"

Ahmed leapt in surprise and immediately smashed his hand down on a wide, flat red button on his control panel. The pallets came to a sudden stop, with the boxes and other items they carried gently wobbling at the sudden cessation of movement.

That is, *almost* all the items wobbled gently. The horse, however, towering precariously on its pallet, rocked violently, and, while all three men looked on in horror, slowly tipped farther and farther to its right, until, with a wrenching, snapping sound, the clamps holding its left hooves in place tore free from the pallet. With a tremendous crash, the horse tumbled forward and onto its right side, smashing down onto the cases of wine and the glass display unit holding the other bronze statues.

The explosive destruction was magnificent. Thick waves of scarlet liquid splashed out from the wine cases, painting the floor and walls in bloody hues. The glass from the display case shattered in an ear-splitting crash, erupting in large shards that scattered across the floor.

The horse lay splayed out on the pallet, nose buried in the crushed wine cases, legs sticking straight out in inanimate paralysis.

"AAAAIIIIIEEEEEEEEEE!" screamed Carrington-Smythe, dropping to his knees in anguish. "What have you done, you fools? You've destroyed my belongings!"

"YOU!" he bellowed, turning and pointing an accusing finger at Tomás, who stood dumbfounded before the tableau of destruction. "You did this!"

"Me?" gibbered the guard. "What did I do? You're the one who screamed at us to stop the pallets!"

"Because they were moving too fast! I merely wanted you to be careful with them – I never told anyone to yank them around like bumper cars in a county fair!

"And now look what you've done! I'll have your jobs for this, I swear!"

Sensing Tomás was mere seconds from strangling Carrington-Smythe with his bare hands, Ahmed came to the rescue.

"I'm the one who did it, sir," he said. "It was me who stopped the pallets. I thought there was something wrong.

"But look, sir," he continued, taking Carrington-Smythe by the arm and leading him over to the pallets. "There's not really all that much damage. We're insured here, and the company will surely cover you for the spilled wine. And the only other damage is the broken display case. It's really not much at all, sir. We can set your horse back upright and get you on your way with hardly any bother at all."

Carrington-Smythe seemed to consider the man's words, and said quietly, "You're right. It's not really the end of the world, after all. You're a good man, my friend. It's not your fault you're forced to work with an idiot."

"Let's get you back on track then, sir. I see your local movers have arrived. Just in the nick of time, eh? We can get you all loaded up and on your way and this will be nothing but a bad memory by the end of the day."

Ahmed pressed a button on his control panel and the pallets came back to life, moving forward once again in an orderly manner. When the third pallet crossed the threshold, however, a series of red lights lit up on the monitors and a persistent buzzing filled the air.

"The system can't verify your pallet," said Tomás. "The weight is off and the scans don't match."

"Are you a complete idiot?" snapped Carrington-Smythe. "Are you somehow unable to see the gallon of spilled wine and sheets of broken glass covering the floor? What part of this picture do you not understand?"

"I understand it all, Mr. Carrington-Smythe," said Tomás smugly. This was his chance to give back a little of the misery that this snotty twerp had been dishing out since he'd arrived. "But rules are rules. We can't release your belongings until we can verify the integrity of the system."

"We don't need to be hardheaded about this, Tomás," said Ahmed, worried that he would be fired for having stopped the pallets and causing this debacle – and with only five months left until retirement! He shuddered to think of the prospect.

"We can override the system. The workaround is there," he said.

"Only if both of us agree," said Tomás. "And I don't. We follow procedure on this one, and all items return to storage pending a full investigation and inspection of all the goods.

"That could take about six months," he added, with a venomous snarl directed at Carrington-Smythe.

"SIX MONTHS?" screeched the man, then strode over until his face was almost touching Tomás's. "I am telling you this as clearly as I am able: if you don't release my belongings in the next ten seconds, I will bring down such a holy hailstorm of shit on your head, you'll be swimming in it. I will call in every favour, harass every one of your superiors, and beat every bush, until you are left unemployed and permanently unemployable for the rest of your natural life. And for a very long time after that, too."

Tomás opened his mouth to tell Carrington-Smythe what he could do with his threats, when he suddenly remembered that all-important letter of recommendation. All that stood between him and the career of his dreams was that letter, and now, Carrington-Smythe, as well.

"Ah, ah…. Um, well, sir, there's no need to be difficult about this, I suppose….

"Ahmed," he said, turning to his coworker, "you're right – why let a little accident spoil this fine gentleman's experience with our company. Go ahead and override the system. We can all have a good chuckle and put all of this behind us, right, Mr. Carrington-Smythe?"

He extended his hand, but Carrington-Smythe turned on his heel and said to Ahmed, "Open the lift door for the movers so they can load up my belongings now." And then he strode out of the facility.

J**ERRY HAD THE PALLETS** delivered to a dead drop, and then immediately picked up again by another moving company, and finally delivered to Petrovsky's warehouse. By the time they arrived, Howard and Suzie had joined Petrovsky onsite, fidgeting and compulsively checking the time every thirty seconds. The only one not visibly wracked with anxiety was Batman, who snoozed contentedly on the armchair beside the stove.

When the shipment arrived, the horse was still laying on its side, as the movers had not wanted to risk standing it upright while in transit. Jerry grimaced in commiseration with Kat, who was surely in the least comfortable of positions inside the horse. He couldn't risk releasing her until they were in safe surroundings, though, so he crossed his fingers and hoped she wouldn't be too upset when she emerged.

It took all three men to stand the horse back upright. Jerry took a thick metal bar and smacked it against the horse in a rhythmic pattern. *Shave-and-a-hair-cut, two-bits*, he tapped out, and the assembled group held its collective breath as… nothing happened.

"Maybe you should tap again," suggested Howard.

"What, you think maybe she mistook it for another signal?" asked Jerry.

"Maybe she—" began Suzie, but stopped speaking as a *click!* and then a soft hiss issued forth from the horse, followed by the saddle moving up and swinging outwards.

Kat popped into view as she pulled herself into an upright sitting position. Her face was smeared with dried blood, and her hair was matted and tangled.

"My God, Kat!" exclaimed Jerry. "Are you hurt? Did you hit your head when the horse fell?"

"Whaaa?" said Kat, then glanced at her hands and realized what they were seeing. "No, no – my head is fine. I cut my hands, is all. I hadn't realized I'd wiped them on my face, I guess. Makes sense. No. Sorry. I'm fine."

Jerry and Petrovsky helped Kat up and out of the horse, whereupon she promptly collapsed onto a nearby chair.

"Owww. My legs are still asleep. Give me a minute."

Glaring at Petrovsky, she said, "Next time, how's about a little more leg room, Myx?"

"You mean there's going to be a next time?" he said.

"You betcha," grunted Kat. "Wouldn't want to deprive my better half of this stellar experience. His time will come, I promise…."

Batman looked up and, spotting Kat, hopped down from his chair and padded over to her, jumping up onto her lap and nuzzling her cheek. "Oh, Batty," she murmured, running her wounded fingers through his fur, "did you miss me?"

By way of answer, the cat merely curled up into a ball on her lap and went back to sleep.

Studiously rooting around in the horse, Jerry triumphantly lifted his hand in the air, clutching a small slab of metal.

"Ladeeeeees and gentulllmennn, I give you… The Disk!"

Every eye in the room focused on the object in his hand. All conversation ceased, and for a moment, everyone held their breath, not even blinking as they stared at the priceless object.

"I can't believe it," said Suzie.

"So this is the precious prize you were chasing," said Petrovsky.

"I always knew you guys could do it!" crowed Howard.

Jerry held out the disk to them for their admiration.

Howard took it from him, turning it over in his hand and peering at it closely. "Still with the Archives holographic seal, too," he chuckled.

Jerry turned back to Petrovsky and Kat, making his way over to her chair while Howard and Suzie oohed and aahed over the disk. Crouching down, he announced, "And I have a little surprise for you, too, baby." He lifted up a small sculpture and offered it to her. "Myx made this for you."

The sculpture was a small onyx and platinum life-size representation of a cat.

"It's Batman!" Kat giggled. "Oh Myx, how sweet! I love it!"

"I can't take all the credit, Diana – it was Bruce's idea. He told me about the little fridge magnet you lost when your ship was destroyed. I hoped this would make up for that a bit."

"I'll say! This almost makes up for the whole ship! Thank you, Je— Bruce. You guys are the best!"

Kat was giving Myx a big hug when their attention was drawn to Howard and Suzie, who seemed to have started arguing.

"What's the matter with you, Howie? I said I just wanted to look at it. Why won't you let me see the disk?"

"Because I said 'no', Suzie. You're not listening to me. As usual. But the time has come for you – and everyone else – to listen to me. Finally."

He looked up at the other three, who were staring at him.

"Do I have everyone's attention? Good. I have some news to share with you.

"This disk," he said, waving the little silver slab around in the air, "is coming with me." And he slipped the disk into his pants pocket.

"But none of you are. I'm leaving. Alone."

"Howard!" cried Kat. "What's come over you?"

"What's come over me? Well, how about: I'm finally looking out for Number One. How's that for starters?

"It started with this one." He gestured viciously at Suzie. "Pretending she liked me, acting all lovey-dovey, when the only thing she cared about was my computer access."

"Howard," cried Suzie, "you know that's not true!"

"I know nothing of the sort, you lying, two-faced, greedy little – – " Howard's voice diminished into a choked gurgle for a moment, but he quickly regained his speech.

"All you care about is scoring a fabulous treasure for your family, so they can rule the galaxy and continue to shit all over honest hardworking people like me. Continue to use us to pad their bank accounts. Continue to—"

"Howard. That's enough," said Kat, in a harsh, stern tone.

"No, that's *not* enough! It's never enough! You and Jerry fell hook, line and sinker for this strumpet's sob story, but I'm not letting you take this disk and just hand it over to her.

"Jerry, you never had any respect for me. You were so shocked to learn I had a girlfriend you were almost speechless. Turns out you were right, I suppose, but we'll see how the worm turns when I'm suddenly the richest man in the galaxy."

Howard pulled a plasma blaster out from under his suit jacket and stepped back a pace.

"Take off those glasses and empty your pockets," he said to Kat. "And you, too, Jerry."

Jerry pulled out a wad of cash and a pocket laser, his phone and a folded sheaf of papers from the storage unit and the movers. All that was in Kat's pockets was a small wedge of silvery metal.

"What's that?" he asked suspiciously, pointing at the silver wedge.

"Our ship's auth token," replied Kat in a flat monotone.

"Hah! Well, I suppose you can keep that as a souvenir, then, for all the good it'll do you now. And don't worry, I have no interest in your Slimlines – I know they're useless to anyone but you."

"Howard," said Jerry, "this isn't you. I've known you a long time, and you've always been a straight shooter. Forget about whatever crazy plans you've made. We'll all go to Earth together and register the planet with equal shares."

"Forget it, Jerry. I'm not the same patsy anymore. The Howard you've always known is tired of being treated like a schmuck. I'm done."

Waving his blaster, he herded the four over to a huge statue of the Minotaur, then removed several pairs of handcuffs from a small duffel bag he had brought with him. He clipped one of the cuffs onto the Minotaur's thick wrist, barely managing to close it around the brawny appendage.

"Suzie," he said quietly, "come here and put your wrist into the other cuff."

"Forget it," she said.

A thick stream of white-hot plasma burst out of Howard's pistol and left a sizzling, molten hole the size of a dinner plate in the pillar she was standing beside.

"If you don't think the next one won't burn a hole in you, you really don't know me as well as you think you do."

"Go ahead, Suzie," said Kat quietly. "Jerry and I are right here with you. Just do what Howard says, and we'll all be okay."

"That's good advice, Sue," said Howard. "You're lucky to have such good friends."

Reluctantly, Suzie moved over to the Minotaur and clipped the dangling handcuff onto her wrist.

"Now you, Kat. Take these and cuff yourself to Suzie." Howard threw her another set of cuffs.

When she was done, he turned to Jerry.

"You know the drill, old friend," he said, tossing another set of cuffs at him.

The last one was Petrovsky, and for the first time, Howard looked a bit sheepish.

"I'm sorry. I don't really know you, but I can't let you just walk out of here," he said apologetically.

"Not a problem, *tovarisch*," said Petrovsky, getting in place beside Jerry. "Toss me a set of those bracelets."

Once the human daisy-chain was all locked to the gigantic statue, Howard said, "I have no doubt you'll all get free within a short time. You're very resourceful people. But seeing as how you have no ship, and I happen to have a charter waiting for me at the Port Depot, I don't anticipate any problem beating you to Earth. By time you catch up to me, I'll own the world. Or at least the most lucrative part of it."

"I'm tired of your crowing, Howard," said Jerry. "How's about you just get on your merry way now and leave us the hell alone?"

"Oh no, old friend. I'm wise to your tricks. You've regaled me enough times with your tales of pulling the old switcheroo on your erstwhile partners in crime. I'm not *completely* stupid, you know."

Howard moved back a safe distance and put down his blaster, then pulled a collection of machine pieces out of his duffel bag and began assembling them.

"In case you're wondering," he said to Jerry, "this is a portable wide-range spectrometer. It scans the entire spectrum of non-optical wavelengths, from gamma rays all the way to the far infrared. And I've made a few modifications to this particular unit, so it can also detect miniscule amounts of photon energy frequencies, like the kind emitted by certain batteries."

"It's not beyond my imagination to conceive of you two con artists preparing a duplicate disk, but even if you have, this baby will find it, no matter where it's concealed."

He waved his instrument at his pocket and its display panel

lit up like a Christmas tree. The machine's speaker screeched out several high-pitched beeps and whines, falling silent only when he removed the wand.

He waved it in various directions around the room. "It has a terrific range. I've set it to detect electronics from as far as five hundred meters away. I can see a few faint indicators on the display, but it appears they are all coming from other buildings on this street. It's awfully convenient you chose a Stone Age-level workshop for our rendezvous point."

"I prefer the term, 'unplugged'," said Petrovsky quietly.

Walking over to Kat, Howard pointed the machine's sensor at her and slowly worked his way from her head to her feet, front and back. Then he repeated the procedure with Jerry, Petrovsky and Suzie. "Can't be too careful, you know."

Satisfied they weren't concealing electronics of any kind, Howard moved over to the horse. He carefully scanned the interior chamber, tugging and flexing the lining to make sure there were no hidden pockets.

He twisted a dial on the machine to maximum sensitivity, and performed one last scan of the entire space they were standing in, completing a painfully-slow 360° rotation.

"Alright," he said finally. "It appears you were playing this one straight for once, Jerry. I guess being your friend was my saving grace. Bet you won't make that mistake again."

"You've got that one right," muttered Jerry.

"And now, I'm afraid I must leave you nice people. Best of luck to all of you in your future endeavours."

And with that as his parting words, he turned and ran out the door, leaving the line of captives standing helplessly beside the towering metallic horned beast.

"Well," said Kat, breaking the silence, "anyone got a bobby pin?"

DESPITE HIS BRAVADO, Howard knew he needed to get off the asteroid fast. Jerry and Kat were not to be trifled with, and he was sure that as soon as they freed themselves, they would be hot on his trail.

Especially Jerry – he was surely steaming mad about being double-crossed. Howard wouldn't feel safe until he had put at least a dozen star systems between them.

Luck was with him, though – a cab was passing by just as he hit the main thoroughfare near Petrovsky's studio. He leapt in and called out his own address. Time was of the essence, to be sure, but he couldn't bear to travel without a few of his favourite devices, and he needed fresh clothes, too.

Suzie had stayed maddeningly close to him all morning, and it had been a superhuman task to assemble just the few items he'd put in his duffel bag without her noticing. They'd agreed to wait on-asteroid for two days after Kat and Jerry had made their escape, so as not to accidentally put anyone on their trail. If Suzie had seen him packing his go-bag, she might have gotten suspicious and blown the whole deal.

He patted the disk, snug in his pocket, and chortled softly thinking about the life of luxury awaiting him. He already knew which planets he would buy. There was one where the ratio of women to men was 8:1. It was also, unsurprisingly, one of the most expensive places to live in the galaxy – if you were a man, that is. He giggled again.

The cab pulled up at his apartment and Howard punched the button for the "wait" protocol. The vehicle would wait for Howard up to thirty minutes, charging his account all the time, of course, before it would give up and move on in search of another fare. Howard didn't intend to make it wait more than five minutes, at most.

He thundered up the stairs and barely broke stride as he waved his fob at his door. He charged inside and had made it perhaps a dozen strides before he noticed the large man sitting at his desk, studiously examining the various papers and notes scattered across it.

He heard the door click shut behind him and he turned to see a second, slimmer man, with greying hair at his temples.

"Buh— ah, what? Who are you? And what are you doing at my desk?"

He tried to collect his wits and assert control. "Stop that!" he shouted at the large man at the desk. "Those are private papers! You have no right—"

Whatever rights Howard was about to deny these two men were left unspecified, as a heavy blow smashed into the side of his head, sending him spinning into a tall filing cabinet.

"Shut up," said the man with greying temples, putting the leather sap back into his pocket. "That was just a love tap, 'cause we need you conscious to answer some questions. But don't test me. We can still be mighty persuasive without sending you to dreamland."

"Take it easy, Tony," said the big man at the desk, strolling over to Howard and smiling warmly.

"You'll have to excuse my partner. He tends to act first and think later. Me, I'm more of a listener, you know what I mean? And I heard you ask who we are. And I'm happy to answer your question, because I know you'll return the favour and answer all of mine.

"My name is Leo. Leo Frenetti. I'm pleased to meet you, Mr. —?"

"Ah, I, I'm, my name, my name is Howard. Howard Gruenbaum.

"I'm the Assistant Supervising Administrator of Asteroid Environmental and Atmosphere Conservation," he added, as though he were in a professional networking meeting.

"There now! That's what I'm talking 'bout! And now that we're on a first-name basis, Howard – it's okay if I call you 'Howard', isn't it? You can call me 'Frenetti', I don't mind. Everybody does. My mother wasted her time giving me a first name. Even she calls me Frenetti. Ain't that true, Tony?"

"Sure is," agreed the man with the greying temples.

"So Howard, help me out here. Can you tell me why an Assistant Supervising Administrator of Asteroid… ah —"

"—Environmental and Atmosphere Conservation," finished Howard helpfully.

"Right! So why would that guy be interested in a one-hundred-year-old computer disk? And be searching through the emails of a recently-deceased member of the settlement's Archives Department? I'm only asking for a friend, you know, but he's my boss, so I really want to give him the right answer."

If it can ever accurately be said that the blood drained from someone's face, this would be that moment. Howard felt the world spinning, and he clutched the filing cabinet to keep from collapsing.

As he teetered against the cabinet, Howard felt a meaningful lump in his suit jacket pressing against his ribcage. The realisation brought new clarity to his thoughts.

"Absolutely!" he replied ebulliently. "I'm so glad you gentlemen have come – I'd almost given up hope. It's been weeks since I submitted my inquiries. You're from the Historical Society, right?"

He casually moved forward and eased his way around Frenetti and walked toward the desk. I've got the docs right here—"

"Not so fast, Howard," said Frenetti, catching up to Howard and putting a meaty paw on his shoulder.

Howard spun and a thick stream of plasma shot out of the blaster he had pulled from under his suit jacket. Twisting out of the way, Frenetti grabbed Howard's wrist. The blast missed Frenetti's stomach by a millimeter, scorching his shirt in the process.

There would be no second blast from the pistol, and when Howard looked down in confusion to try to figure out why he couldn't seem to control his fingers anymore, he saw the last inch of Frenetti's stiletto sticking out of his chest, right about where his heart would be.

The world went dark very quickly, and Howard collapsed onto the structurally-unstable stack of printouts Batman had been sleeping on just a few days earlier. His last thought as he lay dying was to keep his face away from the papers, lest he start sneezing. He was allergic to cats.

Frenetti stood for a moment over the dead man, and absentmindedly rubbed his finger across the plasma burn on his shirt. Bending down, he turned Howard over to retrieve his stiletto, which he then wiped clean on the dead man's clothes.

While wiping his blade, Frenetti noticed a strange bulge in Howard's pants pocket. He gingerly reached in and extracted a small silver slab of metal with a row of interface ports on one end. A holographic label was affixed to one side that read: "Property of the Department of Archives".

"Son of a bitch," murmured Frenetti reverently.

"Hey, Tony," he said, "I think we just made it to Easy Street. The boss is going to pay us so much for this thing we'll never have to work another day in our lives."

?

"Tony?"

Turning to see what his partner was doing, Frenetti saw his body crumpled on the floor, as though he were taking an impromptu nap. A large red stain waist-high on the wall behind him and a dark splash of burned wood in the center made it clear what had happened.

"Son of a bitch," he said again. "Well, I guess you won't be needing your share, Tony.

"Talk about being in the wrong place at the wrong time."

AAAAAAND, THERE! Done!" said Kat, as a sharp *click!* announced the release of the last handcuff lock.

"Thanks, Myx," she said, handing him two thin strips of black metal. "I think I speak for all of us when I say your spider gave its life for a good cause."

The remains of a large metal spider lay at their feet, with its two fangs missing.

Petrovsky laughed and said, "The ultimate sacrifice. We shall never forget."

Jerry and Suzie sat side by side on the new couch Kat had bought in their shopping spree. Suzie was rubbing her wrists and looking haggard. Petrovsky looked positively cheerful, though.

"I love my new furniture, Diana. Are you sure it's okay for me to keep it?"

"Absolutely, Myx. I'm delighted it has a good home. And it won't hurt your feelings if I leave the horse behind, will it? It's a beautiful piece, but I'd advise you to close up that saddle pretty soon. It would look so much better that way."

"Noted. I'm assuming your business is done here now — can I assist you in any way with your transportation? I'm on very good terms with several cargo shippers. I could get you good rates on a trip."

Kat giggled and said, "That's okay, Myx. We've got it covered. In fact, we'd better be hitting the road right now. I think I've had about all I can take of this asteroid."

"Amen to that," said Suzie quietly.

"You should come with us, Suzie," said Jerry. "Kat and I will see you safely back to the Sillestrian Institute."

Myx and Jerry said their goodbyes while Kat and Suzie gathered up their belongings. There wasn't much, as all of Kat's possessions were inside their now-flattened ship. Kat wrapped-up her new Batman sculpture in a heavy sweater Suzie had brought her to change into, and Jerry walked them to the door, holding the new cat carrier, with a little black and white face peering out the cage door.

They took a transit shuttle to the Port Depot, but when Jerry turned toward the commercial passenger terminal, Kat grabbed his arm and said quietly, "Uh-uh, Tonto. This way," and led him over to the Long-Term Storage Hangar.

Kat paused to study a site map, then led Jerry and Suzie into a lift. She waved a small silver wedge at the destination sensor.

As the lift started to move, Jerry turned to Kat and said, "Correct me if I'm wrong, but didn't you leave our ship's auth token with the registration clerk when we first arrived?"

"Uh-huh," she said, eyes watching the monitor as it displayed the lift's progress.

"So what would that other little token be, the one you showed Howard back at the warehouse?"

The lift hissed to a stop and they walked into a quiet hangar.

"Oh, I guess I forgot to mention," said Kat with a twinkle in her eye as a moving walkway swept them along past a row of parked interstellar pleasure cruisers. "When I was in Sarkosian's storage area, I noticed a box with the Royal Outfitters logo, so I opened it to see what was inside."

Suzie looked befuddled, but Jerry was starting to get the idea. Royal Outfitters was an exclusive builder of made-to-order luxury spacefaring yachts. All their ships were meticulously constructed by hand, by a team of the finest craftsmen in the industry. Some components, such as the kitchens and bedrooms, were even signed by the designers.

Mere money couldn't buy you a Royal Outfitters yacht, however. They maintained an inviolable waiting list. It might be several decades before your name came to the top, and they had been known to refuse entreaties, bribes, and even threats from kings and other powerful tycoons desperate to jump the queue.

The fob in Kat's hand vibrated gently as they drew within meters of a gigantic yacht. The ship's lights illuminated and the access door on its side hissed open, extending a short set of mahogany stairs that silently reached out to touch the pavement.

"Sir?" said Kat, stepping off the walkway and extending her arm to Jerry that he might take it in his own. "Would you do me the honour of joining me on my humble vessel?"

Giggling, she led him and Suzie into their new ship, then gasped as she drank in the opulence of the interior.

"Oh, Jerry," she whispered. "I think I'm going to pass out."

Jerry placed the cat carrier on the floor and opened the cage door. Batman stuck his head out and sniffed. He made a beeline to a pristine white couch, jumped up and started flexing his claws into the material.

"Kat, I think we have a seal of approval from The Boss. I suppose you can keep it."

KAT SAT FROWNING at the command console while Jerry and Suzie explored the ship. Her new cat sculpture sat dead-center on top of the main instrument panel. The real cat lay splayed out in repose on a nav console to her right.

"Jerry, according to this ship's telemetry records, it's never been flown. How is that possible? It must have gotten here somehow."

"Probably delivered by the manufacturer using a much larger cargo ship," called Jerry from inside the walk-in pantry.

"Larger than this? It must have been a battleship."

Kat fiddled with a display. "My glasses say it wants us to register our DNA. Once we do that it will burn us new auth tokens – there are two blanks here in a cradle."

"Really?" said Jerry, popping into the cabin. "That would mean it's never been registered anywhere before – a real blank slate."

Suzie called out, "Hey, where are you guys?"

"We're up front, Suzie, on the bridge. Come join us."

"Oh my God," she said, panting slightly as she jogged into the command cabin, "this thing is enormous. I got lost twice just making my way to the stern. I gave up before I was even halfway there."

"Did you notice where they put the hot tub?" said Kat. "Please tell me you found the hot tub."

"Um, yeah," said Suzie. "It's right beside the salt-water swimming pool and the steam rooms."

"Jerry," said Kat quietly, "please don't think less of me if I start to cry."

"Way ahead of you, baby. I'm starting to tear-up myself."

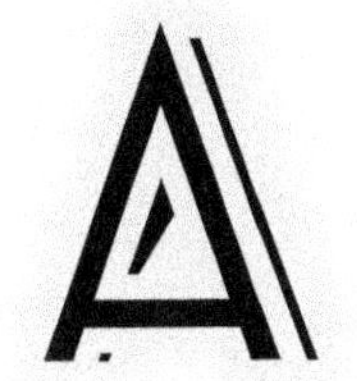

S THEY RECLINED in the command chairs, Suzie sighed from her visitor's seat behind them. The stars glimmered in a breathtaking 180° arc above them, magnificently displayed in the clear shell covering the command cabin. The instrument panel indicated that they were finally past New Terra's solar system, and Jerry was tapping on a series of screens, readying the ship for the main jump into lightspeed.

"You don't sound happy, Suzie," said Kat.

"Oh, well, it's just, you know, losing the disk and everything, I guess it's getting to me."

"Oh, is that all?" said Kat, grinning at Jerry. "I forgot all about that."

Suzie looked at them suspiciously.

"Is there something you guys aren't telling me?"

"Whaddaya say, Jer – think it's time to let her in on it?"

Eyes wide, Jerry feigned innocence. "I'm sure I have no idea what you're talking about, my dear."

Kat laughed.

"Kat?" said Suzie. "What have you and Jerry done?"

"Actually, Suzie, I have no idea, but I know this devious creature next to me so well, I can read him like a book.

Kat lifted up a hand and began ticking off points on her fingers.

"*One*: he's way too cheerful. I know this guy. He's far too pigheaded to accept someone like Howard getting the better of him. If he's this jolly, then that didn't happen.

"*Two*," she continued, "my glasses tell me our present course is *not* for the Sillestrian Institute, but for dear old Planet Earth – you know, the place where they keep the Registry of Planets?"

"What?" exclaimed Suzie. "Jerry, are you trying to beat Howard to the Registry office? Can we even do that?"

"Calm down, Suzie," said Kat. "I'm not done yet. Now, where was I… oh yes—

"*Three*, Myx was all but giggling when we left him. He doesn't have the poker face Jerry does, so I knew right then that something, as they say, was fishy.

"The way I see it, Suzie, is that if both Jerry and Myx have cooked something up – and they obviously have – the only reason for Jerry to include Myx was because he needed something from him."

"But—" began Suzie, but Kat held up a hand to silence her.

"Hold on, Suzie, I'm getting to the finish line.

"Now what, I ask myself, did Myx do for us, besides building a gigantic horse that we ended up leaving behind?"

Kat turned and looked directly at the cat sculpture sitting on the instrument panel. Suzie followed her eyes and gasped.

"But – but that was just a gift, and Myx made it for you long before you were even out of the storage facility. What could it have to do with anything?"

"Myx may have made it for me days ago, but *Jerry* gave it to me this morning. *After* I came out of the horse."

Suzie blinked.

"I'm sorry, Kat, I'm drawing a blank."

"Well then, why don't we just take a closer look at this wonderful little sculpture," said Kat, picking up the cat and turning it over in her hands in examination.

She tugged on its front paws, and then its rear paws. She pulled its ears and pressed its nose. She tried twisting its head, then poked its butt.

Nothing.

"I don't think—" began Suzie, but Kat cut her off.

"*Hush!*"

Kat yanked on the tail, then tried lifting it up, then pressing it down, then pushing it.

"AHA!" she cried.

She gripped the statue firmly with her left hand, and with her right she pushed the tail forward, into the cat's body. While pushing it in, she twisted the tail as though she were winding up a toy.

She'd only made half a revolution when an invisible slot clicked open along the cat's spine, and a small silver slab of metal popped up from inside the statue.

"Oh my God!" shrieked Suzie. Kat looked pleased, and handed the disk to Suzie.

"Merry Christmas," she said.

UT I SAW YOU take the disk out of the horse," said Suzie, stretched out on an overstuffed couch and staring at the silvery treasure she still clutched in her hand.

After the ship had jumped to lightspeed, the three of them had moved to more comfortable surroundings in the observation lounge on the top deck. Thanks to discreet cabin lighting and the wraparound crystal-clear dome above their heads, the lounge offered the breathtaking illusion of sitting atop a rocket as it sped through space.

Reclined in an armchair, Jerry silently scrolled through a tablet detailing the yacht's features.

Kat put her feet up on an ottoman covered in sumptuous Corinthian leather as soft as butter. She took a sip of her drink and laughed.

"You only *think* you saw him take it out of the horse."

"But I did!" protested Suzie. "And it had the holographic seal from the Archives on it, too."

"Yeah," mumbled Jerry distractedly while he examined the ship's specs. "I stole a sheet of those from the Archives when we were there."

"I'm just guessing here now," said Kat, "but I bet the phony disk was part of those 'supplies' you had waiting for us on Menos II."

"Mm-hm," nodded Jerry, concentrating on his reading.

Batman strolled into the lounge and stopped briefly beside the starboard wall of glass to look out at the cosmos whizzing by. After a few seconds he lost interest and jumped up onto Kat's lap, prodding her briefly with his front paws before curling up and closing his eyes.

"Uh-oh," said Kat, "Suzie, you wouldn't have come across any built-in litterboxes during your exploration, would you?"

"No, but we should be okay for a while – I left the door to the botanical garden open, and poured out a bag of cactus sand into a large tray. Just don't grow any tomatoes in it."

"Guys, you've gotta listen to this," said Jerry, suddenly energized. "This ship has an adaptive AI that will fly the ship, run the ship, repair the ship—"

"We get the idea, Jerry," said Kat, laughing.

"No, it gets better. Just listen: the AI also manages and coordinates two hundred task-specific robots on board."

He looked directly at Kat and spoke with great emphasis, "That includes doing the laundry, making the beds, and even *cleaning the litter box*. If we had one, that is.

"And pay attention now, Kat: the kitchen robots will cook all our meals, make us drinks, and serve snacks. And the AI has a library of over 25,000 recipes collected from the greatest chefs of the last three centuries."

"Jerry, don't toy with me. I'm very fragile right now."

"Oh! Oh! It gets better! It maintains an inventory of all our supplies, including food and liquor, of course, and pre-orders anything that needs to be replenished and has it waiting for us wherever we dock."

"Jerry," whispered Kat, "please don't take this the wrong way, but that sounds better than sex."

Suzie giggled. "You guys kill me. Here you are, about to become the wealthiest people in the galaxy, and you're all excited about some silly spaceship."

"Suzie, I'm going to pretend you didn't just say that, and I hope the AI didn't hear you either," said Kat.

"Besides, Suzie, you've got it all wrong," said Jerry. "All Kat and I are keeping is this ship. You're the one about to become the wealthiest person in the galaxy – well, you and your family, of course.

"Kat and I don't want any part of your inheritance."

"I could never allow that," said Suzie, eyes wide. "If I walked away and left you two with nothing, I'd be no better than Howard. Of course I won't refuse your gift, but I demand that you accept at least a finder's fee. How about…."

"One tenth of a percent?" suggested Jerry.

"No. One full percentage. Paid annually, forever."

"Suzie, that's far more money than any human should have."

"Then give it to charity. I don't care. But I'm not letting you walk away from this with less."

"We'll accept your payment, Suzie," said Kat, "as long as you allow us to make one quick stop on Earth, before we return you to your family. Jerry and I need to pay a debt."

"Of course, Kat. I'd love to – I've never been to Earth. Where are we stopping?"

"It's a place called 'Alaska'. We need to pick up a few cases of a certain pink fish they catch there.

"We promised a friend."

Did you enjoy this book?

If you did, then I'm delighted!

And if you'd like to see more like it, there's one simple little thing you can do for me that's worth its weight in gold (metaphorically-speaking):

Scan this code to leave a review!

Your online review will do more for me than you can imagine, and ultimately it will enable me to continue writing more books.

Plus, because I read every review, your review will help me to understand what you liked about my book, so that I can create others that you might enjoy even more!

THANK YOU, in advance.

--*J.M. Holmes*

ACKNOWLEDGMENT

Writing is supposed to be a solitary profession, but the longer one writes, the more one recognizes the need for other people's involvement in a book's creation.

With this book I find myself owing a debt of gratitude to two people, both of whom are Canadian, which, of course, makes them more intelligent than their neighbours south of the 49th Parallel, as those living in the Great White North need to have better blood circulation than more southerly folks, which inevitably leads to greater brain development.

My highly intelligent friend Brian Eldridge gave me minimal advice, but provides moral support with his willingness to fact-check scientific details. Apparently, he is something of an expert in cryptographic technology, but that only brings to mind the quote by Neils Bohr:

An expert is a person who has made all the mistakes that can be made in a very narrow field.

My other collaborator is my erstwhile schoolmate, Lee Zimmerman, who compensates for having very few original ideas by devoting his life to translating the words of others. Luckily for me, he is also a keen writer and editor with a rare grasp of the King's English. Notwithstanding his ruthless butchering of my pristine prose, I freely admit that my writing is dramatically improved with his extensive input, meticulous adjustments and invariably-ignored suggestions.

Thank you to both of these Canucks.

about the illustrator

Francesco La Cerva was born more than half a century ago in Palermo on the beautiful island of Sicily, where he lives to this day.

A childhood immersed in films, cartoons, books and comics inspired him to bring to life drawing – first on the walls of his house, and eventually on sheets of paper – the fantastic characters and worlds of fantasy and science fiction.

Today Francesco supports his family, including three children, by working as an established architect. But between his daily commitments designing houses and other buildings, he still feeds his soul with a regular diet of books, comics, cartoons, and film. And ever faithful to his First Love, he dedicates his free time to illustration, never forgetting the passion that has always inspired him: drawing.

See more of his work at https://www.artstation.com/lacerva_art or https://www.deviantart.com/francescolacerva or find him on Instagram: @francesco_lacerva

Francesco La Cerva nasce più di mezzo secolo fa a Palermo, nella bellissima isola della Sicilia, dove vive ancora oggi.

Un'allegra infanzia passata tra film, cartoni animati, libri e fumetti, lo hanno ispirato a riportare in vita disegnando, prima sui muri di casa sua e infine su fogli di carta, i fantastici personaggi e mondi immaginari di fantasy e fantascienza.

Oggi Francesco sostiene la sua famiglia, compresi tre figli, lavorando come un affermato architetto. Ma tra i suoi impegni quotidiani nella progettazione di case e altri edifici, nutre ancora la sua anima con una regolare dieta di libri, fumetti, cartoni animati e film. Sempre fedele al suo Primo Amore, dedica il suo tempo libero all'illustrazione, senza mai dimenticare la passione che da sempre lo ispira: il disegno.

Per vedere altri suoi lavori visita:
https://www.artstation.com/lacerva_art
o https://www.deviantart.com/francescolacerva
o visita su instagram: @francesco_lacerva

about the cover artist

My name is Bohdan. I grew up in Kyiv, immersed in the vibrant pulse of the city and the dedicated spirit of its cultural richness. I spent my formative years within the walls of the Kyiv Academy of Arts, where I delved into the secrets of artistic craftsmanship.

Beckoned by the virtual realm, I realized that my calling lay in digital artistry, a medium which allows me to depict the world through pixels, merging the artist with technology.

My ambition is to shape a new reality for Ukraine, initially through the avenues of the virtual. I believe that art has the power to reshape perceptions and wield a significant influence on society.

The war, which has spared so few lives, couldn't leave me untouched. My personal contribution — my art — echoes the reverberations of the surrounding reality. Missiles tend to pierce the night sky around the profound slumber of the 3rd hour. These barrages have transformed my creative process into a striking demonstration of resilience and fortitude.

Through my creations, I aspire to illuminate a path into the future, hoping for a virtual world that will act as a stepping stone toward real change.

Мене звуть Богдан. Мої дитячі роки пройшли у Києві, де я відчував пульс міста та відданий дух його культурного багатства. Моє студентське життя пройшло у стінах Київської Академії мистецтв, де я освоював секрети художньої майстерності.

Відчувши дзвінку віртуального світу, я вперше пізнав, що моє покликання — цифровий художник. Це те, що дозволяє мені відобразити світ за допомогою пікселів та об'єднати митця із технологією.

Моя амбіція — створити нову реальність для України, спочатку за допомогою віртуальних витоків. Вірю, що мистецтво може перетворити уявлення та надати суттєвий вплив на суспільство.

Війна, яка обійшла стороною багато життів, не могла залишити мене осторонь. Мій власний внесок - моє мистецтво - відбиває ноти навколишньої реальності. Ракетні обстріли стали важким випробуванням, яке перетворило мій процес творчості на визначну демонстрацію волі та стійкості. Ракети летять, зазвичай, коли глибокий сон загорнув світ у темряву о третій годині ночі.

Сподіваюся, що через мої творіння я зможу засвітити шлях у майбутнє, надіючись на віртуальний світ, який стане кроком до реальних змін.

about the author

J. M. Holmes was born and raised in Canada
and educated in the Classics by Jesuits and nuns.

Renaissance polymath, amateur beekeeper, film historian,
long-distance bicyclist, author, computer whisperer,
and the one person who knows how to fix all the world's
problems, Holmes delights in confounding expectations
and ascribes to multiple, often contradictory life
philosophies.

Especially proud of daughter Sarah and son Alex,
Holmes considers everything else in an admittedly
long and highly rewarding life as mere dross,
agreeing heartily with Ezra Pound, who points out:

> *What thou lovest well remains,*
> *the rest is dross.*
> *What thou lov'st well shall not be reft from the*
> *What thou lov'st well is thy true heritage.*

(Including cats, of course.)

If you'd like to know more about the author,
read about upcoming (or past) books,
or offer your own comments,
direct your browser to:

jm-holmes.com

ICE, ICE, BABY

Don't miss this volume of three exciting scifi novellas

The ice will swallow the whole science station within days if
Vedana, Alice, and their fellow scientists can't find out what's
causing its unstoppable growth.

In the meantime, they're slowly being roasted to death by a
malfunctioning life support system aboard their ship. If they don't
restore the environmental controls they will be forced to evacuate
to the planet's frozen surface.

And while they fight to avoid being frozen or cooked,
a murderous saboteur bent on destroying their mission is killing
them off one by one.

This thrilling scifi tale of two brilliant heroines leading their
comrades in a life-and-death struggle will engage you from the
very first page and leave you hungry for more.

VEDANA COULD HEAR the keypad beeping quietly as someone entered the door access code sequence. A metallic *click!*, a pause, a hiss, and she heard a footstep inside the room.

She would have bet money that her breathing could be heard throughout the whole ship, it seemed so loud to her. She opened her mouth wide and tried to calm her racing heartbeat, which was humming along at around 200 beats per minute.

She heard the footsteps moving quietly about the room, but they weren't wandering around aimlessly. Whoever they belonged to knew where to go and what to do. There was a quiet efficiency at work here. She heard a few little clinks, a quiet hum of some unknown machine, and the ripple of a zipper being opened and then, a second later, closed.

And then… silence.

Vedana froze. Had she done something to give herself away or left some tiny sign of her presence here?

The intruder seemed to be standing still in the dark lab.

Listening? Examining the room? What was he doing?

Vedana wanted to scream, the tension was so extreme.

And then she heard a quiet footstep come closer to her.

Then another.

The footsteps stopped directly in front of Vedana's cabinet.

She gritted her teeth, and waited for the inevitable yanking open of the cabinet door.

from THEY LEFT ME FOR DEAD:

THEY LEAVE ME for dead, lying in a drainage ditch beside the road, and I can hear them as they drive away in my car, just a couple of good ol' boys lighting cigarettes and cracking jokes, as though they're coming back from a fishing trip and not from having just beaten someone to death.

I can't tell you how long I lie here, listening to the rain and the wind and the crickets and all the assorted night sounds that creep back to life after the humans have gone. The stentorian gasps of my own ragged breathing keep time with the persistent rustle of some weeds just off to my left, making me wonder if perhaps some hungry wild creature is assessing my potential as a snack.

I am slipping into and out of consciousness every few minutes, and in a grey recess of my mind I peripherally hope that I will be insensate when the beast finally starts gnawing on whichever part of my body it's going to eat first. Every so often a vehicle shoots by in the night, announcing itself with the quiet hiss of its approach, then gradually crescendoing into a deafening, rattling roar defining its identity as car, pickup truck, or 18-wheeler. The weeds around my head sway and buck convulsively as the vehicle whizzes past my location, and then resume their motionless witness to my suffering.

I have no way to alert the passing drivers to my presence. I can't seem to move my arms and legs, or even turn my head, either because some part of my spine is damaged or because the intense pain from the rest of my body is overwhelming all my other senses. I know that several of my ribs are broken, along with at least two of the fingers on my left hand. My sides throb in excruciating pain, and I assume I'm bleeding internally from several damaged organs. I can't really see at all from either of my eyes, as both are swollen shut and caked in blood. The taste of blood fills my mouth and I can't breathe through my nose.

I lie here, face down in the dirt and muck, and I wait — for death, or the dawn. I wonder which will arrive first.

Literati International is the privately-held parent company of Literati Media, established in 1984 in Toronto, Canada, which comprises Literati Worldwide Publications, Literati Broadcasting Enterprises, Literati International Reporting & Podcast Productions, and Literati Film and Television Post-Production Services.

Literati International has affiliate partnerships and representatives in numerous countries around the globe, including Australia, India, and Brazil.

Check out the full line of Literati-produced books and media at www.literatiinternational.com

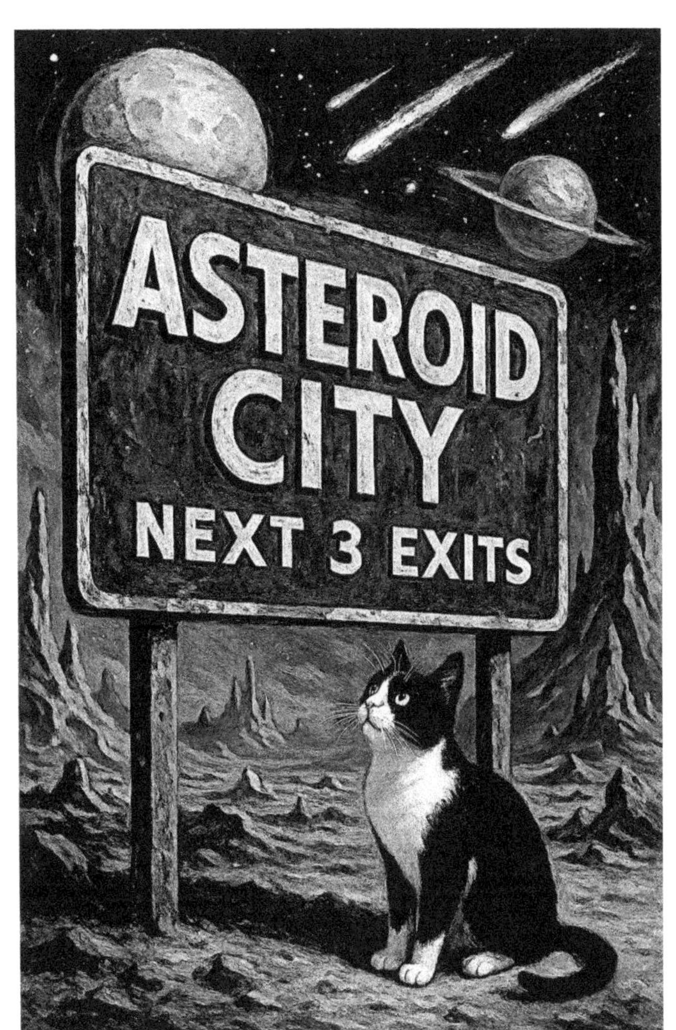

ASTEROID
CITY
NEXT 3 EXITS